# Don't Tell Anyone

Editing by: Allie Bliss from Blissed Out Editing
Proofreading by Sarah Baker from Word Emporium

# Don't Tell Anyone

## BREAKING THE RULES
### BOOK ONE

KA JAMES

# Meghan and Cooper's Rules

1 - Don't tell anyone.

2 - We're exclusive.

3 - If either of us meets someone else we want to date, this ends, effective immediately.

4 - No dates.

5 - No intimacy at work.

6 - No sleepovers.

# Dedication

This book is dedicated to everyone that has supported me throughout the process of writing this book.

But also, to you, the reader, I hope you love Meghan and Cooper's story as much as I loved writing it.

⚖️

P.s. If you are a member of my family or a friend, thank you for supporting me but don't make it awkward when I see you next.

In fact, better yet, just put the book down and walk away.

# Trigger Warnings

To help you decide if this book is for you, I have included a trope and trigger warning outline below. Rest assured, there is a happy ending but to make it interesting for you, there has to be some turbulence on the journey.

This is a contemporary romance.

**Tropes:** Accidental Pregnancy, Office Romance, Boss/Employee, Secret Baby

**Triggers:** Parental Death, Pregnancy, Separation, Sexual Harassment

# Playlist

Listen Here

*Gold* - Kiiara

*Desire* - Meg Myers

*Don't Give Up On Me* - Solomon Burke

*A Change Is Gonna Come* - Otis Redding

*Stronger* - Kanye West

*Rules* - Doja Cat

*Confident* - Justin Bieber, Chance the Rapper

*Body* - Sinéad Harnett

*Do It To It* - ACRAZE, Cherish

*Your Love (9PM)* - ATB, Topic, A7S

*Don't Forget to Breathe (feat Yebba)* - Stormzy

*Birthday Cake* - Dylan Conrique

*Only Love Can Hurt Like This* - Paloma Faith

*Honest* - Kyndal Inskeep, Song House

*Tennessee Whiskey* - Chris Stapleton

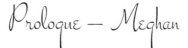

# Prologue — Meghan

**T**he day I met Cooper Jackson will forever be ingrained in my mind. I remember how my breath caught in my throat, how my mouth went dry, and the way my skin tingled at the contact of his skin on mine as he shook my hand.

It was a simple introductory meeting at a job interview. I certainly didn't think it would be something that would change my life forever.

But I should have known, and maybe deep down I did, that it was the start of our story, of how Cooper Jackson and I would come to be more than boss and employee.

*So much more.*

It's a cold, wet January morning, and I'm racing down the sidewalk on my way to an interview with the Human Resources manager of Jackson and Partners. In typical Meghan Taylor fashion, I'm running late.

The position I'm interviewing for is Assistant to the Managing Partner, but I'm not holding my breath on getting it, not with my lack of experience.

I'm very aware of the fact that I'm only being interviewed because of my best friend, Alexandra–or Alex as she prefers to be called–and that my prior waitressing and bar work experience will not help me here. She put in a good word for me and all but begged for her friend—who'd just moved to the city on a whim—to be interviewed.

"Have you got your warm coat on?" My mom worries down the phone.

"Yes, mom. I'm wrapped in layers upon layers." I chuckle as I dodge the never ending stream of commuters.

*Why does it feel like I'm a fish swimming upstream?*

Although my mom says she understands my desire to move to New York, she still worries that her twenty-seven-year-old daughter is going to get hurt or worse—I guess it's her maternal instinct. My mom is the biggest worrier I know and, even though she sometimes forgets that I'm a grown woman, I don't know what I'd do without her.

"I just don't want you to get sick," she clucks.

"I won't, Mom. I promise I'm looking after myself. If I

wrapped up any more I'd be rolling down the sidewalk like the Michelin Man." I laugh lightly and my smile stays on my face when she joins in.

I could understand her worry if this was my first foray out into the world, but when I left home to go to college to study business—which I ended up not finishing—I found my own place and got a job to cover my bills. I know I can make this work, even if New York is a billion times more expensive.

"Good. Did you prepare enough? Have you been eating enough? I worry about you sometimes. How is Alex? Is she looking after herself?" She reels off a list of questions, not giving me the chance to respond.

I pull in a deep breath–slightly flustered at her barrage of questions–and repeat to myself that she's just being my mom as I continue to navigate through the throng of people.

It's in her nature to worry about me, even though sometimes it can make me feel like I'm fourteen again and failing math class—numbers are not my forte.

"I prepared as well as I could. I've been eating three meals a day. And if I don't get this role, it's New York. There are plenty of opportunities out here. And Alex is great." I try to reassure her because I know if I don't, she'll get herself worked up over nothing.

The line goes quiet before she can respond, and I can hear a muffled conversation in the background. There's some rustling in my ear and a smile breaks out across my face as I picture my dad trying to wrestle the phone from her grip. The line clears and I can hear my dad trying to reassure her before he takes the phone and his gruff voice fills my ears.

Briefly closing my eyes, I allow the sound to soothe me and ease my nerves.

"Now buttercup, you show them you're the best person for this job."

"Yes, Dad. That's the plan."

"And if you don't get it, it's not meant to be. There will be someone out there that wants to snap you up," he assures me.

"Exactly. Worst case, I'll come home and let Mom baby me some more."

"We'd have you back here any time. You'll always be our baby."

"I know, Dad. And I'll come home soon, but for now can you tell Mom that I'm fine?" I ask, knowing that's exactly what's going to happen.

"You know it. Go and show them what you're made of, buttercup."

I smile into the phone and say my goodbyes just as the building that houses the Jackson and Partner's offices comes into view.

This is it.

As much as I've tried to reassure my parents, I'm very aware of the fact that I need to get this job. I can't keep staying on Alex's couch any longer than necessary, and this is the first step to my new future.

I stop on the sidewalk, taking in the impressive

building. People move around me, huffing out sounds of annoyance in their rush to get to work. Pulling in a deep breath to regroup, I release it in a rush as I make my way into the building and toward the sleek reception desk.

"How can I help you?" the receptionist asks with a smile.

She looks to be in her forties with her shiny chestnut brown hair pulled back in a restricting bun, and her makeup artfully applied. Her uniform matches that of the three other receptionists—sleek black power suits.

I guess I kind of fit in with my loose, wide-leg black pants, white shirt and black jacket. I've gone for a simple flat shoe on my feet and my blonde hair is pulled back in a bun.

"Hi, my name is Meghan Taylor and I have a nine am interview booked in with Maria Fernandes from Jackson and Partners Human Resources department."

"Of course, please take a seat and I'll let her know you're here." She points me to a breakout area of uncomfortable looking gray couches before typing away on her computer, all but dismissing me.

Taking a seat in the waiting area, I use the time to look around the space. There isn't much in the way of furniture, just a couple of couches similar to the one I'm sitting on.

There's a bakery to the right of the doors, but other than that, the space is empty, almost clinical. Barriers lead through to a bank of elevators and I people watch as workers come through and make their way to their floors.

"Meghan? Meghan Taylor?" A petite woman with gray streaked, brown hair that falls to her shoulders comes toward me. As she gets closer, I can see defined smile lines around her sparkling brown eyes and her straight white teeth as she gives me a warm smile. She's wearing shiny black three-inch heels, a bright red fifties style dress, and a black cropped cardigan.

After seeing the receptionists and having built up an image of her during our email exchanges, I didn't expect her to look like this. She's cute and looks like she's fun to be around. She kind of reminds me of my mom with the air of comfort and openness that she exudes—I guess that quality is necessary if you work in HR.

With a smile to match hers, I stand from my seat and rub my slightly damp palms on my pant legs to wipe away the moisture before extending my hand toward her. *Stupid layers.*

"Ms. Fernandes, it's so nice to meet you."

"Oh, please, call me Maria. I may work in a law firm, but I'm not one for formalities when it comes to names." She flashes me a grin and envelopes my hand in her own, giving it a firm shake.

"We're going to be in the conference room on the twentieth floor for your interview," she states as we walk toward the bank of elevators.

During the swift elevator ride, with stops on at least six floors, Maria chats to me about the firm and asks me how I'm liking New York so far. When the doors open on the twentieth floor, I'm no longer as nervous as when I arrived in the building.

Evenly spaced doors line the walls on each side of the corridor and although there are very few windows, the decor makes the space feel light and open. I can't see anyone, but the low murmur of people working and keyboards being hit as we make our way to the conference room is somehow soothing.

With each step down the corridor, a knot of anxiousness grows and tightens in the depths of my stomach, until I feel like I might be sick due to the nerves that have rained down on me. I don't understand where this feeling has come from. I was fine on the ride up.

*Oh God, I hope I don't throw up.*

Yes, I want this job, but it's not going to be the end of the world if I don't get it. All morning I've tried to pinpoint this... I guess nervousness. It feels like a kaleidoscope of butterflies have taken flight in the pit of my stomach.

I don't normally get nervous.

The last time I had a feeling like this I was humiliated by a girl that was supposed to be my friend and the guy I was dating, at the winter formal. I'd had this exact same feeling in my stomach then and I wish I'd listened to it. I'd been embarrassed in front of everyone and had vowed to remain invisible ever since—although that particular vow had only lasted for one semester.

I'm pulled from my thoughts when we arrive at an

open area at the end of the corridor. In front of us is a door that I can only assume is the conference room where my interview will be held. The blinds are shut, and the door is firmly closed, so Maria gives a courtesy knock before opening the door and taking a step inside.

"Mr. Jackson, our nine o'clock interview is here. Do you need a moment?"

I hear a murmured response, but it's spoken so low that I can't hear exactly what is being said.

Blindly, I follow Maria into the center of the room as she glides toward the mahogany conference table. I had assumed my interview would only be with Maria, which in hindsight was a poor assumption. I'm careful to keep my face clear even as I internally frown at this latest development.

My mind whirls as I mentally go over the correspondence I've received, but when I look up into the most beautiful eyes I've ever seen, my mind goes blank.

From my research this week, I know that Mr. Jackson is Cooper Jackson, the Managing Partner I would work for if I get this job. He's one of the most respected attorneys in New York City and is one of the youngest managing partners at the firm his dad started.

The pictures online didn't do him justice. He looked untouchable, typically dressed in a tuxedo, with a serious look on his face, his hair short and styled and his jaw clean shaven. Right now he looks more approachable, although still as... severe, I guess.

His hair looks to be free from product, with his curls

messy and free, begging to have fingers run through them. A light dusting of stubble coats his chin and his blue eyes are intense as they bore into me.

As I look into his sparkling eyes, the sounds coming through the still open door seem to fade away and he becomes all I see as we stare at each other for what feels like an eternity. I'm vaguely aware of Maria still being in the room.

My breath catches in my throat as he holds my gaze captive. I want to move my hand to my racing heart, but my limbs are frozen. I've never been this caught off guard by a man and I'm sure that if I could tear my gaze away from his hypnotic stare, everything would be moving in slow motion.

*What is going on?*

Blissful silence surrounds us. I'm hyper aware of the cool air from the air conditioning blowing across my skin, causing goosebumps, and the sounds of my labored breathing.

He breaks the silence, shaking his head and diverting his gaze as he seems to snap himself out of the trance moments before me. "Good morning, Miss Taylor. It's a pleasure to meet you." He stands from his seat and makes his way around the table before extending his hand as he stops in front of me.

I place my hand into his palm and a current of electricity jolts through me, causing me to jerk away. Maria clears her throat, penetrating the bubble around us, and I blink up at him before taking a step back.

*Did I move toward him?*

I've never had this reaction to someone before and it's really throwing me off of my game.

"It's a pleasure to meet you too, Mr. Jackson," I murmur, praying he hasn't noticed my reaction to him. The slight narrowing of his eyes and furrowing of his brow however, tells me he most likely did, but that I wasn't the only one affected.

"Please, take a seat." Maria smiles up at me before directing a frown and then a glare at Mr. Jackson.

Pulling out the seat in front of me, I keep my eyes focused on the large table as he moves around the room to his seat. He clears his throat, and the sound causes my eyes to dart to his own before I drag them away and over to Maria.

*She's much safer to look at.*

"Thank you for coming in today, Ms. Taylor." Maria soothes, and I will my rapidly beating heart to slow down. "Let's not keep you too long and get straight into the interview."

"Sounds good to me." I smile nervously, my gaze still trained on Maria.

"Why do you think you're the right person for this role?" The deep rumble of his voice fills the room and I barely resist the urge to close my eyes at the feeling it stirs within me.

Clearing my throat, I turn to him and give the answer I practiced in front of the bathroom mirror last night.

"Although I don't have experience as an assistant, I

have many positive attributes that I believe would be an asset to the role. I am highly organized, I have great attention to detail and I am incredibly flexible, to name a few." At that, his right brow lifts and I feel my cheeks heat with a blush at the implication of my words.

My gaze goes back to Maria and she offers me a reassuring smile before asking me the next question.

For the next hour I try to avoid his gaze and when he asks me questions, I keep my eyes locked over his shoulder, not willing to give into the distraction his proximity seems to cause me.

I leave the interview feeling like there's not a chance in hell that I'm getting the job. How can I, when the entire time I could feel his blue eyes boring into me and I wasn't able to look back? He'd be my boss and as it stands, I wouldn't be able to look him in the eye because he puts me on edge.

Resolute that I'm not going to be offered the role, I go about my day, doing the chores I put off yesterday in favor of prepping for my interview. It's as I'm doing laundry and constantly refreshing my emails that afternoon in the hopes of having secured another interview that Maria's name pops up in my inbox.

My eyes scan over the message and I drop the pants I'd been folding back into the basket when it registers that they're offering me the role. With a ridiculously good salary–considering my lack of experience–and a start date of the next day.

I sit on the edge of my bed, replaying the interview

over and over in my mind, trying to understand why I'd be the best candidate for them. I'm not quite sure how I've managed to land this role and even though I'm happy that I have, I still need to seriously consider if I can work for Mr. Jackson.

I need to pay my bills, yes, but should I take the job when I'll have to work so closely with the man who makes me feel things I've never felt before?

I *need* a job.

Picking up my phone, I pull up the email, reading it over again. I hesitate for a moment before typing out a reply, accepting the offer. I don't send it immediately. Instead, I fold the rest of the laundry, throwing glances at my phone and praying for some sort of sign. When the clothes are folded, put away, and no sign has been sent, I press send on the email.

*I guess time will tell if I made a mistake.*

I place his black coffee with half a sugar on the right hand side of his desk, just above his keyboard.

Making sure it's in the position he likes before I brush a flake of pastry into my palm from the edge of the gleaming surface.

I straighten the papers for the meetings he has this morning before checking my grandmother's wristwatch and then double check everything is in its rightful place.

He doesn't get mad or shout at me, he just likes things how he likes them and it's my job to make sure they're right.

Stepping back from the desk, I observe my handy work, pushing an errant strand of hair back into place. My natural blonde hair, which typically falls in beachy curls to my waist, is pulled back into a high ponytail. For work, my hair is always up to keep it out of my face.

He should be in any minute now, so I smooth my

hands down my thighs as I make my way back to my desk.

*Time to get to work.*

Sitting at my desk, I rub my temples, moaning under my breath as the dull pain of a headache looms in the back of my eyes.

Every morning like clockwork, my mind starts playing a montage of Mr. Jackson. It always starts with him fully clothed, going through the variety of suits he wears.

My favorite is the light gray one, with a matching waistcoat and royal blue tie. It accentuates his eyes and when he takes his jacket off, you can see his bulging biceps and tapered waist to perfection. Seeing him every day is one of the many perks of my job.

The innocent daydreaming quickly morphs into riskier scenes. Him with his sculpted chest bare. Then him in just his boxers. Before he's completely naked and hovering above me. I've never even seen this man naked before, but a girl can fantasize.

I need to concentrate if I'm going to get this report completed on time—I'm not great with numbers at the best of times, let alone with x-rated scenes running through my mind.

Pushing my glasses up my nose, I sit up straighter and stare at the screen in front of me, willing myself to get back into the zone. The numbers jumble on the spreadsheet once again, and as I close my eyes in an attempt to clear my vision, another scene of sweaty, entangled bodies flashes through my mind.

Just the thought of him, naked and losing control, has me shifting in my seat and rubbing my thighs together to ease the ache.

*Shit, pull yourself together, Meghan. You're supposed to be working.*

Coffee... I need coffee. Letting out a sigh of frustration at my wandering mind, I push my chair back from my desk and make my way toward the office kitchen. My desk is on the thirtieth floor of the building and is tucked around a corner, out of sight.

It's quiet at this time of the morning, with most of the associates not getting in until eight am. The offices for Jackson and Partners are open plan, clean, white, and bright spaces. I've always thought it was almost clinical, but you definitely get the whole *Suits* vibe from it.

In the middle of the floor, there's a bullpen of desks surrounded by four walls. One wall houses meeting rooms, another gives a floor to ceiling view of Manhattan, a third wall only has the entrance to the large kitchen area. The last wall has a bookshelf running the length of it, filled with all kinds of law books.

Since working here, my respect for attorneys and paralegals, with all the work that they have to put into a single case has increased tenfold.

My mind wanders back to the man I've been daydreaming about as it often does. Cooper Jackson would *never* look at me the way I fantasize he would, with passion in his eyes and a need to own me. He most definitely wouldn't get me naked and bless my ears with the sounds of his groans.

I've never slept with him and neither of us has crossed the professional line that was drawn when I took the job. If we ever did decide to step over it, I know it would be fantastic based on the way he carries himself, the sexy huskiness of his voice and the dominance he oozes, even in his work life. I know being with him would be the best time of my life.

Or maybe I've read too many romance books. The hopeless romantic in me likes to get lost in romance novels with my book boyfriends.

It's why my favorite area in my apartment is the second hand royal blue loveseat in the reading corner I created, next to the window. I can get lost for hours in a fictional world of romance that I have never had the pleasure to experience in real life.

A conversation I've had many times, in one way or another, with my best friend Alex, comes to mind as I walk to the kitchen. Most recently, I'd been recounting my day to her and when it featured heavily on how Mr. Jackson was dressed and the smell of his cologne, she called me out.

*"Come on, Meghan. I've sat here for the past fifteen minutes and listened to you rattle on about what he wore, ate, how he smelt, and how he looked at you today. You say you want him out of your system, but when I give you advice on*

*what to do, you tell me you can't. You could easily seduce him and then you could move on," she teases me.*

*"It's not that easy. I've worked for him for nearly a year. I swore to myself when I accepted the job that he would be nothing more than my boss," I state, attempting to put some sense of finality into my tone.*

*"And how's that working out for you?" She laughs. "Last time I checked, you haven't been laid since you started working for him and whenever I try and get you to even go on a date with someone else, you come up with an endless list of excuses as to why you can't... I don't buy any of them, by the way."*

*"It's fine. My lack of dating has nothing to do with him. I'm just not ready to date anyone," I murmur, my earlier determination gone.*

*"I say this for your own good..." Alex grabs my hand, pulling my attention to her as she continues. "If you aren't going to make a move with him, you need to move on and get laid. It's not healthy for you to be obsessing over a guy because he made your panties wet one time."*

*"It wasn't one time, and it's not just him making my panties wet. It's the looks he gives me when I walk into his office, it's the hunger I feel for him and think I see reciprocated in his gaze. It's the way the air is pulled out of the room whenever he's near. It's... I can't fully explain it, but he has a hold over me."*

*"I'll say it one last time... Make. A. Move," Alex affirms.*

Pulling myself back into the present, I repeat over

and over in my mind that, as much as I want to experience all of him, I just *can't*.

Too much is at stake.

Based on the sparks that zap through my body when he's near or we accidentally touch, I have no doubt that he would have me screaming his name, forgetting anyone that came before and comparing every man that comes after.

He exudes power and dominance. Whereas, I tend to be shy until I get to know someone—or I've had a few drinks. Alex likes to say fun Meghan comes out to play after about five tequila shots.

Because of my past experiences, I tend to hide away and not draw too much attention to myself, especially when we have certain clients in the office.

Today I'm dressed in a pair of loose black pants, probably a size too big for me, a flowing black blouse, again a size too big, and my trusty cream cable knit cardigan—because it keeps me warm on cold December days. The cardigan may have seen better days, with the color slightly off and worn-looking, but it's one of my winter wardrobe staples.

Without a scrap of makeup on my face, my peaches and cream skin glows from the moisturizer and face oil I applied this morning.

I don't tend to make much of an effort for the office and so I wear some variant of this look every day. It's appropriate business attire, especially when I don't want to draw attention to myself. I much prefer to be inconspicuous and remain in the shadows, although it doesn't always seem to work—*hello creepy clients, who are old enough to be my dad.*

The only person whose attention I want, I would never get, even if I changed the way I dressed for work.

In the kitchen, I rinse out my mug before making a cup of coffee from the machine, turning around to lean against the counter fiddling with my simple chain necklace while it brews.

The kitchen is another modern room, with all the appliances you could possibly need. It also has a variety of breakfast items that are brought in fresh every morning. I go to the pastries that are calling my name and help myself to a croissant before grabbing my coffee and making my way back to my desk.

My steps falter as I walk around the corner and spot Mr. Elijah Jackson, Cooper's dad, leaning against my desk.

*Oh God, I should've checked the calendar before I made my coffee.*

"Good morning, Mr. Jackson. How are you?" I ask, pasting a smile on my face as I go to walk behind the desk to put a barrier between us.

Mr. Jackson Sr. is an older man in his late fifties. He still has a thick head of hair, although it's graying on the sides, but his dull blue eyes hold many secrets I have no desire to unravel. Although he's retired from the firm, he still owns several businesses and, as he puts it, likes to keep his fingers in many pies.

Balancing my coffee and croissant in one hand, I pull my cardigan tight around myself to afford a bit of protection from his leering gaze. I do my best to skirt around him, avoiding his usually grabby hands.

*I wish I'd worn heels.*

My sensible black pumps have him towering over me, and I don't like the way he seems to relish this.

"Well, if it isn't the ever beautiful Meghan," he says as he blocks my path. His tongue darts out to wet his thin lips as his gaze travels the length of my body, looking at me like I'm his next meal. "When are you going to let me take you to dinner? You know I'll treat you like the queen you are." He moves closer, invading my space as he pushes a strand of hair away from my face.

I try my hardest not to recoil at the feel of his fingers on my skin. "As I've said before, Mr. Jackson, it would be against my contract for me to go to dinner with you. Unless my boss was there and I'm needed to take minutes." It's the same excuse I've given him every time he's asked.

"Please, call me Elijah, darling. Nobody would need to know and anyway, your boss is my son. It'll be our little secret," he whispers, his hot breath covering my ear, causing me to cringe as my mind is filled with flashbacks of a past I'd rather forget.

A cough sounds from behind him and he shifts to reveal *my* Mr. Jackson. For a second I can breathe. He's come to my rescue without even knowing it. But then I see the look on his face and avert my eyes from his annoyed stare. A knot of anger forms in the pit of my stomach, and I subtly roll my eyes at him in exasperation. He doesn't have the right to be annoyed at me when it's *his dad* making inappropriate propositions.

"Father, what are you doing here this early?" he asks, taking his dad's attention away from me.

"I came to see my favorite son, of course," Mr. Jackson Sr. replies as he walks toward Cooper.

Once they've gone into the office and the door is firmly closed behind them, I sit down at my desk and relax into my chair, or at least I try to, taking a bite of my flaky pastry. It tastes like cardboard. I sip on my coffee, trying to wash the taste away before signing into my computer and staring at the billing reports I loathe preparing each month. Anything to put the look on Mr. Jackson's face out of my mind. I know the dark cloud that has entered the office with Mr. Jackson Sr.'s presence will remain for a while.

As I'm trying to get my eyes to focus on the spreadsheet in front of me, the office door behind me opens, causing my eyes to dart to the time display on my PC monitor as I frown at the quickness of their meeting.

I brace myself to deal with Mr. Jackson Sr. again, but I release a breath when I feel the hairs on the back of my neck lift and Cooper's signature scent envelopes me. It's a weird mix of being relaxed in his presence but also wired by the way he makes me feel.

When no words are uttered, I slowly turn in my seat. My eyes start at his shiny black Oxfords, traveling up the long solid legs encased in light gray suit pants. I stall at the impressive bulge hidden behind the zipper, causing my tongue to sweep across suddenly dry lips. I continue up his body and look somewhere over his left shoulder, mentally shaking my head to clear the inappropriate thoughts from my mind.

"Are you done?" his deep masculine voice asks as he leans against the doorjamb with his arms folded across his chest. It's his deep baritone that does things to me, and it's becoming increasingly difficult to hide this from him.

I can hear the humor in his tone, I'm sure if I looked at his face now I'd see one of his sexy smirks gracing his delectable full lips. I'm sure he finds it funny that his assistant is checking him out and just the thought of being caught sends a blush across my cheeks.

My eyes grow wide, flashing to his devastatingly handsome face. *My God, he's beautiful.* He towers over my seated five-foot-five frame, standing at nearly a foot taller than me. I struggle to maintain contact with his dazzling eyes and drop my gaze down to his delectable mouth. He's growing out a beard and has just enough stubble to mark my sensitive skin.

*Pull it together, Meghan. He's your boss.*

With much effort, I drag my gaze from his, afraid I might say 'fuck it' and do something stupid like offer myself up to him.

With my focus on his hair, I take in the light brown strands, with hints of natural highlights scattered throughout. It's short on the sides but not shaved, and the longer strands on top are naturally curly. He doesn't load it with product and, on many late nights going over cases, I've watched him run his fingers through it, wishing it was my own gliding into his hair.

"I'm sorry. Did you need something?" I ask, trying to mask my embarrassment behind a professional facade.

"I need the file for Walker..." he pauses, waiting for me to move, which I don't because to move past him I'd need to touch him and I'm not sure my body could handle that. When I make no move, he adds, "Now, please."

"Of course, I'll go and get it for you now," I state, pushing away from my desk and rising from my seat.

He remains standing in the small space between my desk and the corridor and I look up at him, willing him to step back so I can move past. Of course he doesn't. He just stands there, staring at me, daring me.

With my head down I brush past him, sucking in a breath as our shoulders brush before moving toward the file room.

TWO

# Cooper

I watch as she walks toward the filing room, her head down, and her usual shine dimmed. It doesn't take a genius to understand exactly what was happening before I interrupted.

Nothing ever fucking changes with my father—he's never been a dad to me. With her now not in his vicinity, I turn on my heel, walking back into my office.

*The sooner he's gone, the better.*

"Have you fucked her?" he asks, an air of arrogance about him.

"Excuse me?" I ask, affronted as I glare at him.

I walk around my desk, taking a seat as he stands in the middle of my office. I won't be offering him a seat. I need the control and power I get from being in this position with him.

"I said—"

"I heard what you said, and it's entirely inappropriate. Not only for a father and son, but for you to ask me that as her boss."

He chuckles as he takes a seat opposite me and leans back in the chair. "I'll take that as a no then." His gaze moves to the door before he continues, "So she's fair game."

Clenching my fist, I stiffen as his words sink in. I will my temper to calm down. It'll do me no good to attack him and stoop to his level.

"Let me make something very clear to you, *Elijah*," I sneer his name, ashamed that he's my father. "Meghan is my assistant and an asset to my team. Without her, half of the stuff that gets done around here never would be. She knows my next move before I even make it. She takes the time to get to know my clients and what their favorite *fucking* drinks are so that she can be prepared for when they come in. She keeps *me* on track." I press a finger into my chest as I pull in a breath, staring at him.

"It's okay to admit you want to fuck her."

Under my desk I clench and unclench my fists, barely able to resist the urge to lunge for him. How *fucking* dare he?

"I'll remind you one last time to watch what you say about her."

*Breathe, Cooper.*

He might be right, I do want to fuck her, but it's not a fuck her and discard her kind of need for me. I want to... I want to have her and make her mine. But I can't cross that line when she doesn't want it too.

A smirk spreads across his face as he leans back further in his chair. "Come on, son. It's just between us. I can help you navigate this. Protect the firm and get yourself serviced."

"Get out and don't come back," I shout.

I've had enough of his bullshit.

He has the gall to look taken aback at my statement. "Excuse me?"

"You heard me." My voice is laced with venom. "I said, get out and don't come back. If you can't treat Meghan or me with respect, then you aren't welcome here." I stand as he does, ready to take him on.

"You can't do that. My name is on the door."

"I can and I am. When you gave me the firm, it became mine. You no longer have a say in how it is run, and when you disrespect the people who work for me, you disrespect me. I won't stand for you to do either."

"I won't allow this, Cooper. You can't throw me out when you and I both know what I'm saying is the truth. You want to fuck her. You're just pissed that I'm calling you out on it. You'll do well to remember that the apple doesn't fall far from the tree."

It pains me that he's right–the apple really doesn't fall far from the fucking tree.

I need to stay away from her.

I need to not be like *him*.

Without saying a word to him, I pick up my phone and dial the building's security company, waiting for the call to connect. I'm done talking with him.

"Security, how can I help?" the unimpressed voice answers.

"This is Cooper Jackson from Jackson and Partners, I have somebody that needs to be removed on the thirtieth floor."

My father interrupts me, throwing his hands up as he says, "I'm going, Cooper. But if I walk out of that door, don't expect me to help you when you do fuck her and it all goes to shit."

Hanging up the phone without signing off, I level a stare at the 'great' Elijah Jackson. "Goodbye, Elijah."

Momentarily, his eyes flare in surprise, and I take the time to really look at him.

I didn't see him much when I was growing up. He was always too busy with work and fucking his assistants. He's no longer as physically fit as he once was, but overall he's aged well. It's probably why he tries to hit on women young enough to be his daughter.

Occasionally he likes to turn up at the office unannounced and make inappropriate passes at Meghan, that can take her days to get over. I should have dealt with it sooner, but some part of me was holding out hope that he'd change, that he'd treat me like a father is supposed to.

Today, seeing the look on her face and her palpable relief when I interrupted him, it made me realize one thing.

*Enough is enough.*

He stalks from my office and I collapse back into my

chair before grabbing my phone and shooting a text to my mom.

As a kid, whenever I would rebel against my father, he'd take his anger out on her, never physically, but verbally. He was an aggressive attorney in court, and I could see how his verbal attacks always left my mom shaken and withdrawn. She's really come out of her shell since their divorce.

A knock sounds on my door, and I call out for Meghan to enter. She steps through, her gaze darting around the room before resting on me.

"My father won't be coming back," I say, not wanting to go into the details.

"Oh." Her perfect plump lips form a perfect 'O' and I drag my gaze away, pointedly looking at the file in her hand.

Stepping forward, she places it on my desk before moving back toward the door. She hesitates before speaking. "If you don't need me for anything else, I'll get back to the report I was working on."

"Okay, what time is our catch up again?" I ask, my gaze intent on the file in front of me. I'm not taking a single word in, but I can't look at her. Not when I want to pull her into my arms and just hold her. To make everything better.

*Get your head in the game, Cooper.*

"It's at eleven."

"Thank you. I won't need you again until then."

I'm grateful I have a couple of hours without having

to interact with her. It's becoming more and more difficult to remember there is a line that can't be crossed with her. She doesn't say a word as she leaves, but when she's gone, I sit back in my chair and try to refocus my mind.

## THREE

## Meghan

I t's finally Friday and after an... interesting start to the week, I've finally managed to put the interaction with Mr. Jackson Sr. behind me.

I don't know what happened while I was in the file room, but whatever it was cast a shadow over the office, over Mr. Jackson and I, for the rest of the day. He was quiet and barely looked at me during our interactions.

Work has kept me busy with reports, organizing case files and putting the finishing touches on the firm's Christmas party that's happening tonight.

As I'm replying to an email from a prospective client, the sound of an incoming text message chimes from my phone. Finishing the email and pressing send, I pick up my phone and read the message.

ALEX

I've found the PERFECT dress for you.
It's going to look stunning and you're
going to have everyone's jaws on the
floor at the party tonight! I can't wait!!

I re-read it and let out a frustrated groan. Alex has been my best friend since we were five-years-old and she has made it her life's mission to get me to step out of my comfort zone as often as possible.

Alex is full of not-so-bright ideas and constantly suggests I wear clothes that I wouldn't normally wear, even knowing why I choose to dress the way I do.

She thinks I should show off my figure and bask in the attention, but I have no desire to do that. Yes, I'm older and wiser now, but I prefer to be out of the spotlight.

Alex is bold and not afraid to be her true self, no matter what. I'm the complete opposite, always worried about what others will think and how they might judge me or what they might try and make me do.

For unknown reasons, one night when we were having cocktails and a pamper night, I drunkenly agreed to let Alex pick my outfit for the Christmas party.

I'd been telling her—for the millionth time—all about this *thing* between Mr. Jackson and me and how I wished he would initiate the first move because I wasn't likely to.

She told me that I should seduce him with a sexy outfit at work. Stupid, drunk, Meghan had said I should do it at the Christmas party, and now here we are with sober Meghan having to be the responsible one and put a stop to these plans.

If I'm being honest, it was six months ago, and I'd forgotten about it. *More like I wished she had forgotten about it.* But the party's tonight and she clearly didn't forget because she's found a dress for me to wear.

Sometimes I hate that she knows me so well, because if she'd given me more notice, I'd have been able to get out of this. Putting my phone on the desk in front of me, I drop my head into my hands as I try in vain to think of a plan.

Urgh, if I can't convince her it's a bad idea, I'm going to have to wear whatever she's picked out for me and I'm terrified it's going to be a sexy Mrs. Claus costume or something equally bad. I wouldn't put it past her to have picked a costume rather than a dress.

One year, she tried to get me to dress as Catwoman for a Halloween party... latex suit and all. I said no to that idea before she bought the outfit, but if she had, I have no doubt I would've been guilted into wearing it.

Alex is very convincing when she wants to be.

I put the kibosh on any costumes being picked out by Alex going forward after that. Well, that was until the night I agreed she could pick my outfit for the Christmas party.

Picking up my phone, I type out a response.

MEGHAN

It's okay, you can return it.

I think I'll just wear my black dress tonight anyway. It's appropriate for a work party.

Pressing send, I put my phone down as I open the next email in my inbox. The dress I'm referring to is calf length with long sleeves and a collared neck. It's a perfectly suitable outfit for a work function. It doesn't reveal any part of my body except a slither of calf–and calves aren't sexy.

I'll accessorize it with a pair of modest heels, some light make-up, and maybe even wear my hair down. I smile to myself as I get an image of the outfit in my mind.

The sound of my phone vibrating on my desk pulls me from my thoughts.

ALEX

NO!

You agreed to let me pick your outfit.

You told me yourself that it was time you get over this crush you have on him.

This is your chance!

MEGHAN

I vaguely remember this conversation. You surely can't hold it against me?!

I was drunk, Alex!

ALEX

I can, and I am!

> You're wearing the outfit I've chosen
> for you.
>
> End of discussion.

I stare at my phone as the dots dance across the screen, waiting for her message to come through. I'm nervous, not just about the dress but because I've had a funny fluttery feeling in the pit of my stomach nearly all week.

Alex's message comes through and does nothing to ease my nerves.

> ALEX
>
> I promise we will have shots before we
> leave, so you can be drunk enough not
> to care what anyone thinks!

Tapping the side of my phone with my index finger, I take my time trying to think of a way to get her to let me off the hook. If I was having a conversation like this face-to-face with her, I'd pout and flutter my eyelashes in an attempt to get my way, although that hasn't worked for me since we were teenagers and I'd wanted to borrow her favorite winter boots, which I ruined.

Racking my brain for solutions to my predicament, I think over a couple of options. Maybe I can get ready before she comes over... No, that won't work. We'll leave work together because we live in the same building in Brooklyn, so she'll come straight to mine to get ready.

About two months after starting at the firm, an

apartment became available in Alex's building. I'd been searching for a place within my budget for a month, so I had to snap it up. I love that I have my own space and my best friend is just floors away. Although, it's no help right now.

I could pretend to be sick and say I can't go. No, that won't work either. She'd offer to stay home and look after me. I've worked too hard on organizing this event, and it's not fair to ruin her night. I need to show my face.

Before I can come up with an excuse to not wear the outfit she's picked, Alex responds.

ALEX

Got to go, you-know-who is coming.

See you in the lobby at four.

Alex's boss Belinda, or you-know-who as Alex calls her, doesn't tolerate cell phones being used during the workday, even for emergencies. She tried to fire someone once for taking a call when their wife went into labor. Thankfully HR stepped in and put a stop to it.

I release a sigh, resigning myself to my fate, because this is Alex and she's as stubborn as they come. None of my tricks or excuses will work on her. I type out a reply to let her know she'll have no further arguments from me.

MEGHAN

Fine, but there had better be at least ten shots before I even step into it! See you later.

Alex works on the twenty-fifth floor and is an associate in the property division of Jackson and Partners.

We may work for the same firm, in the same building, but we don't get to see each other that much during the day. Because of this, we go to and leave work together most days.

Even though Alex could move out and find a better place closer to work in the city, she's stayed in our rundown apartment building because if she moved we wouldn't see each other as often. I'm lucky to have her as my best friend. She's been there for me through thick and thin.

Putting my phone down, I get back to my inbox with the worry of what Alex has picked out for me in the back of my mind.

I manage to get through half of my inbox before my phone vibrates across my desk, breaking through the quiet in my corner of the office. Glancing at the time on my monitor, I decide I might as well take an early lunch. *Mom* is displayed on the screen, and I snatch it up as I connect the call.

"Hey Mom."

"Hi baby, I just wanted to see how you're doing. Is now a good time?"

"I'm good. You called at the perfect time, I'm just

going to take my lunch. How are you?"

"I'm a bit sick, but otherwise I'm okay, sweetie. Are you busy today?"

"What do you mean, you're sick?" My worry is evident in my tone.

"It's nothing, just a bug or something, so I'm getting plenty of rest."

My brow pulls into a frown and a knot of worry forms in my stomach. She sounds kind of... distant. I don't entirely believe that nothing is wrong. Whenever she's been sick, she's powered on through, taking care of the house and my dad. I make a mental note to call him and get a real answer on how she's doing.

"So long as you're getting rest and drinking plenty of fluids. How's Dad?"

"He's good. Busy with work but you know him, he can never say no. We've been talking about him retiring, but I know how much he loves what he does." She chuckles before breaking into a fit of coughs.

"Are you okay?"

"I'm fine. Just swallowed the wrong way. It's your Christmas party tonight, right?"

"Yeah. Alex brought me a dress and I'm worried what it's going to look like... You know what Alex is like."

"I'm sure she's taken into consideration your feelings. But even if she hasn't, I know she'd only be looking out for you." My mom laughs as she tries to reassure me.

My parents don't know everything that has happened to me. I don't know why I thought it would be a good idea to try and get my mom to see my point. She's always with Alex, trying to get me to live my best life.

We chat for a while longer before she breaks out into more coughing and says she needs to lie down. As soon as we hang up, I shoot a quick message off to my dad.

It feels like something more is happening with her.

Mr. Jackson comes strolling into the office a little before four. His navy-blue suit jacket is draped over one arm, with the other holding his briefcase.

I take a moment to look him over. He really is a beautiful man, with a well-defined jaw, high cheekbones, and a straight nose that gives him model-like features. I could drown in his stunning blue eyes. His hair is messy from having run his fingers through it during his day and is a sign that court might not have gone as well as he hoped.

As he walks past my desk, I suck in a breath and pretend to be typing out an email. My eyes are unfocused as I randomly mash the keys on my keyboard. I'm grateful that he doesn't stop like he sometimes does for a run down of his day. As he walks into his office, I release the breath I'm holding at the sound of the door clicking shut.

Finally able to focus on the screen in front of me, I finish up the report I've been working on all afternoon and load it onto an email to send to the finance team to pick up on Monday. Checking that I don't have any urgent items to finish before the end of the day, I finalize a file for a new client and shut down my computer.

Gathering my belongings, I make my way over to his door, dragging in a deep breath before knocking lightly. Greeted with a muffled call to enter, I open the door and am immediately assaulted by his woodsy, masculine scent as I try my hardest to keep my thoughts focused.

He's busy typing away on his laptop as I walk into the center of the room. I take the opportunity to allow my greedy gaze to roam over him again. His jacket is long gone and the white of his shirt is a stark contrast to his tanned skin tone. I don't know why, but with his burgundy tie tugged loose and his top button undone, the urge to lick the space exposed there is strong.

*My self-control when it comes to him is becoming harder and harder to control.*

Having allowed myself to have my fill, I rest my gaze on the framed photo of the New York skyline that hangs on the wall behind him as I push my glasses up the bridge of my nose.

"I'm heading out now. Do you have a minute to go over the schedule for Monday?" I ask.

"Sure, we'll be quick."

I move toward the chairs in front of his desk, taking a seat and pulling my notebook from my purse. "Okay, at eight you have a conference call with Mr. Evans. The call is to discuss the class action suit that came in on

Wednesday. At ten you have a call with a Mr. Monroe." I push my glasses up again. "He's—"

"He's a friend. I know why he's calling," he replies, almost bored.

"Oh, okay. At eleven I've scheduled you some final prep time for the Dixon and co. trial that starts at two. I've kept you free for the rest of the day." I lift my gaze from the notebook to him. He's staring out of the window.

At the silence that's building, he turns to me. "Okay, thank you. You can head off now."

I stand, my focus on fitting my notebook back in my bag. "Will you be making an appearance at the party?" I have no idea why I just asked him that. It shouldn't be of any concern to me if he comes or not.

I'm met with silence. Begrudgingly, I bring my eyes to his face and am captivated by his striking blue eyes, staring back at me. Studying me. I want to fidget and ask what he's looking at, but my tongue is heavy in my mouth and I can't get a word past my lips.

Sitting behind the mahogany desk, he's leaning back, assessing me, with one elbow on the arm of his chair, his chin resting on his fist. The air is hot and electric as we stare at each other.

The world could end, and I would have no idea that it did. I flick my tongue out over my suddenly dry lips. His eyes dart down to my mouth before he blinks and a slight smirk flits across his face. My eyes are focused on his full lips and when he opens it to talk, his straight white teeth sparkle back at me.

"Yes, I'll see you then," he replies. "Oh, and Meghan? I'm going to need you to book us some flights and a hotel for a week on Monday. We're heading to Miami to meet a prospective client and we'll be gone for two nights."

I nod in response before heading out of his office, making my way to the lobby to meet Alex. In the year that I've worked for him, we've never had to go away for a client meeting. They've always come to us.

Two thoughts run through my head as the elevator descends to the lobby: one, I need to figure out how to book the travel arrangements and two, for two nights, it's going to be just Mr. Jackson and me.

My gut is telling me something is going to happen tonight, but I can't tell if it's a good or bad thing.

FOUR

## Cooper

The door clicks closed softly behind Meghan, and I sit in the silence of my office with her sweet perfume lingering in the air. I lean back in my chair, staring out of the window, luxuriating in the sweet scent of honey and vanilla that she's left in her wake.

Whenever she's near, I've felt some kind of... spark, I guess. I'm certain it's one-sided. I mean, she can barely look at me when we talk, so it's not likely that she'd feel anything remotely romantic for me. I've watched her with other people and she has no issues talking to them.

Is she... scared of me?

I know I can be a demanding boss, but I've never once raised my voice at her or used my size to intimidate her. In fact, I've started to stay quiet on purpose now.

It's become a game of sorts for me, to see how long it takes for her to divert her gaze once it's landed on me.

I'm not in the habit of playing games with my assistants, but for some reason, the fact she won't look me in the eye when she's talking to me kind of irks me.

Women love me—I don't say that to be big headed, in fact it's the reason I had to get a new assistant, but for some reason I get the impression she'd rather be doing anything else but engaging in a conversation with me.

Meanwhile, I'm over here picturing her every time I jerk off. It's fucking with my mind.

*Maybe I should cross the line.*

*No, that's a bad idea.*

As much as I want to feel her wrapped around me, I don't mess with my assistants, not after the drama with my parents and my father's infidelity with his own assistant. And Meghan, is too important to lose.

Maria would kill me if she knew I was even entertaining the idea of fucking Meghan. I was given a stern lecture after Meghan's interview, something along the lines of asking for a lawsuit and that I'd done so well in my tenure as managing partner to not live up to the stereotype the other managing partners had painted of me.

My father's wandering eye was no secret, and much to my annoyance, I've been tarred with the same brush, with zero evidence. You'd have thought a firm of lawyers would know better.

I know that it's not just a sexual attraction—although I am attracted to her. It's the way she scrunches her brow as she completes the finance reports she despises. She was refreshingly honest in her interview about that fact. Or something as simple as how she pushes her glasses up—always with her right index finger.

It's the curve of her neck when she tilts her head when she's being sympathetic and listening to a client in need. Or the way she has no idea how alluring she is. It's like she is completely blind to her own beauty, both inside and out. She has no idea as to the effect she has on me.

Letting out a sigh of frustration, I lean back further in my chair and close my eyes. For the last ten months, I've let my imagination run wild because as much as I want her, I know I can't have her. I'm her boss, for Christ's sake, and I can't put her in that sort of position—especially when it's only based on something as insignificant as attraction.

On occasion, I indulge myself and imagine what she'd taste like. I think she'd taste sweet. Shifting in my chair, I feel myself harden at the thought of her on my tongue. I think that at first, as I devoured her, she would be shy and reserved before coming undone and giving as good as she got.

*Get a grip Cooper, it's not happening.*

Being able to make her feel comfortable enough to be herself with me would be a huge turn on, but it's just not going to happen.

Although, I'm not sure I could hold back again if she looked at me like she had the other day. It was a miracle I stayed only semi-hard when her wet, pink tongue had darted out to flick across her plump lips as she looked at my crotch.

My mind was immediately filled with images of her soft, wet mouth wrapped around my cock. I wanted to lift her up, undress her from those awful clothes and fuck her senseless right there on her desk. But then I remembered why I was asking her to go to the file room and I got mad again.

Don't even get me started on the rage that coursed through my body when I looked up from a file I was reviewing and saw my father *touching* her. The look on her face when she'd seen me standing in my doorway was the only thing that stopped me from launching myself at him. I want to be the man that rescues her, not scare her away.

Running a hand through my hair, I let out a frustrated breath as I look out over downtown Manhattan. Fuck it, I'm going to call Vivian. She's usually available on a Friday and doesn't require romancing. I can fuck her without worrying that she'll become attached, and right now I need to fill my mind with images that aren't Meghan.

Vivian and I have an understanding that we will only see each other when we're both unattached and that we'll never be more than a hook-up to each other. I should've called her the evening of Meghan's interview —and I was going to—but when I'd gone to dial her number, a pair of captivating green eyes flashed through my mind and I couldn't bring myself to press the call button.

*I need to get over this obsession with Meghan.*

Deciding to finish for the day as my concentration is gone, I clear my desk, shut down my laptop and gather some files I'll work on over the weekend. It's been a hell of a week, and I'm ready to unwind. I'll just need to get through an hour or two of the firm's Christmas party before I can meet up with Vivian.

Cracking my neck as I stand, I stretch my body, tired from a long week. For a moment, I consider not going to the party at all, but when I remind myself of all the hard work Meghan and others have put into the planning. I don't intend on staying any longer than necessary because realistically, nobody's going to let loose when the boss is around.

Most years I've skipped any work functions that weren't designated for team building, but a nagging feeling has taken over me the past week and I've always been one to listen to my gut.

Making sure I have everything I need, I switch off the office lights as I make my way to the elevator, calling my driver, Christopher.

For this year's party, we've rented out Passion, a club owned by my good friend Sebastian Worthington. Sebastian—or Seb, as he prefers to be called—is a self-made billionaire from England. He has four clubs around the world. I've known Seb since he opened Passion eight years ago.

We were introduced by our mutual friend, Damien Houston, at a gentleman's club in the city. Initially, I thought Seb was a womanizing asshole that I had nothing in common with. After all, every time I saw him, he had a different woman on his arm.

As our friendship progressed, I came to realize that he keeps people at a distance for a reason. At twenty-two he was overly confident and brash, to my studious and reserved personality–not much has changed.

Normally, Passion would open at ten, but Seb has agreed to open an hour later and so we have the club to ourselves for the start of the evening. I arrive around eight, surprised to see there are so many people here already.

Heading toward the bar, I order a neat Macallan 18, surveying the club as I lean back against the bar. *All I Want for Christmas* by Mariah Carey plays from the speakers and I hum along to my guilty pleasure Christmas song.

Fairy lights are draped around booths and along the bar, adding to the ambience and the light chatter of people mingling broken up with the occasional bout of laughter makes the room feel surprisingly cheerful.

"Cooper, it's good to see you! How are you?" Seb calls as he comes to stand next to me, leaning back against the bar and mirroring my stance.

"Seb, it's nice to see you too, man. I'm okay, thanks. How are you?" I bring my drink to my lips for a sip and let my eyes roam around the crowd looking for her.

I can't feel her presence like I normally can, but it doesn't stop me from searching for a glimpse of her.

"I'm not too bad, business is booming... partly thanks to your booking." He laughs, confirming my suspicion that I didn't get any friends and family discount. I direct a glare in his direction but he continues, oblivious to my expression, "I didn't expect to see you here tonight. Thought it would be more of a *let the worker bees party without the boss* kind of thing."

"I'd much rather be enjoying the company of a beautiful woman." I down my drink, trying to quiet my inner voice as it screams Meghan's name at me.

Turning around, I signal to the bartender for another, resting my elbows on the bar as I wait.

*If I get drunk enough, maybe I'll forget the way she consumes my every thought.*

"I like what your Meghan has done with the place."

"She isn't mine," I grumble.

"She's not your assistant? Did you give into the temptation, Coop?" Seb chuckles as he throws back his drink.

"She *is* my assistant and there's no temptation to give in to." I sigh, because I know damn well she is my temptation and I would surrender myself to her willingly. I throw back my drink and signal for another.

*The sooner I can get out of here, the better.*

Seb and I chat for an hour or so more, catching up since we haven't seen each other for months. He tells me about his plans to open a fifth club and the issues he's having with his legal team, so I invite him into the office, offering up the firm's help.

More people have filtered in and the drinks are flowing freely, before I decide I've been here long enough to make the rounds and check-in before leaving. Although I'm an attorney by trade and making small talk is part of the job, I still struggle with it.

After some painful conversations with people treading on eggshells, I make my way back to the bar, almost wishing I hadn't come. Seb, who has been surveying the club and watching as I've floundered my way around the party, laughs at the awkwardness of the conversations I've had.

"That was entertaining to watch."

"It's not my fault everyone's scared of me. I hardly speak to most of these people."

"That's probably where you've gone wrong. Maybe you need to actually get to know them." Seb smirks like a know-it-all as he takes a sip of his drink.

"Maybe," I grumble.

After a moment of quiet, Seb asks, "I heard Damien is considering a run for mayor."

"Wouldn't that be funny? He's got the charm, that's for sure, but I'm not sure he knows enough about the New York political circuit for the job."

"Can't be any worse than Harry Belrose. It wouldn't

surprise me if there was another scandal in the not so distant future."

"I don't know man. Damien's spent too long in Texas to jump back into..."

My words trail off as my eyes dart toward the entrance, as if drawn to it. My heart skips a beat, my palms sweat and my mouth goes dry as she comes into view behind another woman I vaguely recognize.

I can tell it's her, even with her made up so different to how she is at work. Her blonde hair frames the feminine features of her face and her body is wrapped in a tight, dark pink dress that shows her curves off to perfection.

A spark of jealousy courses through me as I think of the man that will get to have her in his bed, as his woman. I drink her in, as if she's an oasis and I've been stranded in the desert.

"Wow. If she isn't yours, then I'll definitely have to have a taste." Seb steps away from the bar and straightens his shoulders, his gaze is fixed on Meghan.

"If you so much as breathe in her direction, I will end you." My gaze doesn't leave her.

Seb laughs and takes a sip of his drink as I continue to watch her as she slinks through the club.

# FIVE

## Meghan

TWO HOURS EARLIER

Alex and I stand in my living room, surveying the items she's brought with her. My hair is in the rollers she insisted I put in, and I'm dressed in my usual house clothes of sleep shorts and a strappy top. Alex is dressed like she's headed to the gym in a matching burgundy sports bra and leggings.

*The dress* is laid over the back of my second-hand jade green couch, making it look cheaper than it already does, and the dress bag is discarded on the floor by Alex's sneaker-clad feet.

She unveiled it in a flourish, like a proud mother hen and her smile didn't fade, even as my eyes widened and my mouth hung open in shock. I've not been able to utter a single word to her. I'm grateful that she's been content to let me process the scrap of material she's expecting me to wear.

My gaze darts between the dress, the death trap

57

heels, and the matching clutch bag. *This must have cost her a small fortune.* I'm not wearing it. It's all going to go to waste unless Alex wears it, which isn't likely seeing as we haven't been the same size since high school.

The thought of stepping outside wearing it is giving me palpitations and I press my hand to my chest in an effort to ease my racing heart.

When I was nineteen, and working in a diner not far from my childhood home, we had a uniform of tight white tank tops and denim shorts. After dropping out of college, I took the first job that was paying a decent enough wage to allow me to move out of my parents' house and gain some form of independence, like I'd had in college.

I only worked at the diner for four months before I couldn't take any more. Men old enough to be my dad were trying to grope me, and even on occasion waiting for me after my shift.

The thought of being the center of attention causes a physical reaction in me. I know that I need to stop allowing my past to dictate my future, because I'm older and wiser now. I'm just not sure I'm ready for tonight to be the night that I do.

Turning to face Alex, I resolve to try one final time to get out of wearing the outfit she's brought. "Alex, please. I can't wear this dress. Everyone will stare at me, and you know I can't handle that. I'll do anything you want, just don't make me wear it... please." I give her my best puppy dog eyes. I'm about five seconds away from getting on my knees and begging her at this point.

She folds her arms across her chest as if to make sure I can't penetrate her hard exterior with my pleas. "You promised me. You said I could pick your outfit and that you would wear it. No arguments."

"I know, but this is so far from what I'd normally wear, it's not fair!"

She beams at me as she wiggles on the spot in triumph. Oh God, she's going to pull out her ace card. "Do you remember that time I got you out of having to talk to that creepy guy, Dustin, from The Dive? Well, I'm also calling in the favor you promised me then."

*Urgh.*

I know she has a point and I remember telling her that if I say no, she should stick to her guns. And I guess I owe her for the Dustin situation, but... *that's not the point.* I don't want to stick out, not tonight. Not when everyone we work with is going to be there. I'd feel much safer wearing this to a New Year's Eve party or something.

*Why can't she just agree with me and let me off the hook for the promise?*

"I know, but I thought you would pick something more... me." I let out an exasperated breath. I'm panicking now. With one hand on my forehead and one on my waist, I pace up and down my small apartment lounge, careful not to bang my shin on the low oak coffee table.

*I can't wear this dress.*

It's too... sexy.

Too risky.

Too flashy.

Too... *everything*.

I'm close to hyperventilating when a shot of tequila is thrust under my nose. Grabbing it, I toss it back, so distracted with my panic that I don't register the burn.

Alex refills the glass and I throw the second shot back before I start to feel the buzz from the alcohol. Holding my glass out for another, I try to burn a hole in the dress with my gaze.

I know I'm going to end up wearing it tonight.

Ultimately, I do know I need to step out of my comfort zone and stop allowing my past to have such a strong hold over me. I want to be bold and brave enough to wear clothes that make me feel desirable.

"Just try it on and then we can see if you still feel the same way," Alex suggests as she fills my glass up again. Placing the bottle on the side table next to the couch, she rests her hands on my shoulders as I throw back the clear liquid.

I really should've eaten something.

Maybe I can have a snack before we leave.

"Meghan." I lift my gaze to Alex as she calls my name. "You need to realize that you are a beautiful woman who needs to stop hiding her beauty under frumpy, oversized clothes that do nothing for her figure. You have a figure that most women would kill for. I mean, come on, you look like a young Pamela Anderson."

Alex pushes the dress and shoes into my hand and turns me toward my bathroom.

I swipe the tequila bottle off of the side table as Alex pushes me toward the bathroom with a friendly shove to my back. Letting out a heavy sigh, I take a generous swig directly from the bottle before placing it on the counter along with my no longer needed shot glass.

"That's my girl." I hear Alex chuckle through the closed door as I turn on the shower and, even though she can't see me, I roll my eyes at her smugness.

*She hasn't won yet.*

Placing the dress on the back of the door, I sit on the toilet seat lid and stare at it before picking up the tequila bottle and taking several deep swigs.

*Can I do this?*

I stand on slightly unstable legs and nod firmly. *Yes, I can.*

*Yes, I can*, I chant to myself as I shower.

Scrubbed clean and smelling of strawberries, I step out of the shower and dry myself with one of the few luxuries I afford myself, a large fluffy white towel.

Even rubbing the soft material over my body doesn't distract me from the dress that's taunting me on the back of the door. My gaze keeps drifting to it until I turn my back to finish drying myself.

Swiping the bottle from the counter, I take one final swig, because if I drink much more we won't be going anywhere. Blindly, I put the bottle back before I grab the dress off of the hanger and step into it.

The silky fabric rubs over my sensitive skin as I pull the dress up my body before slipping my arms into the straps. Finding the zipper under my arm, I zip myself into the almost skintight dress.

My suspicions are confirmed as I look at my reflection. It's going to be too tight for a bra and will most likely show any visible panty line. With reluctance, I will have to forgo underwear and allow the material to caress my skin.

It's a beautiful dusty pink mini dress with spaghetti straps, and a deep scoop neckline that shows far too much cleavage, if you ask me.

It hugs every curve on my body and cups my chest to the point I'm sure I could jump around and my breasts wouldn't escape. It comes to around mid-thigh and shows far more skin than I've shown in a very long time.

Admiring my reflection in the mirror, I rub my hands over my body, before turning around to view the practically non-existent back.

There's no denying that the dress hugs the curve of my ass, making it look perky and full. I quickly realize I was right about this dress; it's everything I thought it was.

*Too sexy, too risky, too flashy, too everything.*

Slowly opening the bathroom door, I'm greeted by what can only describe as a squeal from Alex. I've certainly never heard her make a noise like that before and for a moment, I forget my anxiousness and chuckle at her silliness.

"Oh my God, Meghan, it fits you better than I could've imagined." She twirls her finger in the air and I turn on the spot as directed. She lets out a whistle and I blush. "Come, let's do your hair and make-up."

"I'm still not one hundred percent sold on this outfit. It just feels a bit too much for a work party."

Alex stops in her tracks and turns to face me. "You look hot. You're wearing the dress. Don't forget we'll be clubbing afterward, plus I have a plan to get you laid. You can't keep pining over a man that barely acknowledges you, Meghan. You could meet a guy tonight and hook up with him, then who knows what might come of it."

*Damn*. It was worth one last shot.

After tonight I'm not drinking with Alex ever again, because apparently I agree to do stupid things when I do.

An hour later, my waist-length hair is curled and combed out, with half of it up in a ponytail and some wavy strands of hair hanging around my face.

My eye make-up is smoky and my lips are coated in a generous layer of lip gloss—Alex said something about guys liking girls with wet-looking lips when she was applying it and who am I to argue?

She's worked some magic to make my cheekbones stand out and finished my face with a light dusting of blush across my cheeks. I hardly recognize myself, but I also feel beautiful and... sexy.

If I'm being honest with myself, I feel like a damn goddess.

I admire Alex's work while trying to keep my face neutral and not give away how confident and sexy I feel. I know Alex well enough to know that she'll have me with a whole new wardrobe come Monday otherwise... maybe that isn't such a bad idea. I could switch up my wardrobe, get some much needed confidence and put myself back out there into the dating world.

*Imagine wearing a dress like this to work...*

Okay, that isn't happening. In fact, it's laughable. It's one thing to go on a night out dressed like this, but it's another thing entirely to wear it in the office.

"Now, you just need to put your contacts in, some perfume on and we're good to go," Alex instructs, her focus on clearing away her things.

It takes longer than I would care to admit putting my contacts in. Unsurprisingly, I'm not that keen on sticking my finger in my eye and so I rarely wear them. Once they're in and I can see clearly, I spray on some perfume and grab my calf-length brown faux fur coat.

To complete my outfit, I slip on the five-inch heels that match my dress and I kind of love how they accentuate my legs, but walking in them is another story.

*This should be fun.*

Placing my ID, credit card, and some cash in the matching handbag, along with the lip gloss and my keys, I turn to Alex before shaking out my hands in an effort to shake off my nerves.

"Megs." *God, I hate that nickname.* She only uses it when we're going out to party. "We are going to have an amazing night, and I'm going to make sure you get laid and break this dry spell you're in."

"I don't need your help getting laid," I chuckle.

She loops her arm through mine as we head toward the front door.

"Believe me, you do. It's been something like a year, right?" she asks, quirking an eyebrow and I'm suddenly curious as to how she knows that. Last time I checked, I hadn't divulged that piece of information.

"How did you know? I didn't tell you when I last had sex..." I furrow my brow and look up at her.

"You didn't need to. I put two and two together and you just confirmed it. So we are going to find a sexy man for you to go home with," she affirms as we make our way onto the street to grab a cab.

As we step out of the semi-warmth of our building, I huddle into my coat as the cold air hits me. Unusual for New York this time of year, we haven't had any snow, but the air is bitterly cold–like chill you to the bones and have you puffing out white clouds with every breath type of cold.

Huffing out a breath but not bothering to argue with Alex because she's right, I glance at my watch as she hails a cab. It's just after seven-thirty, depending on traffic it should take us around forty-five minutes to get to Passion.

The cab pulls up outside of Passion and I can hear Christmas music playing inside as I step onto the sidewalk. Pulling my coat tighter around my body, I wait for Alex as she pays the driver. I take the opportunity to take in the neighborhood.

I've never been to this club before—aside from checking out the venue and setting up the party. During the day, the block was practically dead, but tonight it's thriving with what I'm guessing are successful people.

The building itself is inconspicuous, but the two restaurants with valet parking and expensive cars lining the street tell me the club would typically be out of my price range.

*Thank God for an open bar tonight.*

One bouncer covers the door and since we have the club booked until eleven, there's no queue on the sidewalk when we arrive. Alex, sensing my worry, gave me a pep talk on the ride over and pulled out a small flask of tequila.

With her words ringing in my mind, and the alcohol flowing through my veins, I'm ready to strut my way into the club and have a good time.

We head over to the bouncer and give him our names and that of the firm. Alex flashes him a smile. He throws her a wink, and she responds by running her hand down his arm and squeezing his bulging bicep, before walking inside, an extra sway in her hips.

Not a single word is exchanged between them and I'm left to mutter an awkward *thank you,* as I follow Alex, stumbling in my heels to catch up with her.

Once inside, we hand over our coats and tuck away our collection tabs before we make our way to the door that leads to the party. I inhale a deep breath before blowing it out harshly. My palms feel damp with sweat and I rub them on my exposed thighs in an effort to remove some of the wetness.

The music and chatter of people having a good time dims to a muted sound as it hits me that I'm about to walk into a room full of people I work with, wearing the sexiest outfit I've ever worn. I'm now feeling more self conscious and awkward than confident and sexy.

Maybe I can go back and grab my coat... it can't get that hot in a club, surely? Or, even better, I can just go home, put on my PJ's, and pretend it's any other night.

Sensing my internal panic, Alex comes up behind me and puts her arm around my waist, pulling me into her side. Taking comfort in her gesture, I close my eyes and lean further into her, allowing her to ease some of my worry.

"Remember Megs, no looking at the floor. Go in there and own the room. We'll go to the bar and get you a huge drink, do the rounds, and then find a seat," she whispers in my ear.

I nod in response. "As annoying as you can be sometimes, I do love you, Alex. You're like the sister I never had but desperately wanted. Thank you for pushing me out of my comfort zone... I think."

"Love you too, Megs. Now let's go," she commands, removing her arm from my waist and grabbing my hand, pulling me through the doors into the main area of the club.

Even though I set up the space this afternoon, I take in the room as if for the first time. We've decorated fairy lights around to add a Christmas twinkle and a small tree sits next to the DJ booth—it'll be removed when the doors open to the public.

There are booth tables on either side of the room, with the bar stretching the length of the back wall. A pool of standing tables are well spaced in the area in front of the bar and there's a dance floor taking over a little more than half of the room.

The DJ booth is at the opposite end of the room, next to the stairs that lead to the VIP area, and there's a corridor directly across from us that leads to the restrooms.

My gaze skims the room and, although I see a couple of people lift their eyes to look at us as we enter, it's nothing more than I would expect. Alex leads me toward the bar and as I follow behind her, my eyes find Mr. Jackson, as if they've been searching for him this entire time.

He's talking to the owner, but when his crystal blue eyes find mine, he stops and just stares at me. The look in his eyes is hot... almost lustful, like he wants to strip me of all my clothes and devour me. After a beat, I drop my gaze to the floor, unable to withstand the effect he has on me *and* walk in these sky high heels.

*My body feels like it's on fire.*

Alex nudges her shoulder against mine, pulling me from my thoughts and leans down to whisper to me, "What did I say, Megs? No looking at the floor."

Lifting my gaze to her, I nod, not wanting to get into the real reason for my eyes dropping. Following Alex toward the bar, my head held high, my shoulders pulled back, and my spine straight, I vow to put him out of my mind and have a fun night.

## SIX

*Meghan*

I have had way too much to drink... but I'm having the best time. Other than being hit on by a few of the creepy guys from work—who got the message when I made my lack of interest clear—nobody has paid me much attention. Alex has been so supportive. She's stuck by my side all night and included me in conversations with her work friends.

*Compared to me, she's such a social butterfly.*

Passion opened at eleven and our work party moved upstairs to the VIP area we'd booked. The party is in full swing. The balcony has a great view overlooking the dance floor, and I sit watching the crowd of bodies moving to the rhythm of *Piece Of Your Heart* by Meduza and Goodboys.

Nobody seems to dance up here. Instead, people are hanging out in groups having animated conversations. I fidget in my seat, trying to keep the urge to go and dance at bay. My body is begging to be touched, to be caressed, even by a complete stranger.

*Maybe Alex had the right idea to get me laid.*

At this point, I'd even settle for a gentle graze of my breast.

Taking a moment to survey the crowd, my thoughts are pulled to Mr. Jackson—as they so often are. I haven't seen him tonight aside from the moment when I arrived, and it wouldn't come as a complete shock if it turns out he's already left for the night. He isn't really one for socializing at the office, so I'm not surprised he isn't doing it here.

*It would've been nice for him to come and say hi.*

A part of me had hoped he would stalk across the club and whisk me away to some secret location to act on the need I think I saw reflected in his gaze. Did I imagine the looks he's been giving me recently? *Maybe.* I feel dejected at the fact that he's probably left and didn't bother to say goodbye to me.

"Hi, mind if I take this seat?" a deep masculine voice asks.

"No, of course not," I reply, expecting him to literally take the seat and move away.

"I'm Alfie, do you work for Jackson and Partners too?" he asks, causing me to turn in my seat to face him.

He's holding his hand out to me and I place my own in it as I look him over from head to toe, not bothering to hide my perusal of his body. He's a handsome guy, I guess. He stands about six-foot and has dark blond hair that's cut short. He's got an obviously muscular body based on the way his shirt looks like it could rip with a wrong move, but he just isn't my type.

*He isn't Cooper Jackson.*

"Hi Alfie, yes I do. I'm Mr. Jackson's Assistant, Meghan," I shout over the music before sipping through the straw of my drink. I guess I really do look different tonight, seeing as Alfie works on my floor as an associate.

"You look different... like good different. Have you had a fun night, Meghan?" he shouts back, leaning into me, resting his hand on the back of my chair. I nod in response before he continues, "We're heading to another club, if you wanna come?"

"I'm gonna stay here, but thanks for asking," I reply.

"Maybe next time. We should grab lunch or something soon," he responds. Standing from the seat, he looks down at me as if he wants to say something else before saying goodbye and walking away. He's gone from my mind and sight within seconds.

One of my favorite songs, *Gold* by Kiiara, blasts through the speakers and I glance over at Alex to see if she wants to come and dance, but she's immersed in conversation. I don't need Alex to dance. I've got this by myself.

*I'm going to dance and I don't need Alex to hold my hand.*

Standing on not so steady legs, I make my way toward the stairs that lead to the main floor of the club. The bouncer manning the VIP entrance moves the rope aside and I totter in my heels down the stairs, holding onto the railing as I go.

*Whoever thought it would be a good idea to put stairs in a club is a fool.*

Safely at the bottom, I make my way through the crowd of revelers before stepping onto the dance floor.

Swaying my hips to the beat of the song, my hands roam up and down my body and through my hair as I make my way to the center of the dance floor. It's crowded with people moving as one to the music, bodies crushing against bodies. I lose myself to the music and it's as if everyone else fades away.

*Desire* by Meg Myers comes on and as I'm getting lost in the song, I feel a warm body pressing up against my back. This is different to the crush of strangers that I've been moving to the beat with for the last thirty minutes.

This body feels... connected to me.

The scent from whoever is behind me is familiar, and I close my eyes as the smell I've inhaled for the last year meets my senses. I imagine it's Mr. Jackson behind me; his clean, woodsy, masculine scent envelopes me as our bodies move as one.

It's been so long since I've been sexually satisfied— and I'm so *fucking* horny—that's the only excuse I have for my actions.

I grind into his crotch, feeling an impressive bulge that seems to be growing with every swipe of my ass. A moan rises to the tip of my tongue, begging to burst through my lips.

*I hope he's hot, because I just might end my drought tonight.*

Large masculine hands slide around my waist, pulling me closer, before settling on my hips, pushing me further into his hard cock.

When one hand moves up to cup my chest just under my breast, holding my torso in place. I know I should be worried about the power he has over me, but instead, I relax back into his embrace as we grind into each other.

All of my instincts are telling me this is a safe place to be, that what I've been waiting for is going to be mine tonight.

Lost in the rhythm of the music, I move my hands up behind me into his hair as I tilt my head to the side and bring his mouth down to the crook of my neck, practically begging him to taste me... to do anything and everything.

If he moves his hand under the hem of my skirt, and I'm secretly hoping he does, he will find me dripping wet.

I think I hear him whisper my name, but with the loud music and how much I've had to drink, I can't be certain.

For a brief moment, I contemplate pulling away and asking him what he said, but the moment his tongue comes out and swipes across my neck, my mind goes blank.

When his mouth moves up to nip my earlobe and he releases a growl next to my ear, I'm lost, and honestly couldn't tell you my own name, let alone form a question.

*I feel sexy and... desirable.*

Maybe tonight I can finally get over Mr. Jackson—I just have to work up the courage to burst my own bubble and face the man I've been grinding on for the past thirty minutes. Before I can make a move or any sort of proposition, his warmth disappears and an overwhelming feeling of disappointment comes over me.

*I was so close to ending my dry spell.*

I'm about to groan in frustration when someone grabs my wrist, causing a gasp to escape my lips as a bolt of electricity jolts through me.

Suddenly, I'm dragged through the crowd by the same, oh-so-familiar, muscular hands that had been all over me moments ago.

My disappointment fades, but as we make our way to a secluded part of the club, it dawns on me that I still haven't seen his face.

I follow him down a corridor and through a door that leads into a small room. It's dark, but I can make out a table in the middle with high backed chairs surrounding it. He closes the door behind us before pushing me against the back of it.

There's still no worry or fear in me, but I can't be certain that isn't down to a false bravado the drinks I've had tonight have given me.

I can still hear the music from the club, although it's much quieter now. His hands rest on my hips, and I lift my gaze to his face. It's illuminated by the glow of the green exit sign above us. My stomach clenches and plummets to my feet as I look up.

*Oh God, I'm in so much shit.*

I was practically riding him on the dance floor.

*Okay, maybe it wasn't him and he just pulled me away from a stranger.*

*Come on, Meghan.*

Deep down, I knew it was him. Nobody has caused a reaction in me like he does. *Cooper Jackson.*

"Meghan, what are we doing?" he growls, his voice husky as he moves his body closer to me and I feel his hardness pressing into my stomach.

I release a tortured moan before my tongue darts out and over my suddenly dry lips. I'm fairly certain I'm dreaming—I've had a dream like this once before.

I'm going with it's a dream.

Resting my hands on his chest, I glide them down to his belt buckle before moving lower over his impressive erection, giving him a gentle squeeze.

His moan fills my ears and I rub my thighs together to try and relieve the ache forming in my core.

I'm too busy following the movement of my hands and don't fully register the way his eyes have darkened with lust or that his own hands have fisted at his side in an attempt to not touch me.

As this is a dream, I take my time to think about what I want to do first. My dreams usually end with him devouring me in bed—against a wall will be a new experience that I'm definitely not against.

*I want a kiss.*

Removing my hands from exploring his lower half, I glide them up his chest before throwing my arms around his neck and pressing my body further into his. I kiss him softly at first, my lips coaxing his own open.

This feels like... *coming home.*

"Cooper," I purr against his lips. "You're still here. I thought I'd missed you. Have you come to dance with me?" I say, as I pull back fully from him and smooth my hands down his solid chest.

I barely notice the way his eyes rake over my body or how his jaw is clenched and ticking. He looks sexy in his slim-fit black jersey trousers, white shirt, and dark gray jacket.

*He was wearing this when I saw him in real life.*

I hear him say *fuck* before his hands coast into my hair and he lifts my face to his, crashing his lips against mine.

It's messy, and our teeth clash as we give into our hunger for each other. He nips at my lips, and the sting shoots straight to my core, causing me to moan into his mouth.

My final thought before I give myself up to the sensations he's awakening in me is... *Is this real?*

SEVEN

Cooper

I'm in shock. That's the only plausible explanation for what I did, that and the whiskey flowing through my veins. I lost my resolve and kissed Meghan—*my assistant*—like I've wanted to for a long time.

I dove my hands into the softest locks of hair I have ever felt and crushed my lips to hers, devouring her. I trapped her body between mine and the wall in our hidden room in the club, and when I slid my hands under her dress and found her naked, I knew I had to take her home.

Now we're standing in the corridor outside my apartment as my fingers fumble with the keys to get the door unlocked. Her hands roam over my back, amping up my lust for her, and even though I know I'll probably regret this in the morning, my ability to resist her has finally broken.

*I'm going to have her tonight—if I can get into my damn apartment.*

"Hurry," she murmurs, a pleading note in her voice telling me she wants this as much as I do. The softness of her body presses into the hardness of my back as her hands move around my waist to explore my chest.

Finally shoving the door open, I turn around to wrap my arm around her delicate waist and pull her over the threshold.

Burying my nose into the column of her neck like I've imagined so many times before, I inhale her sweet scent, placing kisses and licking from her jaw to her shoulder.

She lets out the sexiest sound I've ever heard as her head tips back, giving me more access and urging me on.

"Meghan…" I groan, resting my forehead on hers.

I can't go any further if she doesn't tell me she's okay with this. If she wants to stop, I'll tuck her into my spare bed and leave her alone. It'll be the hardest thing I've ever done, but I won't take advantage of her, no matter how much I want her.

"Don't stop now. Please," she begs, answering my unasked question.

*God, I want her so much.*

My mouth crashes down on hers as I bend down, wrapping my hands around the back of her thighs and lifting her up. Her dress rolls up around her hips with the motion, and I vaguely register the sound of her shoes falling to the floor.

Pressing her body against the wall, I continue to

devour her mouth. An overwhelming need to consume all of her runs through me.

She rolls her hips against my stomach and moans into me at the pressure on her core before tearing her lips away from mine. She drags in gulping breaths, our breathing the only sound in the room as I try to get a read on her in the shadows.

I've never had this connection with someone before. I've never experienced a need so strong that it feels like I want to bury my soul in hers. I can't tell where I start and she ends.

Mentally shaking my head to clear away the intense thoughts because this is only one night, I remind myself that if this was more, I'd have felt something deeper than what I did for her over the last year.

"Cooper?" she calls. It's barely a whisper, but her voice is breathy, and I can hear the hint of confusion at the fact that I've stopped.

Having adjusted to the darkness, I stare into what I know are her moss green eyes. I can see they're a little glazed from the alcohol, but there's no confusing the lust evident in them.

Brushing a strand of blonde hair out of the way, I capture her mouth with my own again before parting her lips and tangling my tongue with hers.

*I need to get out of my head and enjoy the woman in front of me.*

My feet move us towards the stairs, dodging the

furniture as we go, my hands braced on her bare ass cheeks with her legs tightly wrapped around my waist. I can feel the heat from her pussy through my shirt, and I growl into her mouth at the thought of what is yet to come.

She breaks the kiss and rests her forehead on mine as I carry her up the stairs. "I've wanted to do this since the first weekend we had to work in the office. When you were dressed in your casual clothes. You looked so sexy," she whispers, her fingers tugging lightly on the hair at the nape of my neck. She nibbles on her bottom lip as her eyes dart around my face. "I always wondered what you'd taste like... What you'd feel like... inside me."

*Fuck.*

Impossibly, I get even harder at her admission and release a groan of satisfaction. Kicking open the door to my bedroom, I make my way to the bed and throw her down. She lets out a yelp of surprise as she bounces on the mattress before letting out a sexy giggle.

Standing at the end of the bed, I look down at this wondrous woman, her dress around her waist, hard nipples visible and calling to me as she rests on her elbows. Her laughter stops as she looks up at me with hooded eyes.

I'm as still as a statue when she turns onto her hands and knees and crawls towards me. She undoes the belt of my pants, pulling it through the loops before dropping it to the floor.

I'm mesmerized by her actions and don't move, even as she unzips my slacks and pushes them, with my boxers, down my legs, causing my painfully hard cock to bob out of its confines. Her eyes look up at me and I see the awe in them, almost like she can't believe this is really happening. I don't blame her.

I can't believe this is happening either.

My fingers dive into her hair as she takes my cock into the warm cove of her mouth and all the way to the back of her throat.

Groaning with satisfaction at the feel of being encased in her wet, hot mouth, I fight the urge to buck into her and instead allow her to set the pace.

I tip my head back as she hums; the sight and feel of her mouth wrapped around me is too much, the vibrations bringing me closer to the edge.

Needing a distraction from her sucking on my cock and twirling her tongue around the sensitive tip, I reach down and find the zipper of her dress, yanking it down in desperation.

Meghan pulls away from me, a *pop* sound echoing around the room as my cock leaves her mouth, and I pull her dress over her head, displaying her curvy body to me. Before I can stop her, her mouth is enveloping me again as she takes me to the back of her throat.

She pleasures me for a few more minutes before I step back, a string of her saliva hanging from my tip and still connecting me to her luscious mouth. Using it as lubrication, I give myself a couple of strong squeezes to slow myself down.

*I refuse to let this end in a matter of minutes.*

Flipping her over so that she's laying on her back and her perfect pussy is on display for me, I drop to my knees at the end of the bed and pull her to the edge by her ankles.

The first lick causes her back to arch off of the bed as her fingers pull on the strands of my hair and she lets out a moan. She tastes fucking amazing. Better that I could have ever imagined and like nothing I've ever tasted before.

"Yes. Oh God... Please... Yes, don't you dare fucking stop," she cries out, causing me to chuckle before carrying on.

I would've never thought she'd be like this in bed—she's so quiet in the office. She grinds on my tongue, and I push her knees up to her chest to give me more control and to spread her further open.

My eyes blaze as I look down at her wet core. She's leaking onto her thighs, and it's the sexiest thing I've ever seen.

"You look so good like this," I murmur, my tongue swirling around her clit as I dip a finger into her tight channel. "Spread out on my bed."

I add another finger and curl them as I move them in and out of her, my mouth sucking on her clit. I devour her like a starved man and her moans become more and more frequent. The sounds urging me on as I increase my speed.

My gaze lifts to take in her glorious body as I continue to suck and flick on her clit. She's laying back, her body arched as she massages her breasts. It's a view I could get used to.

Removing my fingers, I flip her onto her stomach, bringing her up onto her knees. Meghan looks at me over her shoulder, a question in her lust filled green gaze.

"Don't stop, I'm so close," she pleads.

"Nothing could stop me right now."

My hand caresses her ass before I run my finger from the top down to her dripping core. She tenses for a moment as my index finger passes over her tight hole.

*Another time.*

My tongue finds her pussy and I lap her up before returning to her clit as I drive my fingers into her core. I can feel the small tremors racking through her body as she gets closer and closer to the edge.

The pace of my fingers increases with each gasp and moan, my tongue never letting up the pressure on her. It's not long before she comes undone on my fingers, and I slowly remove them as she continues to spasm. My tongue swipes up her come, and I drink it down.

*My little oasis.*

"Please. I can't go again. I'm too sensitive." She wriggles, trying to get away from my tongue.

"You can do it. Just give me another one, baby." My

mouth doesn't leave her clit until I can feel her close to the edge again.

I pull back and tap her pussy. She jumps from the shock of the slap, but it soon turns into a moan as I continue to drink her down. I repeat, tapping her pussy and soothing it until she comes again.

"Good girl," I growl, giving myself one last taste before climbing up the bed.

She moves to the middle and I capture her mouth with mine, giving her a taste of her own release. Settling between her legs, my cock leaks pre-cum at the closeness of her pussy.

*I hope this isn't a dream.*

We spend a moment just tasting each other before she tilts her hips, and the tip of my cock slips through her slit and into her tight entrance.

"Fuck. You feel so good," I breathe out, my forehead resting on hers, my voice husky and unfamiliar as I look down into her green eyes.

I'm sure the need and headiness shining up at me is reflected in my own eyes. Swooping down to capture her mouth again, I move further inside her, swallowing her moans.

I take my time, slowly moving in, inch by inch. I'm in awe at how good she feels wrapped around me. Like heaven.

Once fully seated, I take a moment to catch my breath. Burying my nose in the space between her neck and her shoulder, I inhale deeply as I try to get control of myself.

*Come on, Cooper. Get it together.*

"Please. I need you to move. To fuck me," she whimpers.

Who am I to ignore her pleas? It's now my job to make her feel good, to bring her to release again, and so I move.

My thrusts are smooth and measured. In the back of my mind, I'm aware of how delicate she is compared to me. I'm being gentle with her when, really, I want to pound into her *and make her mine.*

*Whoa! I don't know where that thought came from.*

Before I can think too much, she grabs my face and pulls my mouth down to hers, her lips crushing hard against mine. Her tongue delves into my mouth and tangles with my own.

"I said I need you to fuck me. I don't want to walk straight tomorrow. You can let go," she whispers against my lips.

"You're going to be the death of me," I groan against her mouth.

My thrusts increase. The sound of the headboard banging against the wall, my panting, and her moans fill the room.

I'm getting close.

*So fucking close.*

Rubbing her clit with my thumb, I urge her towards her own release before capturing her mouth. Her pussy convulses around my cock and sends me over the edge with a guttural moan as I come deep inside her.

My eyes lock onto hers and we bask in the moment, the realization of what we've just done sinking in. There's no regret, at least not from me, just awe and contentment.

Meghan's eyes widen for a fraction of a second before she closes them, hiding from me. Dropping to my elbows, I press a gentle kiss on her lips. I feel the tension ease out of her as we take a moment to comfort each other.

*It's going to be alright.*

Pulling out, I collapse to the side of her, careful not to crush her while trying to catch my breath. Turning my head to the side, I'm greeted to the sight of Meghan curled up asleep.

I let out a quiet laugh before heading to the bathroom, where I wash up and grab a washcloth to clean her up.

I'll have to speak to her in the morning about the fact we didn't use any protection. I've never been so caught up in the moment that I've forgotten to use it.

I know I'm clean, but it's not just STDs that we need to be cautious of. I've never really thought about having kids, but I work too much for them to be in my future.

Returning to the bedroom, I pause in the doorway and look at her peacefully asleep in my bed. She looks like she belongs there. I push away from the doorjamb, moving towards the bed where I roll her onto her back and clean her up.

Placing her under the covers, I throw the washcloth in the laundry basket before sliding in behind her and pulling her into my arms.

I half expect her to wake up, but instead she snuggles into my embrace. I fall asleep with a smile on my face and a feeling of excitement at what tomorrow will bring.

## EIGHT

## *Meghan*

I think I might throw up.

Too many cocktails last night have left me with the hangover of all hangovers. Gingerly rolling onto my side so as not to upset my stomach any more than necessary, I feel around for my phone to check the time.

*Urgh, it's four in the morning!*

*Why am I even awake?*

Shoving it back on the side table, I roll onto my back to be met with an unfamiliar ceiling. A frown creases my brow as I lean up onto my elbows to look around the entirely unfamiliar bedroom and the sheet slides down to reveal my bare chest.

Something isn't quite right.

Even taking out the fact that this isn't my room, I don't ever sleep naked.

There are no mementos, or family photos, or…

anything, just furniture. The room is practically bare, with white walls, dark side tables, a bed and a chair in the corner.

*Have I gone home with a serial killer?*

There are three doors in the room, one I assume leads to the bathroom, one to the hallway and the other, which is slightly ajar, looks to be a walk-in closet. There's artwork on the walls, but with the lights off and the floor-length curtains closed, it's hard to be certain what they are of.

There's a warmth radiating from beside me and I close my eyes, praying to God that he's at least hot. Sucking in a deep breath, I turn my head to the right where the sleeping face of none other than Cooper *fucking* Jackson greets me. I smack my hand over my mouth, internally screaming at myself as my eyes grow wide.

*What the hell happened last night?*

*Why the hell am I naked in my boss's bed?*

As soon as I ask myself the question, a montage of images flashes through my mind. They start at the club with me kissing him, then pulling away. Him devouring my mouth like a starved man. In his car, with me straddling his lap in the back seat.

*Oh God.*

I sucked his cock.

*I'm going to have to quit my job.*

He ate my pussy, and I begged him for more.

*Yep, definitely quitting my job.*

Realizing I need to get the fuck out of dodge, I slowly lift the covers to get up. My damn eyes betray me and dart over to his body, as if trying to get one last look at him.

*Shit.*

My teeth dig into my bottom lip to stop myself from moaning, both at my predicament and the fact that temptation is lying next to me. He's semi-hard, but even so, his cock is impressive as it lays heavy against his stomach, thick in girth and long in length.

Moving my eyes up over his taut abs, I can tell he works out but doesn't spend hours upon hours in the gym. My eyes settle on his face as I slowly settle the blanket back against his sleeping form. As quickly and quietly as I can, I slip out of the bed.

I'm going to have to dissect last night when I get home, or at least out of this building. Grabbing my phone as I search the dark room for my dress, I'm grateful for the slivers of light sneaking through the gaps in the heavy curtains. I wish I had more time to stop and take in the glimpse of the man I work for. Correction, worked for, because I can't carry on working for him. Not now.

As I'm about to make my way to the door, my dress clutched to my chest, there's movement from the bed. Freezing in place and trying to hide in the shadows of the room, I glance toward him as he rolls over onto his stomach. I hold my breath for fear that he will hear my breathing in the silence of the room and I'll be forced to address... this.

As soon as he's settled, I race across the room as quietly as I possibly can, praying the door I've chosen isn't the door to the bathroom. With my hand on the doorknob, I fall still when I hear another moan and more movement coming from the bed.

"Meghan," he murmurs.

*Please, don't make me do this, not right now.*

"You like that, baby?" he moans.

*Thank God,* he's just dreaming.

But also... what the fuck? He's dreaming about me? I'm going to have to pack that away for later.

Stealing one last glance over my shoulder, I open the door and slip out, closing it behind me. My heart races and my palms sweat. I feel like I've just got away with breaking out of the White House.

In the hallway, I step into my dress and smooth my hands down the front before searching for my shoes and purse, both of which I locate near the front door. Checking that I have everything I *think* I came with, I place my hand on the doorknob and take one last look around.

Wait, where's my coat?

I don't remember picking it up from the cloakroom and a quick glance in my bag for the token confirms I didn't.

*Great, I'll have to freeze my ass off waiting for an Uber.*

Opening the door, I step into the safety of the corridor, before closing it quietly behind me. I move down the hallway before stopping to put on my shoes, not daring to make a noise on the hardwood flooring.

At the elevator, I request an Uber and pray it'll be outside by the time I reach the lobby before pressing the button to go down. Much like Cooper Jackson, the building is suave and gives off a 'rich vibe'.

*How much must I stick out?*

I can imagine I'm giving off *Pretty Woman* vibes, with my too short dress, makeup that must be long gone and hair in desperate need of a brush. The flooring in the hall probably cost more than all the furniture in my apartment, and that thought alone causes me to clutch my purse even harder.

*Maybe I should've put my shoes on outside.*

When the elevator arrives, I step inside and catch a glimpse of myself in the mirrored walls. I look like I've been well and truly fucked. It's just as I predicted; my hair is a tangled mess and my makeup is pretty much non-existent other than the smudges of mascara under my eyes and some patchy eyeliner.

My lips are swollen from kisses and there's a slight rash across my chin from his stubble. I lift my hand to my lips, running my fingers over them, tracing the marks he's made on my body. A need builds in my core and I rub my thighs together in an effort to ease the ache the memory of last night causes, berating myself for still wanting more of him.

I'm still staring at my reflection, lost in my own

thoughts, when I reach the lobby. The doors open behind me and are about to close again before I snap myself out of my haze. Rushing through them, I make my way across the lobby.

Thankfully, it's quiet, although I make brief eye contact with the elderly concierge before I divert my gaze and rush through the double doors. I breathe a sigh of relief when I see my Uber sitting at the curb. A perk, I guess, of needing a ride at four in the morning.

Sitting securely in the back, I can finally take a minute to comprehend what has happened. The Uber is cruising down the streets of Manhattan when the gravity of what I've done hits me.

*I slept with my boss.*

*How could I be so stupid?*

I bring my hand to my mouth in an effort to muffle the sob that is trying to break through. How could I jeopardize my livelihood over something as silly as getting laid? I guess I only have myself to blame for making such a stupid mistake. I shouldn't have drunk so much. Or kissed him.

I'm going to have to find a new job, or move back home if I can't find one. It was a mistake and there's no getting around it. I can't leave my job straight away, so I'm going to have to face him on Monday with my head held high and tell him it was a mistake and we should forget it happened. Maybe then I stand a chance at not completely ruining my life.

I had the best sex of my life with the one man I've

wanted for months. That doesn't seem like a mistake... except he's my boss.

Argh! *He's my boss.*

I don't sleep with people I work with. He was supposed to be unattainable.

My mind continues running over last night and before I know it, I'm home, rehydrated, showered, in my PJs and climbing into bed.

Lying back against my pillows, I close my eyes in an effort to get some more rest and sleep away the rest of the alcohol still coursing through my veins. Flashes of vivid memories from last night play out behind my closed eyelids like a movie. I didn't even know it was possible for me to come that many times in a row.

Mr. Jackson. *I guess I can call him Cooper now.*

The feel of his warm, rough skin on mine when he'd dragged me across the dance floor. Cooper thrusting his hands into my hair, cursing under his breath before his lips crashed into mine as he pressed me against the wall in our dark space.

*I need to get some sleep.*

Maybe when I wake up, it will turn out this is actually a dream. Or if it isn't, I can at least have a clearer head and be able to come up with a plan—like finding a new job.

Punching my pillow, I turn over and banish the images from my mind.

Or, at least I try to.

In the distance, I can hear a banging noise, like someone's smacking a nail with a hammer but constantly missing and hitting the wall. Turning over and burrowing further into the covers in an attempt to ignore it, I give up the pretense when it gets more insistent and wakes me up fully.

I'm going to hunt down whoever it is and make them pay for waking me up. Don't they get that I'm trying to sleep away a night of mistakes?

Wiping the sleep from my eyes as I sit up in bed, I realize the banging noise is coming from my front door. Is someone hammering something into my door? I climb out of bed, and grab my robe from behind the bedroom door as I head toward the noise. Maybe I can get whoever it is to quit with the noise and get some more sleep.

Looking through the peephole, I'm greeted to the sight of Alex, with her fist raised to bang on the door again. Pulling it open, I paste a smile on my face, if only to hide my hungover state.

*Thank God I showered when I got home.*

"You look like crap. Where did you disappear to last night?" Alex declares as she breezes into my apartment.

I close the door before turning to face her. "I... uh... I wasn't feeling great, so I decided to call it a night," I lie.

There's no way I can tell Alex that I had sex with our

boss. She's a great friend and I have no doubt that she would be super supportive, but something tells me this is something I should keep to myself. Nobody besides me and Cooper needs to know about our little... indiscretion.

"Are you feeling better now?" she asks, her eyes roaming over my face.

"Oh yes, I just needed some sleep."

"Good. You should've said something. I would have left with you." Before I can respond, she continues, "After I couldn't find you, I went out to grab a cab. I figured you'd met someone or something, and I got to talking to that bouncer. Oh my God, Meghan, he's so funny..." Alex continues on about the bouncer as she leads the way into my kitchen.

*Did she not drink as much as me last night?*

She's way too perky for my liking this morning.

I know my friend and something seems off, but I can't quite put my finger on what it is...

My galley kitchen is barely big enough for me and Alex to have a coffee and a chat. The cabinets are white, with light oak-colored handles that match the countertops, and at the end of the room is a window with a view of the street below. I try to keep my space, as small as it is, as free of clutter as possible—so the counters only have the basics on them, allowing me room to cook.

I'm half listening to what Alex is saying, while making us both a drink and grabbing myself something to line my stomach. I'm hungover, and in the back of my mind I'm having a panic attack at the thought of what I've done.

*Was it a mistake? Yes.*

*Would I do it again? Also yes.*

*Am I angry at myself for having fucked my boss? No, not really.*

I'm in this weird sort of place where I know we shouldn't have done what we did but I feel like it was bound to happen at some point.

It was inevitable.

I just wish we could have made a plan before we crossed the line.

"Coffee?" I ask, grabbing mugs from the cupboard as I make a pot, trying to distract myself.

"Sure. So... did you have fun last night, before you went home sick?" Alex asks.

"I did. I had a really good time. It was the most fun I've had in ages. Did you have a good night?"

"I did. We should go out more often. I liked the club. Maybe we can go again."

"Sure. Maybe your bouncer boyfriend can get us in," I joke.

"Umm, yeah. I'll see what I can do," she murmurs as I hand her a mug of hot coffee.

There's definitely something she isn't telling me. I guess we're both keeping secrets from each other today.

"Are you excited for the Miami trip?" Alex asks.

"Honestly?" She nods, encouraging me to continue. "I'd rather not go."

"What? Why? It's Miami. I'm jealous that you get to go."

Thinking on my feet, I say, "Well, it's not exactly going to be warm, and he's probably going to make me work the whole time, so I won't even get to enjoy it."

Alex's face scrunches in disgust before she responds, "Urgh, that's so true. Okay, I was jealous, but not anymore."

Alex doesn't stay for long, and she leaves with a promise to see me tomorrow for our regular Sunday dinner. I spend the remainder of my Saturday trying to sleep off the hangover from hell and ignoring the fact that I don't see or hear from Cooper at all. My anxiety over whatever may wait for me come Monday morning only increases over the weekend.

I have a million questions running through my mind. Do I want him to act as if nothing happened? Ask why I left? Or do I want him to demand that I give him a chance? In a perfect world, I would choose option three. But this isn't a perfect world.

One thing I do determine is that I can't work for a man that would see me as just another notch on his bedpost.

Over the Christmas break, when I'm back home with my parents and away from the noise of New York, I'll evaluate my next steps and look for a new job.

## NINE

## Cooper

Water cascades down my back as I rest my forehead against the cool tile in the shower. I came home with Meghan on Friday night and when I woke up she was gone.

I've not heard a peep from her all weekend and, instead of calling her, I've stewed in my own thoughts. I tried to work, to focus my mind somewhere else, but it was pointless.

Every thought I have is of her. Her taste. The scent of her pussy and the sounds she made as we fucked. How her pretty little mouth felt wrapped around my throbbing cock.

It all plays on repeat in my mind.

I've laid in bed or stood in the shower and stroked myself to the thought of her, and if I concentrate hard enough I can still feel her hot, wet, mouth on me. I've never had a woman affect me like this before.

Now I'm standing here in the shower, washing my body, trying in vain to calm the frustration that's rising inside of me.

*How dare she leave without a word?*

The thing that's getting to me the most is that she could have called me or at least left a note to say... something. I thought after what we experienced, she could have at least communicated with me, instead of running away like a coward. I've left the ball in her court and she's just walked away from it.

*Fuck.*

This can't continue. I swore to myself that I wouldn't ever sample the company pool.

*But that was before her.*

It doesn't matter, I need to end this.

*I'm no better than my father if it continues.*

As much as it pains me to say, he was right when he told me the apple doesn't fall from the tree. The only difference is, I don't have a wife and kid waiting for me at home. I can't believe I fucked up so monumentally.

I go through the motions of dressing, having breakfast and heading to the office, all with her occupying my thoughts and a burning curiosity at how she's going to handle this. Yes, we need to work together, but I'd be lying if I said I didn't want another taste of her.

I won't give in.

*I can't.*

Not again.

She's sitting at her desk when I walk in, her focus on

the screen of her computer with her fingers furiously flying across the keyboard. As I go to walk into my office, I look down and see a document with a bunch of gibberish written in it open on the screen.

My brow pulls into a frown and I lift my gaze to her. A rosy blush steals across her cheeks and she drops her chin in embarrassment before lifting it in defiance.

"We should talk," I declare.

Standing from her chair and moving toward my office door, she says, "Yes, we should. You have time now."

I follow her into my office, closing the door behind her as she walks to the chair in front of my desk.

"Obviously we had sex and it shouldn't have happened," she rushes out.

I freeze in the process of hanging up my coat. Even though I know what she's saying is true, it doesn't stop the ache that starts building in my chest and the feeling of regret that pools in the pit of my stomach.

*Come on, Cooper.*

I was about to say the same damn words to her. This shouldn't be causing any feelings, let alone this feeling of... loss.

Slowly turning to face her with my coat still in my hands, I assess her for a moment. She looks stunning, with her hair pulled back in a ponytail and in an over-sized cream and navy sweater. Although her chin is lifted, her gaze is on my shoulder. She's trying to be brave and strong, but for some reason she can't look me in the eye.

Turning back to hang my coat away, I respond. "I agree. I'm sure we can both be professionals about it. And just so you know, I'm clean and have never forgotten about protection before."

"Of course, I can be professional. I won't be telling anybody. And I... uh, I'm also... clean. I'm on the pill too."

I move to my desk, looking over the files as I reply, "Good. I'd understand if you wanted to mention it to HR, but I hope we can just let it go and put it down to a drunken mistake."

Pushing her glasses up her nose, she gives me a small smile. "I think that would be for the best. To put it down as a drunken mistake. Well, if there isn't anything else, I should get back to work."

She rises from her seat, smoothing her hands down the front of her pants before moving toward the door. I tear my gaze away from watching the subtle sway of her hips.

"I'm glad we got this resolved," I mumble to her retreating back.

Sitting in the silence of my office, I replay the conversation in my mind. I should be relieved that she wanted to draw a line in the sand, and I guess on some level I am. But I'm also disappointed that I won't get to have her again, even though I know it's for the best.

Yes, I had the best time I've had in a very long time,

and if she was anyone else, I'd want to keep seeing her, but I refuse to become my father.

She needs to remain nothing more to me than my assistant, no matter how hard she is to resist.

I'm standing by the check-in desk when I see her step through the doors. Trailing behind her is a small carry-on suitcase and I take the time to drink her in unobserved. She's dressed casually in a chunky cream knit sweater and blue denim jeans. Her parka coat is undone and winter boots adorn her feet.

The column of her neck is exposed as her hair is in a ponytail and I have to remind myself that it's not acceptable to bury my face in the space there.

It's been nearly three weeks since we agreed to call what happened a mistake and resume our professional relationship—and it's been the hardest three weeks of my life. I swear she knows the effect she has on me.

I've found myself watching her as she does the most menial of tasks, like answering the phone or reading through a document. She's been nothing but professional with me, acting like nothing has changed, but I've found myself craving her attention and living for the small snippets I get. For the first time in a long time, I'm not entirely sure how to handle my feelings toward a woman.

"Mr. Jackson," she greets.

I nod my head, biting my tongue to keep from asking her to drop the formalities. "Meghan."

She leads the way over to the desk and takes charge of getting us checked in. The process is smooth and before I know it, we're heading through security. We don't have to wait long for our gate to open and we both busy ourselves with responding to emails and making phone calls.

Meghan spends the three-hour flight briefing me on the client we are going to see and although I know everything she is telling me, because we went to college together, I don't stop her.

Jamison Monroe is a tech giant in Miami. He's looking to move his operations to New York, and that's where I come in. I'll be giving him some legal guidance around the move, as it will most likely result in people being laid off.

She's been in work mode since we met at the airport. Although a part of me is grateful that it's not awkward and we can move past what happened, another part of me is pissed that she can be so unaffected by something that is consuming me day and night.

We take a cab from the airport to the hotel and when I step out of the confines of the air conditioned cab I pull in deep lungfuls of the salty sea air. In comparison to New York, the weather is perfect and I congratulate myself on planning in half a day to relax on the beach.

It's been a stressful year.

Meghan leads the way to the reception desk, her suitcase rolling along behind her. She'd taken it from me when I'd lifted it from the trunk, refusing to hand it over as we walked into the hotel. I'd be lying if I said I didn't take the opportunity to watch the gentle sway of her hips as she strides in.

The reception area of the hotel is modern and sleek with lighting that gives it an almost moody atmosphere. There is plenty of seating and the space is filled with people, either checking in or out or meeting up with people.

"Good morning, ma'am. How are you today?" the receptionist asks as Meghan approaches the desk that sits directly in front of the main doors. He's a slender guy with tanned skin, dark hair and dark eyes. His uniform is pressed and fits in with the prestige of the hotel.

"Morning, I'm good thank you. I have a reservation for Mr. Cooper Jackson for two rooms for two nights," Meghan responds.

"Of course, Mrs. Jackson, let me just get your reservation up."

"Oh, I-I'm not Mrs. Jackson," Meghan mumbles.

A small smile graces my lips at her flustered state. I'm not looking to settle down or get married, not after the disaster that was my parents' marriage, but I've got to admit, the thought of Meghan being Mrs. Jackson doesn't make me want to run for the hills. The sound of Meghan on the edge of panic snaps me out of my reverie.

"What do you mean, we only have one room on the reservation? I booked the rooms myself and had confirmation that the booking was for two."

"I'm sorry, ma'am. It looks like there was an error on our end and your second room was canceled. Unfortunately, we don't have any additional rooms due to a medical conference in the hotel this week. I can see if I can source a hotel for one of you?"

Meghan drops her head into her hands and mutters something unintelligible before pulling in a deep breath and standing straight.

"Does the room you have available have one or two beds?" She asks, a touch of her frustration showing through.

"It has two, ma'am."

Turning to me, she utters, "I know it's not ideal, but would you be okay with sharing a room? We can take turns in the bathroom and I swear I don't snore."

"I know you don't snore." A blush steals across her cheeks and I mentally berate myself for saying it. "If you're fine with it, then so am I. We're professionals."

Turning back to the grimacing receptionist, Meghan states with her resignation clear in her tone, "It's okay, we will share the one room."

"Thank you for being so understanding and please enjoy breakfast on us in the morning. It's served until ten in our fine dining restaurant," the receptionist responds, his shoulders visibly relaxing as he points to the restaurant to the right of the entrance.

With our keys in hand, we make our way to the bank of elevators to the left of the reception desk. I can't help but lean into Meghan, whispering in her ear, "I'm sorry for my comment. I'll be more careful with what I say going forward."

She's tense, but I can't tell if it's down to my proximity or that there is only one room.

I'm sitting in the only chair in the room, that just so happens to face the two queen size beds and bathroom door, waiting for Meghan to get ready for our business dinner with Jamison. She's been in there a while and I'm starting to get worried.

As I'm contemplating knocking on the door, she pulls in open and is framed in the doorway. She looks beautiful. Her outfit's the perfect mixture of business and pleasure.

"It's too much, isn't it?" she whispers, staring down at herself.

She's wearing a black, form-fitting dress that showcases her curves to perfection, and on her feet are a pair of open toe strappy heels.

"No..." I clear my throat and sit up straighter in the chair. "You look... beautiful."

The compliment causes her to blush, and she tries to hide it by busying herself around the room, filling a small clutch with items. Tucking her hair behind her ear draws my attention to the long blonde locks that are cascading down to her waist in loose curls.

"I had another dress in my suitcase, but my friend must have switched it out... well, it actually looks like she switched out everything... including my underwear, if you can believe that," she rambles on. "It's just like her to do something like that."

Standing, I move toward her and place my hands on her hips, turning her toward me. A jolt runs through my fingers at the contact. It blows my mind the effect such a simple thing has on me. Her lips part as her breathing turns shallow, and her eyes widen as she stares up at me. In all the time we've worked together, I have never once touched her in this way and the fact we are in a room with a bed, alone, adds to the intimacy.

"You look perfect," I murmur, my eyes dropping to her lips as her tongue darts out and swipes across them. My gaze roams freely over her features and I notice the natural look she's gone for with her makeup.

"We should get going," she states as she pulls back from me and turns toward the door, throwing an over-sized black blazer over her shoulders as she does.

"Um, yeah."

I grab my wallet from the sideboard and follow her out of the door.

The cab ride to the restaurant is uneventful, and she barely says two words to me, opting to stare out of the window at the passing scenery. I hold the door open for her as she steps onto the sidewalk. Placing my hand at her lower back, we walk toward the entrance of the restaurant Jamison has picked.

It's not until we're being shown to our table and I force my gaze away from her that I notice the eyes of nearly every man in the restaurant tracking her.

I've made a mistake. A very grave mistake.

I should have ripped that *fucking* dress off of her the moment she walked out of the bathroom.

I'm more certain of this as I sit opposite Meghan and Jamison, watching them flirt like I'm not even here. Thankfully, I guess, they didn't start until business was done, but the urge to punch him and throw her over my shoulder like a caveman only seems to be building. I knock back my whiskey and signal to a passing waiter for another one.

We're in a booth at the back of the restaurant. The setting is intimate with dim lighting and secluded booths, but the food, though expensive, is delicious and well worth the cost.

I made the mistake of having Meghan seated in the middle of the booth with myself and Jamison opposite each other.

Throughout the evening, he's scooted closer to her and his arm is now casually draped behind her. Every time he leans in to whisper something to her my fists clench.

Unlike when my father got in her personal space,

Meghan doesn't seem phased by Jamison. She's laughing at his jokes and, on more than one occasion, has leaned into him and rested her hand on his thigh. The waiter returns with my drink, and I gulp down half of the contents as Meghan releases another husky laugh.

"Do you want to come and party with us, Cooper?" Jamison asks, a sly smile on his face.

Party? Us?

*What the hell have I missed?*

I narrow my eyes at him, hoping it conveys the message I want before saying, "No, Meghan and I need to get an early night. We have a call in the morning at 6 am."

Out of the corner of my eye, I can see Meghan's brow pulling into a frown at my statement. She knows we don't have a call in the morning—tomorrow morning is my planned beach time.

"Surely you don't need Megs with you. She deserves a break after working for you for so long." Jamison chuckles.

*Megs?* They've known each other a whole two hours, and he's already got a nickname for her.

"I'm not paying her to be on vacation," I state, more forcefully than I intended.

My eyes dart over to Meghan as she sits up in her seat, sobering up.

*Fuck.*

Why did I have to go and say that? What I should be doing is letting her go off and have a good time. The

111

problem is, I can't. She's *mine*. I stand from the table and hold my hand out for Meghan, my eyes not leaving Jamison. Reluctantly, she takes it and shuffles around to exit the booth, throwing her blazer over her arm.

"I'll be in touch regarding the move soon," I say, before throwing a couple of hundred dollar bills on the table.

"It was nice to meet you," Meghan states, her voice husky as she holds her hand out to Jamison. He stands from the booth and pulls her into his arms, whispering something I don't catch in her ear before handing her a card. "Of course, I'll see you soon."

She walks past me and I turn on my heel to follow, my hand going to the small of her back. I'm aware that I killed her mood, but the feeling festering inside of me couldn't be tamed.

We're sitting in the back of the cab and she's looking out of the window when she speaks, "What is the call we have in the morning? I don't remember putting anything in."

I'm flicking through my emails on my phone, unable to look her in the eye.

"We don't have a call." I don't expand on it and she doesn't ask me any further questions. Neither of us utter a word after that as we head back to the hotel.

We get ready for bed in silence, taking turns to use the bathroom. The lights are off and we're in our own beds. I can hear the sound of the ocean outside and it soothes me as I pull in a deep breath before breaking the silence.

I need to clear the air with her, because the conversation we had in my office didn't do shit to make me forget the line we've crossed.

"We should talk about what happened the other week."

## TEN

# Cooper

She doesn't respond for the longest time and I start to wonder if she's fallen asleep before her husky voice cuts through the silence filling the room.

"There isn't much to talk about. We agreed that we would remain professional."

"I beg to differ. There still seems to be a giant elephant in the room. It's all well and good having a five minute conversation, but it's not really resolved anything."

She releases an audible sigh, as if I'm irritating her by bringing it up again. Maybe she's been able to move past what happened and I'm nothing but a distant memory, but I'm struggling to forget.

I hear her moving around in her bed before I see her figure sit up, turning to look over at me. A sliver of moonlight shines upon her and casts a soft glow over her features. I interlock my fingers together, placing them behind my head, as I feign nonchalance.

Anything to stop from climbing from my bed and claiming her mouth with my own.

With a hint of annoyance in her tone, she asks, "What do you mean?"

I release a breath, preparing to be open and honest with her. No matter what her response may be. "I still find you attractive." She doesn't speak, so I continue, "Don't worry, I'm not going to act on it. I agree, we need to be professional and I don't want to cross that line again, but I can't have you flirting with my clients like you did tonight."

With a resigned sigh, she says, "No matter how either of us feels, we crossed a line that shouldn't have been crossed. If you can't handle me being my normal *friendly* self with clients, then maybe I should resign." Her words come out strong and sure, catching me off guard before she powers on. "It's not what I wanted because I love my job, but if we can't move past it, I'm not sure I will have any other choice. And while we're on the subject of remaining professional, you also don't get to be jealous if I do want to flirt with other men."

A knot forms in my stomach at her threat to leave. Ignoring it, I grit my teeth and utter words that don't strip me bare, because I've already been too honest with her tonight. "You can flirt with whoever you want to, just not on my dime."

"It... *we* won't happen again," she assures me after a lengthy pause.

"I know."

I try to keep the resignation and disappointment at this realization out of my voice. I'm not sure I succeed as she looks at me in the darkness for a moment. When she nods and lies back down, turning her back to me, I release the breath I'd been holding.

I lay awake until the sunrises before giving up and going for a run along the beach. The slightly warmer Miami weather does nothing to relieve my mood. My beach morning was spent wondering what she was up to as I answered emails on my phone, unable to take a break from work even for a few hours.

I'm reunited with her that afternoon, and for her at least, everything seems to be back to normal, whereas I spend the remainder of our time in Miami trying to ignore the way she makes me feel.

For the past two weeks since we returned from Miami, Meghan has continued to occupy my thoughts. No matter how much I tell myself that she wants nothing to do with me, or how many times I tell myself I can't have her, my mind just won't let it go.

It won't let *her* go.

Leaning back in my chair, I stare out at the Manhattan skyline as I indulge myself with replays of the

Christmas party—after all, it's the only time I'll get to have her. Despite her kissing me first, I'd been the one to take it a step further. We could have left it at two kisses, but one taste, no matter how brief, has snapped something inside of me and I haven't had enough self-control to stop myself.

*I couldn't resist her.*

I'd wanted her for so long, and at that moment she'd wanted me too.

When she'd brought her leg up and wrapped it around my waist, grinding herself into my already painfully hard cock, I knew I was going to take her home. When I slipped my hand between us and I found her bare and soaked for me, I'd barely resisted the urge to drop to my knees and devour her against the wall.

I should be grateful that she wants to forget about it, that her immediate thought wasn't to report me to HR or quit her job. Instead, I'm not grateful. I'm frustrated that she's stopped anything more from happening.

*I can't have anything more happen.*

So why am I so worked up over the fact that she wants what I should want?

*Christ, Cooper. Get it together.*

Today she's wearing a corduroy shirt that comes to mid-thigh, an oversized sweater and thick wool tights. It's a simple outfit, definitely not sexy, but I want nothing more than to call her into my office and tell her to strip out of her clothes. To bend her over my desk and make her squirm as I devour her.

*Once wasn't enough.*

Looking out of my window at the view of the city, I contemplate my next step.

*I can't carry on like this.*

I've always been able to plan out a course of action; it's what has made me so successful as an attorney. Right now, though, I don't know what to do. I don't know how to get her out of my mind. I've never been one to become obsessed with a woman, but that's exactly what she is—an obsession.

I know I could call Vivian, or any other woman, but the thought of being with anyone else doesn't turn me on. Not like she does.

*I crave Meghan.*

Letting out a sign of frustration, I press the intercom button on my desk to call her.

"How can I help, Mr. Jackson?" Her soft, breathy tones float down the line and straight to my cock causing it to twitch. Shifting in my seat, I swallow the sudden ball in my throat.

"I need you to stay late tonight, Meghan. I'm going to need your help to sort out the Dexter files." I pray that my tone comes across as authoritative but professional. It's not like this is the first night we'd have to work together after hours.

"Of course, Mr. Jackson. Shall I order dinner?"

"Please. Maybe Yang's around the corner," I suggest.

"Yes, Mr. Jackson," Meghan responds, completely unaffected, before she disconnects the call.

I go back to staring out of my window until Meghan knocks on my door with the files we need to prepare for court next week.

There are documents strewn across the large table in the boardroom. It's long since gone dark outside and the office has cleared out. We have most of the files ready by the time the food arrives and so we eat in relative silence, with Meghan occasionally providing me updates on things she's been working on this week. I know I'm being unusually quiet, but being this close to her is torture even as I do my best to respect the boundaries she's clearly put in place. Having finished eating, Meghan clears away the takeout boxes as I stand over the documents, reviewing the file order.

With the food cleared away, she moves next to me. Her sweet perfume fills my nostrils and the words on the page in front of me blur with my effort to remain focused.

*I must not touch her.*

I reach over to point to a slip of paper. It's on the tip of my tongue to ask Meghan to hand it to me, but as my hand brushes her arm, I hear her breath hitch. I move to pull away, but she turns to face me at the same time that I turn to her, an apology forming on my tongue. Her eyes have darkened with an unmistakable desire that most likely matches my own.

I don't know who moves first, but before I know it, the silky strands of her ponytail are wrapped around my hand, and our mouths are fused in an almost punishing kiss. She tenses for the briefest of moments and just as I'm about to pull away thinking she's changed her mind, she kisses me back, more than matching my desperation.

Using her hair to tilt her head back and expose her neck, I leave the paradise that is her mouth and trail kisses and nips down the column of her throat. She lets out little mewls of pleasure, urging me on. An overwhelming urge overtakes me and I find myself sucking on the sensitive skin of her neck.

*Marking her as mine.*

"Cooper," she pleads.

I don't stop, not until a faint bruise appears on the pale skin of her throat. I haven't given a woman a hickey since I was in high school.

Briefly, because I can't keep my hands and mouth off of her for long, I admire my handiwork before I return to her mouth, my tongue tangling with hers.

My hand leaves her hair, as I slide them both down to rest on her hips before smoothing further down and under her ass. Grabbing a cheek in each hand, I press my pelvis into her stomach, grinding my hips into her softness, causing her to let out a low moan.

*I want to be buried in her.*

*So deep that we don't know where I end and she begins.*

Releasing her ass, I move my hands to the hem of her

skirt, dragging it up until it's over her hips, sitting bunched around her waist.

Reluctantly breaking contact with her lips, I look down at her, my gaze roaming over every inch of her. The raggedness of her breaths match my own. Pulling down her tights and panties, I help her step out of them before returning to her mouth and backing her up to the table. She shoves the papers out of the way, causing most of them to flutter to the floor as I lift her onto the edge. Our movements are rushed, a sense of urgency taking over us as we try to satisfy our hunger for each other.

In this moment, I don't give a fuck about the documents. My only thoughts are that I'm going to get another taste of her, and that she wants this as much as I do.

Her hands are splayed across my chest and as they slide up to push my suit jacket down my arms, I remove my hands from her hips. Shucking off the jacket, it drops to the floor, instantly forgotten. Breaking our kiss, I rest my forehead against hers, our breaths mingling in the small space between us before I remove her glasses.

As soon as they're gone, I capture her lips again, unable to resist.

Her delicate fingers remove my already loose tie and then move onto the buttons of my shirt. She struggles with them, her fingers shaking, with what I hope is her need, so I brush her fingers away and make light work of undoing and discarding the shirt.

Standing between her legs, with my shirt off and her

hands fumbling as she undoes my belt, I stare down at her, moving a strand of hair out of her face. Her eyes lift to mine in question, her hands still, and she sucks in a breath.

*I could look at her all day.*

She's a vision with her skirt around her hips and her perfect pussy glistening up at me as it drips onto the polished wood of the table. I want to touch and taste every inch of her.

*I don't want her to regret this.*

I want her to want me as much as I want her.

It's my turn to fumble with the buttons of her blouse now, like a teenager about to get his first touch of tits. *Perfect tits. She has perfect, perky tits.* Halfway through undoing her shirt, I give up and pull it apart, causing the last few buttons to fly off. My need for her has grown, and it feels like everything is happening far too slowly.

She gasps at the unexpected move before releasing a soft giggle and going back to her task of pulling my belt through the loops of my pants. Underneath her shirt, she's wearing a camisole top and in my desperation to touch her, I pull it down–along with her bra cups. Taking a second to commit to memory the plump, perfectly round breasts in front of me, I cup them and roll her erect nipples between my thumb and finger.

Meghan lets out a deep, guttural moan of satisfaction as her eyes flutter closed and her head tilts back. Resting on her palms, she presses her chest further into my hands, arching her back. She looks like a goddess, with a flush setting across her cheeks and her mouth open in a perfect 'O' shape.

I've never been more grateful for the fact that we're alone in the office.

I lower my mouth to her right nipple and suck on the engorged tip before flicking it with my tongue, moving on to her left before I go back to the right one. She squirms on the table, trying to find her release. I'm in no rush, wanting to savor the moment, and so take my time playing with her breasts and turning her nipples into sensitive little buds.

"Your breasts are perfect. I could get off just playing with them," I murmur while palming them.

Meghan brings her hazy eyes to mine as I scrape her right nipple with my teeth before soothing it with my tongue. Her fingers slide through my hair, gripping the strands, encouraging me to continue.

Unable to resist the urge to feel her, and wanting to give her a little relief, I glide one hand down her smooth, flat stomach toward paradise. She lets out a barely audible whimper as I run a finger through her slit and over the sensitive nub of her clit. Momentarily, her grip tightens in my hair as her head drops forward onto my shoulder and she rolls her hips, begging for more.

"You're soaked for me, baby."

Sliding a finger into her tight pussy, I give her a moment to adjust to being filled before I pump in and out of her. She covers me with her arousal, giving me enough lubrication to be able to add another finger.

Squeezing around me, I place my thumb on her clit and begin moving it in circular motions, as my mouth captures her nipple, grazing it with my teeth. A breathy gasp escapes from her swollen lips.

*Damn, she's so tight.*

"Please..."

Pulling away from her chest, I stand to my full height, looking down at her glazed eyes. "Does that feel good? You like how my fingers fill your tight pussy?"

She nods in response as our eyes remain locked and her tongue darts out to swipe across her parted lips. My fingers continue the slow in and out motion into her slick pussy. It's like time has stood still and I can finally breathe—she's given me the strength to breathe.

"Don't stop," she rasps, pulling herself out of our trance.

My thumb continues its movements, slowly increasing the pressure on her clit. My fingers twist in and out, stretching her. Getting her ready for me.

"I'm so close..."

Capturing her mouth with my own, I swallow down her now muffled scream of release. As she comes on my fingers, her walls clenching around them, I realize I can't wait to be inside her anymore.

I make quick work of unzipping my trousers and push them and my boxers down, releasing my achingly hard cock. Her eyes are focused on me and the movement of my hand as I pump myself twice in an effort to bring myself back from the edge.

Stepping between her spread legs, I run the tip of my cock through her slit, watching in fascination as it becomes wet with her arousal.

"I'll go slower and give you more next time, baby... right now, I need to be inside you," I say, my voice rough and breathless as I look down at her.

I pump myself once more before moving her now loose hair out of her face and leaning down to capture her luscious mouth. The gesture is intimate, probably too much for a quick fuck on a conference room table.

*It's not just a quick fuck though.*

It has to be.

That's all we can ever be.

Our tongues tangle as I slowly enter her. Moving my right hand from her thigh, I pinch her nipple before continuing on my journey to lightly grasp her throat. Pulling away from her mouth, I release her throat and look at the mark I made on her neck.

Some sort of primal need builds inside of me and I barely contain the need to pound on my chest and shout out that she's mine. Instead, I cover the mark with my hand again, and maintain eye contact with her so I can react straightaway if she doesn't like it. Her eyes are heavy and filled with nothing but pleasure and the little whimpers she's making as I thrust in and out of her at a steady pace, tell me she's enjoying this as much as I am.

Briefly breaking eye contact, I look down at where our bodies meet, watching my cock go in and out of her wet, hot core. Her liquid is glistening on my bare cock and it ignites an almost primal feeling in me as my pace increases.

A flicker of something passes through my mind as I watch where we're joined, but it disappears before I can grasp it. Seeing us connected is probably my new favorite thing, and it's hard for me to think coherent thoughts when I'm deep inside of her. My heart rate kicks up with every thrust.

The feelings she ignites in me, not just when we're fucking, are so different to anything I've ever experienced before. It's maddening the effect she has on me. How my gaze seeks her out in a room, how I always want her near, and how I feel a crazy amount of anger toward any man who so much as glances in her direction.

When her eyes flutter closed, I move my hand from her throat to grab her chin and kiss her. With an arm around her waist, I bring her closer to the edge of the table, my chest pressing to hers. The feel of her hot, slick skin against my own ignites a fire inside of me and I part my lips, forcing hers to open. Her tongue darts out to tangle with my own again, as we kiss in a frenzy.

It's as if this is the only way we can survive, me buried deep inside of her and our mouths fused together.

"Eyes on me, baby. I want you to feel every—" *Thrust.* "—Part—" *Thrust.* "—Of—" *Thrust.* "—Me." *Thrust.* I growl against her lips, holding eye contact. With my hands on her hips, I'm pounding into her forcefully and the sound of skin slapping on skin fills the room.

"Please... Cooper... I... I need to... Oh God, I'm... " Meghan gasps.

"Say it again... say my name," I breathe out as a command. My voice is gruff and demanding.

"Cooper..." she exhales in a whispered pleading breath.

*Fuck, I think that's my new favorite sound—my name on her lips.*

Taking my thumb, I move it to her clit and start rubbing her gently, bringing her closer to her completion. I can tell she's nearly there and that it won't take long for the combination of my thrusts in and out of her and the circular motion of my thumb to tip her over the edge.

I can feel the little spasms of her pussy clenching around me as I thrust into her.

"Who does this pussy belong to?" I demand, slowing my pace right down, so it's almost agonizingly slow.

She looks up at me in confusion. I shouldn't have any demands over her body, but I need her to say that one word.

I want all of her to belong to *me*.

"Tell me," I growl as I remove my hand from her clit and stop thrusting completely. I rest my forehead on hers as I hold her gaze, my hands in fists resting on the table top.

"Cooper, please... I'm so close, don't stop now," she begs, her gaze searching mine as she rolls her hips, urging me to move.

My jaw clenches as I tell myself to calm down. "Then tell me who you belong to." I rasp the command, my cock still buried inside her tight, hot pussy.

*I honestly had no clue I had this much self-control.*

"You... I belong to you," she whispers, with no reluctance whatsoever in her tone.

"Good girl," I praise and resume my movements. Rubbing her clit as I kiss her plump lips, I work her up again, the pace of my thrusts building.

It doesn't take long to bring her back to the edge.

I could never have enough of *this*.

Never have enough of *her*.

She lets out a strangled moan as she comes and her pussy grips my cock in a stranglehold, setting off my own as I shoot my come deep inside of her. My teeth dig into her shoulder with the force of my orgasm and I pray that I've left another mark on her.

*Made her mine.*

Resting my forehead on her shoulder, I gulp in lungfuls of air as I try to bring my breathing back to a regular rhythm. My body's covered in a layer of sweat and my legs feel weak from the force of my orgasm. I place a soft kiss over her already bruising skin, trying to keep my smug smile at bay.

Unsure of what I'll see on her face when I pull away, I suck in a breath and steel myself for her reaction now that we're out of the moment. I'm expecting she's going to be pissed at the marks I've left on her skin, or at least still in her post-orgasmic haze.

What I don't expect is for her to not even give me a chance to ask if she's okay, before she shoves me away from her and gathers her clothes.

"I'm sorry. We shouldn't have done that," she mutters as she runs from the room.

I stay rooted to the spot as she runs away.

*Again.*

## ELEVEN

*Meghan*

**W**hat did I just do?

I can't believe I could be so stupid. One minute we were working and then before I knew it, he had my clothes off and his delicious cock was buried deep inside of me.

If this has proven anything, it's that I *definitely* need to quit my job. All it took was one accidental touch and I'm spread on a table ready for him to fuck me.

In Miami, when I said it wouldn't happen again, I didn't mean to lie. In fact, I *hate* lying. I honestly thought I could control myself around him. I mean, I've done it for the last year, so why can't I do it now?

*Because I've had him.*

I haphazardly throw on my clothes as I run back to my desk to collect my things as quickly as possible, before hurrying down the corridor toward the main bank of elevators.

I'm not risking hanging around when he could come after me at any moment. The last thing I want is for him to ask questions I don't have the answer to. Jabbing the button furiously, I curse the fact that we're on the thirtieth floor, all the while throwing glances behind me to make sure he isn't following me.

Breathing a sigh of relief when the elevator arrives, I step inside and press the button for the lobby before repeatedly pressing the close door button. The faint sound of another elevator arriving on the floor has my stomach plummet at the fact that we could have been caught. Trying my best to hide in the corner of the elevator, I hear someone walk past as the doors slide closed, not daring to take a peek. I'm so angry at myself for giving into my most basic needs.

Using the time the elevator takes to descend to the lobby, I freshen myself up the best I can. I don't want to be seen as a woman who sleeps with the boss and tries to use it to her advantage. Even if that isn't what's happening here, people will come to their own conclusions if they get a glimpse of my disheveled appearance.

Letting out a defeated sigh, I pull my coat around my body and try to cover the fact that my shirt has been ripped to shreds and my legs that were covered when I arrived are now bare.

The elevator dings, signaling I've reached the lobby, as I release a heavy breath. When the doors glide open, I step out, ensuring I keep my head down as I rush toward the exit and out onto the quiet street. It's late and in this area of Lower Manhattan, which is predominantly businesses, it's always quiet after eight. It's not ideal, but it means I'll have to walk a little to grab a cab.

Walking a couple of blocks until I hit a busier area, I spot a cab and hail it to take me home. It's worth the cost —getting on the subway looking as disheveled as I do right now probably isn't the best idea. Settling into the back of the cab, I pull out my cell, switching it to silent mode as I make a mental plan for when I get home.

*A long soak in the tub with candles.*

*My homemade oat and honey face mask.*

*Comfy PJ's.*

*And a couple of episodes of a show before bed.*

I'm going to need to stop for snacks and something to take the edge off of my nerves. That's a given.

My heart hasn't stopped racing and butterflies are in full flight mode in my stomach. If I'm being honest with myself, nobody has ever made me feel the way he does. Nobody has ever stolen my breath with a simple touch or made me a quivering mess just from being near them.

*All of this is why I shouldn't keep working for him.*

I spend the remainder of the cab ride replaying the events of tonight in the conference room over and over in my head.

I'll admit it's electric between us when we're together. I love how he takes control and praises me when I do something that pleases him—I never knew that was a kink of mine. Part of me wishes we could have met in a different way. That he wasn't my boss.

But he is, and this giving in to whatever the hell is going on between us, it needs to stop.

I'm flustered, turned on and annoyed with myself even more by the time the cab pulls up outside of my building. Paying the driver, I sheepishly climb out and allow the cold December air to cool my heated cheeks.

Taking my time on the icy sidewalk, I head in the direction of the bodega at the end of my block for my much deserved snacks and alcohol. After the events of tonight and what I'll have to face tomorrow, I think I should have at least a pint of ice cream and a bottle of wine. Or maybe I'll get some whiskey to pour over the ice cream.

*Thank God it's Friday tomorrow.*

My phone vibrates in the bottom of my bag as I'm browsing the shelves of the store. Searching through the depths of my bag, I grasp my phone. As I pull it out, *Mom* flashes across the screen and I press the green button to connect the call.

"Hey Mom, how are you?" I ask, trying to inject some cheer into my voice.

"I'm okay, honey. Still a bit sick, but I wanted to check in with you."

"Mom, we literally spoke yesterday, nothing has changed since then," I chuckle as I pick up my favorite treats—whiskey and salted caramel ice cream—before carrying them to the cash desk to pay.

*Nothing, other than being unable to keep my hands off of my boss.*

"Are you sure? When my mom-alarm goes off, you know I know something is amiss."

"I'm sure. I was working late and I've just stopped at the store for a snack. I'm going to pay and then head home," I reassure her.

"Okay, if you're sure." She coughs, and as I wait for her to finish, I time it with my watch.

She's getting worse, not better. My dad assured me she's doing everything she can to get better, but I feel like they're both being vague.

"What has the doctor said about your cough?" I ask.

"Oh, don't you worry about me, pudding. I've got to go. Call me on Saturday, okay?" It's just like her to ignore my concerns but expect me to answer hers.

"Okay. I love you."

"Love you too, sweetie." With that, I disconnect the call and pay for my treats.

Walking back to my place, I vow not to tell her come Saturday that I've had ice cream for dinner, although I'm sure she has some sort of sixth sense when it comes to what meals I eat.

Inside my apartment, I switch some lamps on as I move about, before putting the ice cream in the freezer and removing two ice cubes. Placing them in a large tumbler, I pour over a generous helping of whiskey. It's not top-shelf, but it will do.

In the bathroom, I put my glass on the side table next to the tub, turning on the faucet and filling it. Sitting on the edge, I pour in a generous amount of lavender bubble bath, inhaling deeply as the comforting scent fills the room.

It's been an eventful few weeks and I need to regroup.

Leaving the tub to fill, I stand in front of the mirror and take in my crumpled appearance. Peeling off my blouse, I inspect the damage before throwing it in the trash. It's beyond repair.

My eyes snag on the red purplish colored bruises he's left on me, and I run my fingers over the first one, reliving his mouth on me. *Marking me.* It's on the side of my neck, and I'm certain I'll have to wear a turtleneck to hide it. The other bruise is on my shoulder, and I run my fingers over the tender skin as I remember him coming deep inside me, the spasms of my own orgasm racking through me as his guttural sounds filled my ears.

*Come on, Meghan.*

Shaking my head to clear away the images, I turn away from the mirror, unable to look at my body for fear of finding more reminders of him. Once naked, I pull on my fluffy, oversized white robe, before lighting some candles and turning off the overly bright overhead light.

In the soft glow of the candles, I remove my makeup with a reusable face cloth before slathering on my home-made face mask. As I connect my phone to my bluetooth speaker, I press shuffle on my *Soul* playlist, and the smooth sound of Solomon Burke's *Don't Give Up on Me* fills the room. With my robe hanging on the back of the bathroom door, I step into the hot, scented water.

I relax to the sounds of some of my favorite soul legends, replaying mine and Cooper's encounter in my mind, taking generous sips of whiskey.

It was like we couldn't have stopped ourselves, even if we'd wanted to. At the same time, I know it shouldn't have happened and I refuse to let it happen again. I have to be strong. Tomorrow I will sit down with him and affirm what we have already agreed. I know now that if there is even a hint that we're going to lose control I need to resign.

I end up staying in the bath until my fingers turn wrinkly and the water has long gone cold. I pull the plug, watching for a moment as the water swirls away, before grabbing my towel and patting myself dry.

Moving to the sink, I rinse my mask off and go through my bedtime skincare routine before smoothing my favorite shea butter lotion all over my body. Naked, I walk to my bedroom, before getting dressed in my usual PJs—a strappy camisole and booty shorts.

With my glasses on and my hair brushed out and tied into a messy bun on top of my head, I walk the few steps to the kitchen and serve myself a large bowl of ice cream. At the last minute, I pour over a generous helping of whiskey. Unable to resist, I scoop up a spoonful and savor the coolness of the ice cream paired with the warmth of the whiskey, moaning in delight.

Snacks in hand, I stroll to the couch where I settle down to watch the latest episode of *Grey's Anatomy*. I'm about thirty minutes into the episode when there's a knock on my door. I frown before pressing pause on the TV and walking to answer it. I'm not expecting anyone and it's kind of late, so I assume it's Alex on the other side.

"Alex, I'm going to bed soon..." I announce as I pull the door open.

Only, it's not Alex.

## TWELVE

# Cooper

I don't know how long I stand in the boardroom, stuck in a trance of disbelief that she's run, *yet again*. But by the time I snap myself out of it, I'm certain that she's left. As I'm gathering the papers that have been strewn across the floor and table, a cough sounds from behind me.

Spinning on my heel, I come face to face with my father, a smirk on his face as he stands in the doorway.

"What are you doing here? Security shouldn't have let you in."

He walks further into the room, coming to stand next to me as I continue to collect the documents. "I came to see if my son had come to his senses and it seems you have. Going by the smell of sex in here and the fact that I saw your assistant looking more than a little disheveled, I'm guessing you finally gave in and fucked her."

Clenching my fists I drag in a calming breath, gritting

my teeth before responding to him. "Regardless of what may or may not have happened here, I told you not to come back. Why are you here?" I hiss.

"Come on, son..."

"As far as I'm concerned, I'm not your son. Now, please leave."

Holding up his hands, he backs toward the door, a slimy smile spreading across his lips. "Just remember, you can fuck the girl but that's it. She's not Jackson-wife material."

He barely finishes the sentence before I rush at him, grabbing his collar and pushing him against the wall. The soft thud of the back of his head hitting the plaster fills the room and mingles with my heavy uncontrolled breathing.

I'm so fucking mad.

Madder than I've ever been before.

We stare into each other's eyes and I direct all of the hate and anger I have at him.

"Who I fuck, fall in love with, or even marry is none of your goddam business. I told you to get the fuck out and never come back. You should heed my warning, *Elijah*," I roar, certain that the vein in the side of my neck is about to burst.

Releasing his collar, I step back and watch as he straightens his appearance before walking out. He doesn't utter a word, but the look on his face tells me I won't be seeing him again.

*Fuck.*

I'm just like him, unable to keep my hands off of a woman that should be unattainable. I'm all the things I thought he was as I was growing up; weak, pathetic, a man with no morals.

This can't keep happening, we... I can't keep doing this back and forth. Every time I say I won't become my father, I do something that makes me just like him. Like fucking my assistant on a conference room table. Enough is enough. We need to talk about what is happening, agree to a plan and stick to it.

She can't keep running from this.

*From me.*

More importantly, I need to stop losing control. I'm not a man that loses control easily, but with her I seem to have none.

Walking into my office, I make a beeline for my private bathroom—I need to prepare for the conversation I'm going to make her have with me tonight.

The lights glare down on me, showing my disheveled appearance, and I run my fingers through my hair in an attempt to smooth it out.

Pulling in a deep breath before releasing it in a slow exhale, I crack my neck and lean my hands on the counter. With my chin on my chest, I take a moment to just let my mind reset.

*Come on Cooper, treat it like a court case.*

Lifting my gaze, I look myself in the eye as I figure out what to say.

"Hi, are you okay? I don't like that you keep running

away from me. I enjoy having sex with you, but we can't keep doing what we're currently doing. Let's go back to how it was before."

It could use a little work.

*Jesus, why does she have me so tied up?*

"Hi, are you okay?"

This shouldn't be this hard.

"I'm sorry, it shouldn't have happened and..." No, that sounds like I regret it, which could not be further from the truth.

*Let's try this again...* "Hi, are you okay? We should talk about what happened and get this sorted, once and for all." Okay, this is a better start.

"I think we should agree on a plan to reduce the risk of us slipping up again, because we can't continue like this. You're my assistant and, as your boss, I don't want you to feel like I'm taking advantage of you."

I think that's a good foundation.

A good start, I can ad lib when I'm in front of her, see what she has to say.

One thing I know for certain is, this can't wait for tomorrow and it needs to be somewhere she feels comfortable. I'm going to have to go to her home.

*I won't touch her.*

Moving to my desk, I login and pull up her personnel file.

*What's crossing one more line?*

Standing on the street outside Meghan's apartment building, I take in its worn and unwelcoming appearance.

I don't like that she lives in this neighborhood.

Literally anyone who lives in the New York area knows this isn't the safest borough and I don't like the thought of her living here by herself. All the buildings on this block look like they've seen better days and there are people loitering around, sitting on stoops looking shady.

As my eyes dart up and down the block, I vow not to have her working anymore late nights and, if we absolutely have to, I'll be making sure she gets home safely.

*It's not my place to be this worried about her.*

I'm just looking out for a valued employee. It's not like I'm acting like her boyfriend. If I did, she'd be living in a nice apartment, somewhere safe.

*What if she has a boyfriend?*

I quickly get rid of that thought, because I know her well enough to know that she would have stopped whatever we are, if that were the case.

Satisfied that I'm not about to walk in on Meghan with a boyfriend, I look up at the building in front of me and count the windows until I see what I think is her apartment. The lights are off and I hope that she's just in bed rather than not home—she should be back by now.

Nerves settle deep in the pit of my stomach as I

contemplate whether I should have come or not. I'm not one for second guessing my actions—why would I when I can argue my way out of pretty much anything—but where she's concerned, I don't want to do anything to scare her away.

That realization has me questioning what I'm doing here, what my grand plan is once I get inside. Yes, I have an idea of what I want to say, but where is this going?

Taking a steading breath, I walk up to the front door and realize that I need to buzz her apartment and, given tonight's events, it's highly unlikely that she'll let me in.

Just as I'm contemplating my next move, an older woman comes struggling through the door pulling a cart, a lit cigarette clenched between her teeth. She's dressed in dark leggings with a Black Sabbath t-shirt that has multiple holes in it and a parka coat. She smells like a wet dog, and I try not to retch as the overwhelming odor travels up my nose.

Taking this as my way in, I hold the door open for her with what I hope is a smile, but could very well be a grimace on my face.

"Thanks, doll," she rasps, pulling her cigarette from her mouth and glancing up at me, baring her yellow teeth in a smile.

I nod in response while holding my breath, so I don't throw up, and slip through the door, making my way to the elevator. An out-of-order sign greets me, so I redirect to the stairs and climb up to the second floor, a sense of urgency taking over me.

Before I know it, I'm standing outside Meghan's apartment door and taking a deep breath as I raise my hand to knock before resting my hands on either side of the door.

"Alex, I'm going to bed soon..." she announces as she throws the door open, her words trailing off as her wide eyes lift to mine.

*Who the fuck is Alex?*

I grind my teeth and clench my fists in... anger. It takes all of ten seconds for me to remember her friend... a girl... who works for my firm.

Alex.

*Breathe Cooper.*

Relaxing my jaw and unclenching my fists, I look at Meghan as I push away from the doorjamb. My eyes roam over her from head to toe. I've never seen her look more alluring.

She's wearing short, skin-tight cotton baby pink shorts. They hug the curve of her hips and I'm sure if she turned around, the bottom of her ass cheeks would be on display for me. She's paired the shorts with a camisole top similar to the one she had on earlier, and with no bra on, I can see her nipples poking through.

Her blonde hair is piled on top of her head in some sort of messy bun, her face is free of make-up and a pair of glasses are perched on her nose. She has a bowl of ice cream in her hand and it's swimming in some brown liquid that smells a lot like whiskey.

*I won't be able to look at her in the office without picturing her like this.*

To my surprise, she doesn't immediately try to shut the door in my face. Instead, she stares up at me, her mouth slightly agape. If she didn't blink, I'd think she was a statue. Shaking her head, she seems to come out of whatever trance she's in.

"Do you always answer the door dressed like that?" I admonish her.

She looks at me with confusion painted across her beautiful face. "What do you mean? Like what?"

I gesture with my hand to her body. "In your underwear."

She glares at me as she folds an arm under her chest, giving me a perfect view of her ample cleavage. "These are my PJ's."

"I'm guessing you didn't even look through the peephole."

"Why are you here, Mr. Jackson?" She asks, looking away sheepishly.

*I was right, dammit.*

*Why isn't she looking out for herself?*

"Cooper. My name is Cooper, Meghan. You were moaning it not that long ago," I remind her. For Christ's sake, she was crying it out, telling me she belonged to me, not even two hours ago.

"Why are you here... *Cooper*?"

It's better, but I still don't like the tone. It's nothing

like when she was in the throes of passion and begging me to make her come.

"I wanted to see you... to apologize and make sure you were okay." It's not really a lie, but it's also not entirely the truth.

Yes, I'm sorry that she felt it shouldn't have happened, but I'm not sorry that it did.

"You don't need to apologize. I could have stopped you if I wanted to," she responds, her teeth dragging over her bottom lip. She lifts her heavy eyes to mine, and I'm a goner.

She's my kryptonite and everything I wanted to say goes out the window.

Stepping into her apartment, forcing her to move away from the door, I take her face between my hands. She doesn't say anything, but she doesn't push me away either. Instead, she places the bowl on the table next to the door and grabs onto the lapels of my coat.

Capturing her lips with mine, I back her further into the apartment, kicking the door closed behind me.

Meghan is curled up next to me with her head on my shoulder and one palm resting on my bare chest. The sheet is draped over my lower half, barely covering her curvy ass, and she has a leg resting over my thigh as she snores softly.

She dozed off almost immediately after we both came and I'm thinking that might be her 'thing'.

The room is shrouded in darkness, even with the curtains open but a slither of light from the street lights beams across her smooth skin and her golden locks, which are spread out over the pillow.

As I lay awake, my hand smoothing over the soft skin of her hip, a thought occurs to me: *I could get used to this.*

Her warm and soft body curved into the side of mine, with her scent all around me and her taste lingering on my tongue. It's what dreams are made of. She feels a lot like home and it dawns on me that I could fall for her—like really fall for her.

As that thought flits through my mind, another comes to the forefront; I need to leave. I shouldn't have kissed her again. *Or fucked her again.*

What is wrong with me? I shouldn't have come here.

I shouldn't have chased after her.

I shouldn't be seeing her as anything other than my assistant.

This thing between us—whatever it is—it can't go anywhere.

No.

It *won't* go anywhere. *I won't allow it.*

I'm not capable of giving her everything she wants, needs or deserves. I'm just like my father and too committed to my job.

*I need to leave.*

As I ease Meghan off of me, she stirs, her lashes fluttering as she wakes, revealing dazzling but slightly confused green eyes.

"Where are you going?" she asks. Her voice is husky as she rubs at her eyes to remove the heaviness of sleep before sitting up in bed, pulling the sheet with her.

"I'm heading home."

Her eyes coast over me as I pull on my clothes and she lifts her hand to her lips before she speaks. "Oh, okay." She looks lost and confused and all I want to do is climb under the covers, pull her into my arms and wipe that look from her face.

Turning away, I pull my pants up as I push through with what needs to be done. "Look, thanks for today. You were great, as usual."

She huffs out a laugh of disbelief, turning her gaze toward the window, and I close my eyes as I realize how my words could be taken. It's for the best that she's misunderstood me. Maybe this is what we need to resist each other.

"I think it's best that this stops here, before one of us..." I stop to look at her, the sheet clutched to her chest, and her chin held high—she's fucking stunning. "Forgets this is only sex."

*Before I forget.*

I don't think I'll ever forget the taste of her or having my nose buried in the curve of her neck as I breathe in her unique scent—honey and vanilla.

Fully dressed, I walk to the door, before turning to

face her. I take one last mental picture. *God, she's beautiful.*

"I'll see you in the office tomorrow." I walk from the room, internally screaming at myself to turn the fuck around.

I don't stop until I get back to my quiet and cold penthouse.

Heading to my bedroom, I change into my workout clothes before making my way to the gym I have set up in one of my many spare rooms. Loading up a playlist on the surround sound system, I press shuffle and the sound of *Stronger* by Kanye West blasts through. On a bench with a set of dumbbells, I start a workout, pushing myself to the limit.

I need a distraction and to detox Meghan from my thoughts.

## THIRTEEN
## Meghan

After Cooper left, I laid in bed and cried myself back to sleep. *Stupidly*. Why am I crying over a man that has made no commitment to me and instead has told me things I was already telling myself?

It feels like my heart is being trampled on.

Why would he do this?

Why would he walk out like he did?

He *fucking* thanked me.

I just don't understand. He's the one that came after me.

*Oh God, I hope he didn't see my tears.*

I don't think he did since he barely looked at me as he dressed, but they definitely escaped while he was still in the room. I'm going to have to go to work knowing this man has been inside of me and that he's just going to forget about it and move on.

*Argh! Fuck him.*

*Fuck him for making me feel this way.*

I call in sick the next day and wallow in my self pity. I'm a coward, but I couldn't face him, not so soon after everything. I end up staying up late Friday night, drinking whiskey, ignoring my phone and eating junk food until I pass out, not waking up until late afternoon on Saturday.

Climbing out of bed, I make my way to the bathroom where I catch my reflection in the mirror. If I wasn't so upset, I would laugh at what I see reflected back at me.

My complexion is pale and my hair looks like a contestant on *Shear Genius* has styled it. Red-ringed and puffy eyes look back at me and I wonder if it's possible to cry in your sleep.

Averting my eyes from the horror show that is my reflection, I brush my teeth and rinse my face with cold water before making my way back to bed.

I love my bed. It's large, fluffy like a cloud, and sits proudly with the headboard against the wall in the middle of the room. When I moved in, I painted the walls an eggshell blue and then accessorized with a white chest of drawers against one wall and a white cushion-topped chest at the foot of the bed.

I'm just climbing back into my queen-size bed, pushing down the large puffy comforter, with a single solitary tear rolling down my cheek at my foolishness, when there's a knock on my front door, which causes me to freeze.

*Surely, he wouldn't have come back.*

I take a moment, convincing myself he wouldn't be stupid enough to return, before climbing off of the bed and heading toward the front door, making sure to peek through the peephole. I'm not making the mistake of opening the door without checking again. My shoulders relax when I see that it's Alex on the other side and I rest my forehead to the back of the door, contemplating my next move. If I open the door, she'll know something's wrong–it wouldn't take a genius to figure it out.

*But I need my friend.*

That fact wins out and I decide to open the door. As soon as I do, Alex lets out a loud gasp of surprise as her eyes settle on my disheveled appearance.

"What happened?" she demands and I can tell that she's ready to fight whoever might have hurt me.

I go to open my mouth to speak, to explain, to say... anything, but my eyes well with tears and I break down, letting out an ugly sob. Pulling me into a tight hug, she leads me into the living room, kicking the door closed behind her. Forcing me to release my hold on her, she sits me on the couch before taking a seat next to me, grabbing my hand and rubbing circles on my back, giving me the comfort I desperately need.

"Tell me what happened, babe."

"I... Oh God, I don't even know why I keep crying," I murmur, angrily swiping at the tears tumbling down my cheeks. "I–I–I slept with... Cooper," I say, hiccuping my way through the admission.

"Cooper?" She looks at me quizzically. Her eyes widen and her jaw goes slack as she realizes who I'm talking about. "Cooper, as in *Cooper Jackson*, your boss? *Our* boss?"

"Yes," I whisper reluctantly, the shame of what I've done overwhelms me and I blink back tears that threaten to fall.

"Okay, let's park that revelation for a moment. What did he do to make you cry?"

She continues to rub my back, but I drop my head, unable to look her in the eyes when it feels like such an overreaction. *I'm definitely blaming being a Cancer for these emotions.* That and my hurt feelings. I wish I didn't feel this way.

Taking a deep breath in, I lift my head and because I'm going to own up to what I've done, I answer Alex. "He came over last night... after I ran out on him because we had sex on the boardroom table. We ended up having sex again, and I fell asleep in his arms. I thought everything was... I didn't think he'd try and leave while I was asleep. I thought the fact that he came to my house meant we would... I don't know, try and move past the whole—" I wave my hand in the air, unsure how to label what we had. "—thing. Maybe give dating a try, which, in hindsight, was foolish of me to think. He accidentally woke me when he was trying to leave and told me I was great, as usual, and then that we should stop before one of us forgets it's just sex. Then he left, like he hadn't just sucker punched me, saying he'd see me the next day."

"And why did you run out on him?" she asks with no judgment in her tone.

"I'd just slept with my boss, Alex," I exclaim. Even though Alex wouldn't ever judge me, I try desperately to justify my actions. "I was scared. I really like him, but he's my boss. What will people think?"

"Oh, babe." She pulls me in for a side hug before continuing. "First of all, wow. Second of all, I don't know why he ran out, but maybe this is, and I mean this in the nicest way possible, what you needed to get over him. He's not the Prince Charming you built him up to be in your mind," she tries to reassure me.

I shake my head at my past self's foolishness, admonishing myself for spending so much time fawning over a man that's treated me like I'm nothing but some easy lay.

Leaning back on the couch, I bring my knees up to my chest, wrapping my arms around them. Alex sits back with me and rests her shoulder against mine, the connection letting me know she's not going anywhere. We sit in a comfortable silence for what feels like an hour but is probably more like fifteen minutes.

With my mind made up, I ask Alex, "Can you help me with something?"

"Anything for you."

"So for a while I've been thinking about how I'd like to, maybe, switch up my wardrobe a bit." I turn to face Alex and find her eyes on me. "I think I'm ready to get back to my old, confident self. Who I was in college. Can we go shopping? And maybe get my hair done? And nails?"

Alex lets out a chuckle as she throws her arm around my shoulder and pulls me in for a hug. "I thought you'd never ask."

I need the confidence of the dress I wore to the Christmas party. Going shopping with Alex will guarantee that I come home with outfits that boost that dwindled confidence.

Standing from the couch, Alex turns to face me before holding out her hands and pulling me up, then pushing me in the direction of the bathroom.

With a pang of regret, I realize I can still smell him on me. Subconsciously, I think I still wanted a part of him on me—aside from the slight bruising on my neck and shoulder from the hickeys he gave me.

"You get in the shower and I'll make us coffee."

Following Alex's demand, I walk into the bathroom and turn on the shower before stripping out of my PJs and throwing them in the laundry. I take a moment to check out my reflection.

I look like crap.

I've shied away from putting myself on display ever since I came to the realization that men will take advantage of you, but maybe it's time to step into my villain era and be the bad bitch Alex is always telling me I am.

Turning away from the mirror, I step under the now warm spray of the shower, allowing the water to cover me before I squirt a generous amount of my favorite strawberries and cream body wash onto a loofah and scrub my body. I watch in fascination as the water carrying his scent flows down the drain.

*If only I could wash away the memories this easily.*

Finally clean, I step out of the shower and wrap my fluffiest towel around me before slathering on my lotion. When Alex knocks on the door, I'm feeling more human and less like a neurotic mess.

"Your coffee's ready. Do you want it in there?" she calls through the door.

Taking one last look in the mirror, I call out, "No, I'm coming out now."

Wrapping myself up in my robe, I walk toward the kitchen where I find Alex typing away on her phone. She hands me a mug of steaming coffee and I lean against the counter, patiently waiting for her to finish.

"Thank you for being here," I say before taking a sip and looking down into my mug, hiding my face from her. I feel ashamed of my actions, of sleeping with my boss and allowing him to mess with my emotions to such an extreme degree. I know I shouldn't feel ashamed; we're both adults after all, but his rejection hurts.

"I wouldn't be anywhere else," she assures me, as she pulls me into a side hug. "Now, let's get you dressed so we can get this show on the road. I've booked you in to see Maxine for a trim and blowout. We don't need to do anything drastic with your gorgeous hair."

Alex happily chatters as we go into my room and I dig

out a pair of comfortable jeans and a warm sweater before getting dressed.

In the bathroom, I run a brush through my hair, smoothing out the tangles caused by Cooper's fingers and sleep, before throwing it into a messy bun. I perch my glasses on my nose, titling my head as I come to the realization that I hate that I use my glasses as a shield, as if they can provide me with some sort of protection. I should wear my contacts more often.

Starting today, I will be a brave, confident, take no shit woman. With one last look at my reflection and a nod to affirm my vow, I meet Alex in the hallway.

Grabbing my crossbody bag and throwing on my parka coat from the closet next to the front door, I pull on a comfortable pair of sneakers before opening the door, signaling for Alex to leave first.

We make our way down the stairs, stepping out onto the bustling street, and bundled in our coats, we walk the block and a half to Alex's hair stylist.

*Makeover, here I come.*

# FOURTEEN

## Meghan

After a day and half of shopping, pampering, and pep talks, Monday morning still seems to come around far too quickly. I'm nervous and almost afraid to go into work this morning. This is despite Alex getting ready with me, which I guess was to make sure I didn't revert to my usual ways, and to give me affirmations and pep talks for breakfast.

Today, I've opted for a red ruched midi form fitting dress with spaghetti straps—when I say *I* opted, what I actually mean is Alex chose it for me.

We've paired it with Alex's black *Louis Vuitton Lockme Shopper Bag,* a pair of five-inch black patent leather court shoes, and an oversized black blazer that I'm not allowed to put my arms in the sleeves of and I'm only to remove when at my desk.

*Insert eye roll here.*

I'm going to freeze my nipples off, but, according to

Alex, fashion comes at a price—that price being no nipples, apparently.

My hair is down with my newly cut bangs parting like curtains and we've somehow managed to recreate the blow out I got on Saturday.

I've kept my make-up simple, but the new rose-gold creamy eyeshadow we picked up from *Saks* really makes my eyes pop. A dusting of bronzer and blush across my cheeks make my face look snatched, according to Alex, and accentuates my cheekbones.

We're packed like sardines on the subway heading into Manhattan when Alex mentions Cooper. I can tell that she's been thinking of a sensitive way to bring him up, the cogs of her mind clearly turning. With how close we're stood, it's been impossible to ignore the sound of her mind whirling.

*Should I go back to calling him Mr. Jackson now?* I guess I should.

Although I don't want to talk about our situation, I know I'm going to have to face him soon and that I'll need all of the encouragement Alex can give me, so indulge her.

"I'm glad you're looking better than when I came over on Saturday," she starts off tentatively, side eyeing me as she moves closer for more commuters to board the cart.

"I am. Thank you for taking me out. I needed it. Now that I've had time to reflect on it, I know I need to get over this silly crush and move on. Maybe find someone new." I shrug like it's no big deal and I'm not still crushing on my boss.

It's not going to be as easy to get over him as I'm making it out to be.

"Are you sure?" Alex asks, one of her perfectly arched brows raised in question—sometimes I wish she didn't know me so well. I'm certain she can see through my facade.

"I'm positive," I reply with a wide grin that I'm sure doesn't fully reach my eyes.

"Well, you need to remember a few things for today," Alex states, lifting up her gloved hand as she ticks off her fingers. "Remember, you are a goddess and it's his loss." *Tick.* "Stop looking away from him because you're a *Boss Bitch* and you should be using your eye contact to intimidate him." *Tick.* "He won't ever get to have you again." *Tick.* "Own it. So what if you slept with him? You got your needs met and now you can move on."

"I've got this," I assure her as I take hold of her outstretched hand and squeeze it, letting out a low chuckle.

I don't know what I'd do without her, because I honestly don't know if I *have* got this.

*Fake it til you make it, I guess.*

We make it to the office in record time, which is just typical. When I'm wanting to drag the commute out or wish for a broken down train, the gods have different plans and get me to work early.

Stepping into the elevator, Alex takes advantage of

the busy carriage by whispering words of encouragement in my ear. "Remember to keep your head held high, make eye contact, and don't let the fucker get to you. You are a *Boss Bitch*, remember that."

The elevator arrives at the twentieth floor and Alex steps out, holding the doors open as she turns to convey her message to me through her eyes—ignoring the glares of the passengers still waiting to get to their floors. Stepping back, she lets the doors close and I drop my head, chanting her words underneath my breath while rubbing my sweaty palms on my thighs.

*I've got this... right?*

It seems to take an eternity to reach the thirtieth floor, but when the doors open, I step out and head to my desk, keeping my head held high as I sashay my way through the office.

Once at my desk, I set my belongings down before removing my jacket and hanging it on the coat stand. *Okay, this is going well so far.* Grabbing my mug, I make my way to the kitchen—I'm going to need a sugary treat to get through this morning.

I'm feeling good... confident even. With Alex's words running through my mind, I feel like I'm going to be okay. *It's all going to be okay.*

"Are you new?" A deep masculine voice asks. My back is to whoever has asked the question and I finish stirring my coffee before turning around with a smile on my lips.

"Meghan? Wow. Um, you look... good," Alfie stutters.

I've never once considered Alfie as anything more

than a colleague. Then again, I've been preoccupied with my stupid crush on my boss. Maybe it wouldn't be such a bad idea to flirt a little and put myself out there.

"Hey, Alfie. Did you have a good weekend?" I ask in my most sultry voice. It probably sounds creepy instead of sexy, but I've got to work with what I've got. I flutter my lashes at him, the lick of mascara I put on this morning having exaggerated them.

"Uh, yeah, it was good. I—wow, where—what—what did you do?" Alfie stutters.

*Maybe it did sound sexy.*

It's almost comical how flustered he seems to be over my appearance. Tilting my head to the side, I look at him for a second before walking to the doorway he's stood in, purposefully swaying my hips.

His eyes dart to my breasts before dragging down my body, watching the motion of my hips as I walk toward him. Coming to a stop just slightly off to the side of him so I can pass by, I reach my arm out and rest it on his bicep. His eyes flick to my hand before coming up to my face, his breath hitching.

*I feel absolutely nothing.*

*No flutters.*

*No excitement.*

*No need.*

*Nothing.*

"Nothing much, just a bit of shopping," I say breathlessly before squeezing his arm and sliding my hand off of it. Running my tongue over my lips that look plump from the lip-gloss I've coated them in causes a flicker of need to light in his eyes.

*Still nothing.*

My body tenses as I get the sense of being watched, and it's like every inch of my skin is on fire as it prickles with awareness. My gaze swings across the sea of booths and meets the stormy gaze of Cooper Jackson.

His jaw is clenched, the muscle in his cheek is ticking, and I can practically see the grinding motion of his jaw from my spot in the kitchen doorway. If I didn't know any better, I'd say he looks pissed off.

Why though, I'm not quite sure.

Tilting my head, I sweep my gaze over Cooper's body before grinning up at Alfie as I say goodbye and sashay back to my desk. A triumphant smirk slips across my lips —maybe I have got this after all.

*Suck on that, Cooper Jackson.*

## FIFTEEN

# Cooper

W hat in the actual fuck is going on? Have I walked into the *Twilight Zone*? I've got a blonde haired Jessica *fucking* Rabbit working for me now, apparently.

I'll admit, Meghan looks amazing, she's got her curves, that dip in all the right places, on full display and a confidence I haven't seen in her since the Christmas party—and I'm certain that confidence was down to the alcohol.

I felt her before I saw her and because I wasn't expecting her to look the way she does. It took me a moment to realize the stunner in the red dress was her.

From my position across the office, I've watched her flirt with an associate and by the way my body is now tightly wound and my fingers are digging into the palms of my clenched fists, I'm going to say I don't fucking like it.

*I might actually need to fire this guy, which I'm not entirely adverse to doing.*

Breaking eye contact with me, Meghan turns to the guy, a sultry smile spreading across her luscious lips as she says something to him before walking away.

Her voluptuous hips sway from left to right in a mesmerizing motion, and I catch myself staring at her ass as she makes her way back to her desk. With great effort—because I don't need to get hard standing in the middle of the office—I tear my gaze away from her.

Rubbing my hand over the back of my neck to relieve some of the tension I feel building, I think of anything to rid my mind of images of me bending her over her desk and fucking her until she screams my name for the world to hear.

*It's going to be a long day.*

Shaking my head brings me back into the room, which is abuzz with people chattering and the eyes of nearly every male staring at the hypnotic sway of her hips. I cough to draw their attention away from what's mine—even if she isn't, really.

Well, she is my assistant, so they shouldn't look for that reason alone, right?

When Meghan's out of sight, I follow in her wake back to my office. As I walk toward her, my eyes greedily roam over her. It doesn't escape my attention that she's covered the marks I made on her with make-up. You wouldn't be able to see them unless you knew to look for them.

An overwhelming urge to drag her to a bathroom and make her wash it off rushes through me, causing my steps to falter. Walking past her, I don't utter a single word or acknowledge her presence. I need to get myself together before I rip that dress off of her and fuck her in the middle of the office. *Then they'd all know she's mine.*

I'm supposed to be forgetting about our indiscretions but how can I do that when she's taunting me with her body?

*What game is she playing?*

Sitting at my desk, I stare out the window, not seeing a thing. My leg bounces, my still clenched fist atop it, as I try to calm my restless energy. I know my mind won't be able to focus with her out there.

*So close, yet so far.*

Men have been crawling out of the woodwork all morning coming to talk to *my* assistant.

*Seriously, where the hell are they all coming from?*

We rarely have visitors to our end of the floor, and if we do, it's always with an appointment. Not once has she buzzed through on the intercom to tell me someone needs something from me.

I'm certain they're social visitors for her and, let's be honest, who can blame them? She was beautiful before, but now... now she's a damn knockout and it's not just her body—her confidence is shining through.

The same guy from the kitchen is now sitting on the edge of Meghan's desk. It's his second visit of the day and it's only two in the afternoon.

I swear I'm not spying on her.

She's beaming up at him, as if he's the most riveting man she has ever laid eyes on. I can barely contain this feeling inside of me that is trying to claw its way out of my chest. When her hand rests on his thigh and she leans forward, letting out a laugh, my own hand reaches out of its own accord and presses the intercom button on my desk phone, buzzing through to her.

"Meghan," I growl when she connects the call.

Her eyes dart to mine through the glass window, the surprise at my tone quickly hidden away, before she holds my gaze as she speaks.

*Where's the woman who avoided making eye contact with me?*

"Yes, *Mr. Jackson*?" she asks, her voice comes out breathy, making my cock twitch and my jaw clench at the same time. I shift uncomfortably in my seat as I try to control my libido.

"Can you come here, please?"

"Why?" she asks.

"Because it's your damn job," I grind out through gritted teeth.

The jackass sitting on her desk is gazing down at the cleavage she has on display, and it takes all of my self-control to not call him in and fire him on the spot.

"Of course. Coming right now, *sir*."

And then she fucking salutes at me through the window, one corner of her kissable mouth lifting as she does. I watch as she puts the phone down and turns back to the associate. I think his name's Arthur or Alfred, something like that.

*It doesn't fucking matter.*

She smiles at him as if she's been completely oblivious to his lecherous staring. An irrational part of me wants to go out there and destroy him, because her smiles should only be directed at me. He stands with her and as she walks to my office, his gaze doesn't leave her ass.

"How can I help you?" she asks, coming to a stop in the middle of my office.

Rounding my desk, I stalk toward her, unable to halt my movements and not caring if someone might see us. My hands lift to cup her face and I bend my head to capture her mouth, grazing my lips over hers.

Even the lightest touch feels like heaven.

Moving my hands down to her waist, she brings hers up and I feel the pressure of her pushing against my chest.

"What do you think you're doing?" she hisses at me, her eyes darting to the door.

"I'm kissing you. What does it look like?"

Folding her arms across her chest, she levels her stare at me. "Without my permission. You called me in here, for what reason exactly? To kiss me? To humiliate me one more time?"

"I didn't call you in here for that."

"Then why?" she practically shouts.

"Meghan, watch your tone."

"Or what, you'll write me up? Jesus Christ, Cooper." She tears her gaze away from me as she looks out of the window. Her jaw is clenched and she's furiously blinking.

*Why do I keep fucking this up?*

"I'm sorry, okay? I can't seem to help myself when I'm around you."

"Well, you're going to have to. Whatever this is won't be happening anymore."

Running a hand through my hair in frustration, I turn away from her and walk to the chairs in front of my desk, gesturing for her to take a seat. "Please, can we just talk about this?"

## SIXTEEN

## Meghan

"Please, can we just talk about this?"

I stare at Cooper for a moment, taking in his features, the way his eyes are filled with apology and... regret. Shaking my head, I tentatively make my way to the chairs, taking a seat in the one furthest from him—which was pointless since he steps between the two chairs and sits on the edge of his desk, his legs crossed at his ankles.

*God, he's so sexy—get it together, Meghan.*

Today he's wearing a navy-blue pinstripe suit with a crisp white shirt. He's gone without a tie and left the top two buttons open, exposing the thick column of his throat. Just thinking about licking his neck and leaving little bite marks has my mouth going dry and me wriggling in my seat to ease the ache I feel building.

I'm instantly annoyed at myself for feeling this way

toward him after last week. A low throaty chuckle sounds from Cooper, causing my eyes to dart to his.

*Dammit, why does he always see right through me?*

"I'm not sure what there is to talk about," I reply, lifting my nose in the air. At my statement he looks away and I can see his jaw clench as if he's annoyed that I dared to pretend everything is business as usual.

"Meghan," he warns in frustration, his eyes begging me to defy him and see what happens. The brat in me wants to do just that.

Leaning back in the chair, I fold my arms over my chest, causing my breasts to lift and Cooper's eyes to drop to them. It's not creepy like when Alfie did it in the kitchen or at my desk. Instead, I feel empowered, like I've got this man's attention and he's mesmerized by me. For extra measure, I uncross and recross my legs, eliciting a barely audible moan from him as he shifts position.

"As far as I am concerned, what we've been doing should end—just like you said. Before one of us... how did you put it exactly?" I press my finger to my chin, pretending to think of what he'd said as if it isn't playing on repeat in my mind. "Aha, yes, that's it. *Before one of us forgets it's only sex.* To be honest, Cooper, I'm not sure when I gave you the impression that I thought it was anything more." I tilt my head as I wait for his reaction.

But what he says catches me off guard.

"Is that really what you want? Because if it is, then that's what we'll do," Cooper says, making me wonder what he would say if I asked him to be mine.

*No, that's silly. I don't want him to be mine. Do I?*

We stare into each other's eyes, each trying to get a read on the other. His are showing me nothing. His face is a mask, and I can't help but wonder if he's being sincere. Is he just telling me what he thinks I want to hear so he can get between my legs?

I fear that what I want is written all over my face. The conversation I had with Alex over the weekend comes to mind—I need to stop putting other people before me, and I need to do what I want to do.

Right now, I want to keep doing what I've been doing with Cooper.

*Well, not exactly that, because that just led to heartache.*

With my mind made up, I sit up straighter and utter, "If we do this, we don't tell anyone."

For a split second, his eyes flair in surprise before he schools his features and I smirk at the fact I was able to get a reaction out of him. Even if it was only small and he recovered quickly.

He nods as he clears his throat and I take this as my opportunity to put down a few ground rules. Rules are good, rules will help me keep clear boundaries, because he was right; I probably would have forgotten that it was only sex.

I need to not have him treating me as anything more than someone he fucks occasionally. *As a friend with benefits.*

"I have some more rules, so we're both on the same

page," I state, looking down at my hands, suddenly nervous to voice them.

"Go ahead," he responds soothingly, as if sensing my nerves and causing me to lift my gaze to his own. His patience is evident and it gives me the courage to continue.

"Rule number one..." I'm truly flying by the seat of my pants, so I pause as my mind goes over options. "Well, obviously, rule number one is that we don't tell anyone... and I mean anyone. I won't tell Alex, and I usually tell her everything." I pause, waiting for his agreement and take the time to think of the next rule.

"If that's what you want, then nobody will know," he agrees with a shrug of his shoulder, as if it's no big deal. I guess to him it might not be. I mean, for all I know, he's probably sleeping with half of Manhattan. Okay, that brings me to my next one.

"Rule number two..." I pause, unsure of how he'll take this one. "Sleeping with anyone else while we are sleeping together isn't allowed."

"Agreed," Cooper responds almost instantly.

It's my turn to school my features as my brow pulls into a frown. I really did think that would be a deal breaker for him. My romance books have clearly skewed my perception of single billionaires.

"Good. Umm... Rule number three... we can date other people but see rule number two," I state, thinking his answer will be a quick agreement again. It's not like he's going to want to pin all of his hopes on me. He's still going to want to find a woman to marry and have a family with—someone used to fancy parties, penthouses and chauffeur driven cars.

His tone is commanding and I can see his shoulders tensing up as he speaks. "No. Not a chance. If I'm fucking you, you aren't going on dates and kissing or flirting with other men. It's just not happening, Meghan."

"Why not?" I ask, my brow furrowing in confusion as I fold my arms across my chest. He's supposed to be happy that I'm not expecting him to romance me, not looking like he's going to hulk out and smash up the room.

"Because you'll be mine and nobody touches what's mine," he growls, his cheek ticks as the annoyance rolls off of him in waves.

"If I can't date other people, then the same thing goes for you. Are you okay with that?" I ask. A sense of triumph builds inside of me and I roll my lips together to hide my smile.

He probably didn't consider that he wouldn't be able to date either.

"I don't care, you'll be meeting my most basic needs," he throws out casually and it stumps me because he's right. If he doesn't want marriage and kids, I'll be giving him the only thing, other than companionship, that he could want or need.

"Fine." I say, caught off guard. "Let's amend rule three then. If either of us meets someone else we want to date, this ends—effective immediately," I compromise.

I'm not going to put my life on hold for someone that's essentially going to be a fuck buddy, especially when I'm a romantic at heart. It's just asking for more heartache and disaster.

*I can't fall for him.*

If I see him as just a means to an orgasmic end then I can walk away when it's time.

"Agreed," Cooper breathes, his shoulders visibly relaxing.

"Rule number four... we don't date. This is just sex. We don't go out for dinner other than where work requires us to, we don't see each other socially. If we want to see each other it's just going to be to itch a scratch."

"Okay." He shrugs.

"Rule number five, in order for this not to become public, we should refrain from any intimacy at work."

"Okay."

"My last rule is that there will be no sleepovers. No matter how tired you may be, you have to leave afterwards, and I'll do the same."

"Fine," Cooper grumbles, as if it pains him to not be able to hold me at night.

*What a ridiculous notion.*

He's probably just thinking about all the morning sex he could have scored. *Dammit*, now so am I.

I really hope this isn't a mistake.

"Well, I'm glad we got that sorted. If we think of any more rules, we can reconvene this. I'm going to get the

Wilson file. You have some prep time blocked out this afternoon."

Standing, I head toward the door, feeling his gaze on me as I walk across his office. It should feel creepy, but as with everything Cooper Jackson does, it just makes me feel sexy and wanted.

## SEVENTEEN

## Cooper

I watch her as she walks out of my office, bypassing her desk and heading to the file room. A smile spreads across my face as I stay leaning against my desk, replaying our conversation in my mind.

Yes, we have some rules, but I get to have her and no more of this back and forth. *She's mine.* The rules were actually a genius idea, because now neither of us will try to cross the line to make this more than what it is.

*God knows I'm tempted.*

Standing from my desk, my feet carry me across my office, through the door and in her wake. Before I know it, I'm opening the door to the filing room.

Stepping inside, I softly shut and lock the door behind me. Taking a moment, I briefly consider returning to my office. I know I shouldn't have followed her, but I just can't stay away. I've done nothing but think about her all weekend.

The file room is windowless and holds the files for all our current and past cases. Walking along the edge of the room, I look down each of the ten rows of filing cabinets to make sure the room is empty before stopping at the end row where Meghan is. Her back is to me and the curve of her ass is more prominent in her crouched position while she searches for the Wilson file in the bottom drawer of a cabinet. I lean against the wall, my hands in my pockets as I wait for her to finish.

Having found the file, she closes the drawer and stands, smoothing her hands over her dress. As she turns around, she notices me leaning against the wall and lets out an audible gasp, dropping the file on the floor as she brings her hands up to her chest.

"Cooper, what are you doing in here?" she whispers, looking down at the papers on the floor.

I don't know what I planned to do when I came in here, maybe subconsciously it was to have her. *I'm breaking the rules already.* It's when she whispered my name that I realized I am a weak man, a *very* weak man, because the moment it leaves her lips, I want her again.

Screw the inappropriateness of it all.

Stalking toward her, the sound of paper crunching under my feet brings her focus back to me and I force her back until she encounters the wall at the end of the row. My hands instinctively thread into her hair as I tilt her head up, giving me better access to her delectable mouth.

Before this goes any further, I need to know she wants this as much as I do.

"Tell me to stop. Tell me you don't want this and that I should turn around and leave," I plead, my chest pressed to hers. My eyes are fixated on her lips, praying the words I've asked her to speak don't leave them.

Her ragged breaths mix with my own in the small space between us.

"Meghan... tell me to stop." Tilting my mouth down further toward hers, barely an inch away, I plead with her one last time. Giving her a second to tell me no, to push me away, to do anything, before I crash my mouth to hers.

Her hands come up to rest on my chest under my suit jacket, and for a brief moment I think she's going to push me away, causing an emotion I don't care to identify to flit through me. It's soon washed away without another thought as her delicate fingers grab onto my shirt and her lips part, allowing my tongue to sweep between them and get my first taste in three *fucking* days.

*Three days too long.*

My hands leave her hair. One travels down her body to her slim waist and the other lightly captures her throat. With my thumb resting on her jaw, I turn her face and break our kiss, licking her throat and sucking on the sensitive skin, a twisted part of me hoping that I mark her again.

I want to wipe away the makeup she's used to conceal the mark I left on her last week. I want her to walk out of here, with my mark visibly on her. She lets out a whimper as her fingers dive into my hair and she holds my head still.

*Interesting.*

"You like that, baby girl?" I murmur into her neck, my teeth grazing her delicate skin again. A guttural moan releases from her and if I wasn't enjoying the sounds so much, I might worry that people will hear her.

The hand that was holding her waist smooths up to cup her breast through her dress. I can feel the pebble of her nipple through the material. Her dress is tight like the one she wore to the Christmas party, and I pray that she's gone commando again.

"Cooper... more action, less talking," she demands, her breath coming out in pants.

"Whatever you want, darlin'," I reply, dragging my hand from her breast to the hem of her dress before I realize it's too tight and release her throat so I can use both hands to lift it. I bury my face in the space between her shoulder and the column of her neck, kissing, licking, and nipping at the sensitive flesh.

My cock is painfully hard, causing me to adjust myself in order to relieve some of the pressure the confines of my pants are causing.

With her dress now sitting on her waist, I look down at her soaked panties and the barely there G-string covering paradise. I understand how addicts feel because, much like one, I crave another hit of *her*.

*And I think I always will.*

Dropping to my knees, I lift her right leg and place it over my shoulder. There's so little fabric to the G-string that I don't bother taking it off. Instead I pull it to the side and drag my tongue through the slit of her pink, glistening pussy. She lets out another loud moan that can most likely be heard in the office, but at this moment, I really don't care if the whole city can hear. Her moans are music to my ears.

Circling my tongue over her clit, I slip a finger into her pussy, as my free hand moves up her body and I slip a finger into the warm wetness of her mouth. She sucks on my finger as I move it in and out of her mouth, in sync with the one in her tight core. She swirls her tongue around my finger and I imagine it's my cock she's tasting.

*I could eat her for breakfast, lunch, and dinner.*

I flick my tongue against her clit and she rolls her hips, greedily rubbing her pussy against my mouth. Growling in satisfaction at her demand, I slip a second finger into her pussy, stretching her out. She's so fucking tight. Keeping a steady rhythm, going in and out, I try not to rush her. I want her to enjoy this as much as I'm enjoying the taste and heat coming from her.

Pulling my fingers from her core, I gently lift her leg off of my shoulder, smoothing my hand from the back of her knee to her delicate ankle. She looks down at me with a mix of confusion and disappointment on her beautiful face, but it's soon erased with my next words.

"Turn around, bend over and brace yourself on the

wall, baby. I'm not done with you yet," I instruct, my voice thick with lust.

She does as I command, slipping her panties off as she goes, and then I'm presented with a perfect view of her pussy and puckered asshole. Burying my face in her pussy, one hand wrapped around one of her thighs, the other comes up and cracks against her ass cheek as I spank her.

"Cooper..." she groans.

"You like that, baby?" I ask, my voice is muffled as I continue to devour her. She wiggles her ass at me in response, begging me to do it again. "I'll do it again, but you have to promise no noise. You make a noise and there *will* be consequences and you won't like them," I rasp.

"I promise," she gasps out as my tongue flicks over her sensitive clit.

Barely giving her time to finish her declaration, I bring my hand down and connect it with the other ass cheek, not hard enough to leave a mark but enough to have her moaning in pleasure. She keeps her promise and muffles her cries with her fist as I alternate between her bouncy cheeks.

When they're nice and pink, I grab her cheeks in a hand each and fuck her pussy with my tongue. I can tell she's struggling to keep the volume down and it's turning me on even more. Moving my tongue to her clit, my index finger dips into her pussy, taking her wetness, and using it as a lube, I rub my finger around the puckered hole of her ass before I apply pressure and end up with the first knuckle inside.

"Cooper, please... I'm going to come." She moans as I slip my thumb into her pussy and continue my ministrations with my mouth on her clit. My finger and thumb fuck her ass and pussy in tandem and as I feel her orgasm build, an idea forms involving me fucking her pussy and a toy filling her ass.

We're in this position when she comes, her body shuddering at the force as my mouth covers her clit, my thumb is buried in her tight core and my finger is deep in her ass. She collapses against the wall, her cheeks are flushed and she has a post-orgasmic glow on her face and a dazed look in her eyes.

Pulling a handkerchief out of my pocket, I wipe her up as best as I can before picking up the panties that have fallen out of her grasp. I put them in my pocket—I have no idea what comes next but I'm taking these as a little memento. I pull her dress down and turn her around so her back is to the wall, standing as I do so. She looks down at my visibly hard cock, then back up to my face, before going back down again.

"Don't worry about me," I whisper as I move a strand of hair away from her face, before placing my hands in my pockets.

*God, she's beautiful.*

"Are you okay?" I ask.

She opens her mouth to respond, before closing it and giving me a nod. A smile of satisfaction playing on her luscious lips, I take this as my sign to leave, placing a soft kiss on her lips before stepping back.

"Thank you."

*What the fuck, Cooper?*

I nod to her, ignoring her confused gaze as I smooth my hand down my tie and turn and walk out of the file room, back to my office. At this moment, I'm grateful for the half-walls protecting my lower half from anyone that might see me crossing the office.

For the first time since we first hooked up, I don't feel an overwhelming sense of shame. Instead, I feel... excited for what's to come, because although we've put these rules in place, I don't plan on sticking to them all.

In my office, I walk straight into my private bathroom and with the door securely locked behind me I unzip my pants and pull out my throbbing cock. I stroke myself a pitiful number of times, before I come all over my sink, the taste of Meghan on my tongue and the sounds of her moans in my ears.

## EIGHTEEN

# Meghan

y labored breathing is the only sound filling the room as the door clicks shut behind Cooper. I'm still leaning against the wall where he left me, my mind trying to comprehend what the hell just happened.

With legs that feel like jelly from the force of my orgasm, I don't think I can move right now and I'm worried that if I try, I'll just melt into a puddle on the floor. I rest my fingers on my lips in an effort to hide the smile tugging at the corners.

*That was probably the hottest thing I've ever experienced.*

Having given myself five minutes to collect myself, I push away from the wall and crouch down to start collecting the papers from the Wilson file. Prints from his shoes mark some of the pages and others have tears in them from where my heels ripped them.

Releasing a sigh as I stand, I amble on not-so-strong

legs back to my desk, praying nobody heard my screams in the main office. Making it back to my desk with no stares or whispers directed at me, I sneak a glance into Cooper's office through the window, only to stop short when I can't see him.

*I wonder where he's gone.*

*Surely he hasn't left the building.*

There isn't much I can do about it, but if he has, I will be so disappointed. Taking a deep breath to calm my nerves, I open the Wilson file in front of me and try my best to concentrate on putting the documents back in the correct order.

I really hope nobody heard us.

In truth, all I can think about is what just happened and a goofy grin I fail to tamper down spreads across my mouth. Then I remember that he might have left, and it falls away.

Alfie appears like a bad smell at my desk as I'm about to go in search of Cooper—I swear I've spoken to Alfie more times today than I have in the whole time I've worked here. Surely all of this attention can't be down to my appearance.

*I'm still the same person for goodness sake.*

"You okay, Alfie?" I ask, smiling up at him. My mom raised me to always be polite, even when I'm frustrated with the person I'm talking to.

Right now, I'm frustrated with Alfie for following me around like a lost puppy and Cooper for doing a vanishing act.

"Hey Meghan, just wanted to see if you wanted to come for a drink after work?" Alfie asks, leaning against the edge of my desk. I must take too long to answer him as he rushes in to add, "A bunch of us are going, if it makes you feel more comfortable."

"Oh, sur—" I don't get to finish my response before Cooper has his office door open. It dawns on me that he must have been *taking care* of himself, and a blush flourishes across my cheeks at the thought.

Cooper's voice is gentle when he asks me to bring him the Wilson file, but his eyes are hard and fixed on Alfie. With a quick, apologetic grimace to Alfie, I stand and walk the folder over to Cooper. My intention is to hand him the file and go back to my desk, but my plans go out the window as Cooper steps back from the door and motions for me to enter. Releasing a relieved sigh, I follow his silent command.

"We need to talk," he flicks his eyes back to Alfie before continuing, "About the Wilson case."

I pull back my outstretched hand and walk past him with the file clutched to my chest, making my way over to the chairs in front of his desk.

Sitting in the seat I was in not even an hour ago, I set the folder on his desk and fold my hands onto my lap. I'm brushing a piece of lint from my crossed legs when I realize I forgot a pad and paper.

I'm halfway to standing, when Cooper puts his hand on my shoulder, causing me to jump at the unexpected contact, the carpet having muffled his approach.

"Are you okay?" he asks, his blue eyes searching my face.

"I'm great, never been better." I grin up at him, causing him to release a chuckle.

"Okay, well, let's go over the Wilson case."

And just like that, we get back to work as if everything is normal, and he didn't just give me the best orgasm of my life.

Cooper and I see each other every night for the remainder of the week, but come Friday we've made no plans, so when Alex suggests a night of cocktails and dancing at Passion, how can I say no?

I've somehow got through a week of wearing the clothes that I picked up on my shopping spree with Alex and although I was hoping the attention would die down, it doesn't seem to show any signs of doing so.

This means that when Alex suggested our night out, it was in front of Alfie and a couple of other associates and has now turned into a work night out. I can't say I'm excited by the prospect of a night clubbing with the same people I've been trying to avoid all week.

I've just finished putting on my make-up and curling my hair when Alex knocks on my front door. For my make-up, I've chosen to go with a simple light pink shadow blended into the crease of my eye and black-winged liner. On top of my foundation, I dusted over a baby pink blush, contoured to sculpt my features and coated my lips with a red lip stain, leaving them with a matte effect. I take a moment to admire my handiwork before I hurry down the hallway to answer the door.

Alex comes barrelling in, a dress bag in hand, as I pull the door open for her. Taking a second to appreciate the dress she's chosen to wear tonight, I give her a once over and wolf whistle as she twirls in the hallway. Although it looks conservative, with its high neckline and long sleeves, the dress stops just below her ass and has no back. We break into a fit of giggles, both clearly having had a couple of shots before meeting up.

"I may have taken it upon myself to get you a dress for tonight," she says sheepishly as our laughter subsides.

Thrusting the bag into my chest, she walks past me into the living room. Shutting the door, I follow behind her, pulling the belt of my robe tighter as I admonish her for having brought me yet *another* dress.

"Alex. Seriously, you didn't need to buy me a dress. I have plenty I could have picked from."

"They aren't really for going out though, are they? Don't forget I was with you when you brought them. I got you something sexy. Plus, you never know, you might go home with someone tonight." She wiggles her eyebrows at me as she moves into the kitchen.

I follow in her wake, watching as she helps herself and pours us both a glass of wine before sliding mine across the counter.

"Are you going to look at it?" she asks, nodding her head toward the bag before bringing her glass up to her mouth to hide her smirk.

*Okay, now I'm worried.*

Unzipping the garment bag, I reveal the tiniest dress I've ever laid eyes on—and Alex is a fan of wearing very little, so I've seen some tiny scraps of material.

It's gorgeous, but literally everything will be on display. The dress is a white sequin mini dress with a deep V-neck. It has spaghetti straps and as I remove it from the bag, I can see it's backless.

"Alex... I don't know if I can wear this," I murmur as my eyes roam over the fabric.

"Of course you can. You are going to look sexy as hell, and we *are* going to find someone for you to go home with," she declares, like it's her personal mission to send me off with someone.

*Dammit.* I haven't told her about the agreement I made with Cooper and yet I don't *want* to break the agreement with him by telling her.

Realizing I have no choice but to play along with Alex's plan to an extent, I change into the dress she's picked out. I accessorize it with a cute sequin clutch and strappy heels that wrap around my calves.

My plan is to tell Alex that nobody was doing it for me and then come home alone. Returning to the kitchen with the dress on and a plan in place, I grab my wine glass off of the side and clink it against Alex's before downing half of the contents.

*Let's get this show on the road.*

Coats tightly wrapped around us, we step from the cab and walk up to the entrance of Passion, bypassing the queue. I hear the bassline of a popular song from the sidewalk and the alcohol I consumed earlier has me ready to dance.

Alex flirts with the bouncer, a different one from the last time we were here, and so it doesn't take long for us to get through and deposit our coats at the check-in.

We make our way through the door and toward the bar. Bodies are crushed on the dance floor, moving as one to the rhythm of the music and strobe lights slash through the darkness, illuminating them. I don't recognize the song, but it has a sultry, sexy beat to it and I get flashbacks of the Christmas party and dancing with Cooper.

At the bar, Alex orders us a round of shots, handing me two tequilas that I drink down before she hands me a pink cocktail. I have no clue what's in it but I take a sip, enjoying the sweet and fruity concoction.

"Come on, let's go find the others," Alex shouts over the music, and I internally groan at the idea.

Taking her hand, she leads us through the crush of people and toward a group of tables. My stomach tightens and a prickling sensation creeps across my skin from head to toe. I feel like I'm being watched.

*He's here.*

I look around, desperately trying to see over the crowds before lifting my gaze to the VIP area. Cooper's leaning over the railing and his eyes connect with mine from across the darkened club as a well-timed strobe light flashes across us both. He's wearing a white shirt that fits like a glove to his toned body, paired with black jeans that encase his muscular legs.

*He looks edible.*

Just as I'm about to wave up at him, a smile forming on my lips, a woman who looks like a damn supermodel approaches him. Her hands roam over his arm and shoulder, yet he makes no move to get her off of him. *He should be pushing her away.* She leans in to whisper something in his ear and when I think he's finally going to tell her to go away, he breaks eye contact with me, places his arm around her waist, and leans in to listen to whatever it is she has to say.

My stomach clenches with a feeling I'm not quite ready to acknowledge—it's a cross between hurt, jealousy, anger, and embarrassment at his blatant disregard for the rules we agreed to.

I suppose it's better that I've seen this now, before I'd been fucking him for a while. *Before I've fallen for him.* It certainly didn't take him long to get tired of me.

Shaking my head, if only to get rid of the image, I continue following Alex toward the table. Did I seriously think that a man like Cooper Jackson would want *me*?

Before I know it, we reach the booth that Alfie and

two other guys I don't recognize are sitting in. I'm guessing the others are either doing their own thing or decided not to come.

*I wish I was anywhere else but here at this moment.*

"Meghan. You look amazing," Alfie exclaims as he stands from the booth, slurring slightly.

His hand rests on my hip as he leans in to kiss me on the cheek. I don't bother to push him away, too stunned by what I've just witnessed. I vaguely register that he smells good and the voice in my head that is telling me I need to be open for something with someone else, especially after what I just saw with Cooper. My jaw clenches in anger and I down the remnants of my drink as I reply to Alfie.

"Thank you. You look good too, Alfie," I reply, kissing him back on the cheek.

Alfie greets Alex in the same manner before taking his seat and I'm grateful that he doesn't seem to have the wrong idea about me, even though his eyes haven't left me the whole time. Alex and I take our seats on the ends of the booth sitting opposite each other.

"This is Wesley." Alfie points to a beautiful man with short ash blond hair, plump lips, mysterious brown eyes, a nose that looks like it may have been broken at some point and a sharp jawline dusted with a hint of five o'clock stubble. There are sleeve tattoos on his arms and one of a rose on his hand. From across the table, he smiles at me, his gaze intense, causing me to wave back shyly.

"...and this is Charlie." Alfie points to another gorgeous man.

*Does Alfie only hang out with models?*

Charlie has a shaved head, dark features, and the most striking blue eyes with long thick lashes any girl would be envious of. Charlie tips his chin in greeting and throws Alex a wink, causing her to blush.

*Interesting.*

"It's nice to meet you both," Alex and I shout in unison over the music, giggling at our synchronization.

*I think the drinks have started to go to my head.*

"Come on, let's go dance," Alex demands.

Not being one to deny Alex anything, I stand and sway my hips to the beat of the music. *Do It To It* by ACRAZE and Cherish comes on, so I grab Alex's hand as I shimmy my hips and she leads the way to the dance floor. We're followed by the guys and one look behind me sees them all staring at each other, whispering conspiratorially.

We start with Alex and I dancing together, while the guys create a semicircle around us, blocking out the other nightclubbers. It isn't long before Alfie's hand is resting on my hip as I grind into his crotch with Wesley dancing in front of me, his hand on my other hip and his leg between mine.

If I hadn't had so many drinks, I wouldn't have dreamed of doing this but I'm feeling in a *fuck it* mood. A *fuck* Cooper mood. Alex is dancing with Charlie, making very extreme eye contact as they gyrate to the music. We stay like this for the next few songs, grinding on each other on the crowded dance floor; the bodies around us forcing us closer and closer together.

"I'm going to get a drink," I shout over my shoulder to Alfie.

"Want me to come with you?" he asks, and I shake my head in response.

*I need a break.*

Wesley steps back as Alfie's hand drops from my waist. I break away and make my way through the throng of people to the bar.

I'm leaning over, trying to catch the eye of the bartender when I feel a warm body press against the back of me. I can smell his signature scent and as two muscular forearms come around either side of me to cage me in, I don't panic.

I know who it is and had I not seen what I saw, I would have been excited that he found me. I would have leant back into his solid embrace and begged him to take me home. Instead, he's about to ruin my night and just the thought has me blowing out an exasperated breath.

"What are you doing, Meghan?" Cooper demands, his voice gruff as his hot breath skates across the shell of my ear.

I close my eyes at the feeling he elicits in me and the shiver that skates down my spine. I can't help my physical reactions. A hot pool of desire sweeps through my body and I barely resist the urge to turn around and

195

claim him as mine in the middle of the crowded club, not giving a damn who sees.

"Getting a drink... or trying to," I reply with as much innocence as I can inject into my voice as I lean even further onto the bar, my ass pushing out into his crotch.

Trying to be nonchalant around him is getting harder and harder every day.

He growls in response... *literally*. If I were wearing panties, they would be soaked through. I love it when he makes that sound. It usually happens when he's buried deep inside me though.

Closing my eyes, I try to find some form of self control. My resolve is truly being tested right now as I fight with all my might to not moan and press even further into my hardness.

*I'm pissed at him. Don't forget what you saw him doing.*

"That isn't what I'm talking about, and you know it. Why are you dancing like that with those guys?"

Is he jealous? Surely not, that's a laughable idea and I can't contain the laugh that erupts from my lips.

Turning around in the cage of his arms so that I can attempt to get a read on him, especially when I confront him over what I've seen, I fold my arms over my chest. He doesn't get to act all possessive over me when he had some woman touching him and whispering sweet nothings in his ear.

*He isn't yours.*

But I want him to be. Tears well in my eyes, and I look down at my shoes while I compose myself. I want to stamp my foot in frustration because how dare he make me feel like this.

It's like a damn roller coaster of emotions and I hate roller coasters.

"I could've asked you the same thing, but seeing as you're my boss and I'm not at work right now... I don't think you have any say in what I do or do not get up to outside of the office."

His eyes go stormy with my declaration, but I don't care at this precise moment. I'm turning back toward the bar, my focus back on getting drunk, when he takes hold of my arm and proceeds to drag me across the club.

He's heading to the same dark and secluded corridor that started all of this mess. I try desperately to yank my arm out of his grasp because I'm not going anywhere with him, especially there. He lost the chance for sex in public places when he let another woman put her hands on what's mine.

As I'm being dragged across the club, I come to the conclusion that when we made our agreement he was clearly saying what he needed to in order to get what he wanted. He didn't know I was going to be here tonight and so he probably thought he would get away with his plan to fuck around and have me waiting around for whenever he fancied something different.

"Cooper, stop it," I shout over the music.

I don't want to go with him.

I don't want him to touch me.

*I want to cry because he's hurt my heart.*

He stops in the middle of the club, whirling around to answer me. "Now it's Cooper?" he growls before laughing in my face, shaking his head. *Personally, I don't see what's funny at all.* "I thought I was Mr. Jackson to you?" He doesn't give me a chance to respond before he's turned back around and continues marching toward the corridor, the tension in his body clear for everyone to see.

"Let go of me. I'm going home," I practically scream as I try once again to get my arm free of his grip.

"I'll take you home," he shouts back, but only to be heard over the pounding bass.

"I don't want you to take me home. I'm going to go with my friends."

He comes to a stop and I crash into his back before he turns to face me once again.

He's deathly quiet. "You either go home alone or you come home with me. Rule number two, Meghan."

As if he's just tried to throw a rule at me. *How dare he?*

"Don't tell me what the rules are... were, Cooper. You had another woman all over you," I shout back at him.

He doesn't move or say a word, he just looks into my eyes as if he's seeing into my soul.

"Then I chose to go home... alone," I affirm.

Our bodies are pressed together and it would take minimal effort for me to lean forward and press my lips to his. *No, Meghan, no kissing.*

I should be scared, or more annoyed, but if anything I'm turned on by his take-control attitude and what I've now identified as jealousy rolling off of him. He changes direction, heading toward the entrance, his grip still firm on my arm, but I'm no longer trying to tug free.

We stop at the coat check and he helps me into my coat, ever the gentleman. Taking my hand this time, he intertwines his fingers with mine as he leads me out of the club.

Opening the door of a black car stopped at the curb, he nods for me to get in. I stare up at him. A part of me wants to turn around, go back into the club and enjoy my night. But something in his gaze has me moving into the back seat without argument.

*I'm just going home. To my home.*

*I will not sleep with him*, I chant.

## NINETEEN

## Meghan

Cooper closes the door and moves around the car to climb in next to me. He instructs his driver to take us to his penthouse. The fight has left me and I don't bother to argue with him about taking me to my place, instead I pull out my cell and bring up Alex's messages thread.

I'm not entirely sure what to say to her. I hate lying. I drag my lip into my mouth, nervously nibbling at it as I stare out of the window at the passing city, contemplating what to text her. If I think about this for much longer, she'll have noticed I'm missing and get worried. I type out a message to her.

MEGHAN

> Not feeling well. I've gone home. I'll call you tomorrow.

I delete that text. I can't use the excuse of feeling sick again. She won't buy it for the second time in a row.

*Think, Meghan.*

I can feel Cooper's gaze on me as I type out another message, but I ignore him.

MEGHAN

> I saw a guy I met a few weeks ago. I've gone back to his place. I'll call you in the morning.

Deciding that one might actually work, I press send before I can change my mind and put my phone back in my clutch.

The rest of the drive is silent, the rumble of the car and sound of the city outside the only noise. Even though I can feel his eyes on me, I don't look at him. I can't. If I do, I might close the distance between us and beg him to want me as much as I want him.

As we pull up to Cooper's building, I get flashbacks to the morning I ran out of here looking like a disheveled mess. I'm lost in the memory and all that has happened since when the sound of Cooper's voice breaks through my pondering. I know that tone—he's still pissed.

"I'll get the doors, Christopher. We won't be needing you for the rest of the night. I'll see you in the morning," Cooper informs his driver before he gets out of the car and makes his way to my side.

*I guess I'll be getting a cab home.*

"Thanks for the ride, Christopher. It was nice to see

you again." Our eyes connect in the rearview and he gives me a soft, apologetic smile. I wonder what he's thinking about this situation. After all, he knows that Cooper and I work together.

"It was nice to see you again, Meghan," he replies.

As I go to grab the handle of the door, it swings open and a scowling Cooper is impatiently waiting on the sidewalk.

"I see the drive didn't get rid of your shitty mood," I say under my breath, or at least I had intended to but I'm guessing by Christopher's choked laugh and the smirk that Cooper's unsuccessfully trying to hide, that I didn't.

"Oops, sorry," I say with zero remorse as I get out of the car and strut toward the front of Cooper's building, an extra sassy sway to my hips.

Cooper catches up to me and places his hand on the small of my back, the familiar zing of electricity traveling up my spine from his touch as he guides me to the bank of elevators. I don't move away and instead I luxuriate in the contact of his hand on me and the way the heat radiates through my coat.

We walk across the lobby and when we arrive at the elevator, Cooper presses the call button, and the doors open almost immediately. Stepping inside, he presses the button for his floor and leans against the back wall, surveying me with his hands in his pockets. I'm momentarily distracted.

*When did leaning become... sexy?*

Pulling myself out of my own dirty thoughts, I step into the cart and turn my back to him. We don't say a word to each other on the ride up. The tension builds within us and not just from our actions earlier in the night, it's an awareness of each other that only comes with intimacy. As the doors open on his floor, I lead the way along the corridor before moving aside to allow him to pass.

At his door, he unlocks it with none of the fumbling from the last time he brought me here, and we step over the threshold into his apartment. I move to the middle of the living room and survey the white walls with colorful artwork hanging on them. Even though I've worked for him for the last year, I haven't stepped foot in his personal space aside from the night of the Christmas party.

With the front door at my back, I'm facing the floor to ceiling windows that give the perfect view of the Upper East Side. The lights of the city shine bright and from this high up, it's hard to connect the bustling city with the fairytale laid out beyond the window.

Dragging my gaze away from the sparkling skyline of Manhattan, I take in the living room. In the middle of the room is the comfiest looking gray couch facing a huge TV mounted on the wall. In front of the couch is a low glass coffee table with remotes and magazines littered across it, making the space look lived in. If they weren't there, it would look cold, almost... clinical.

I turn to face Cooper, who's observing me with his

hands in his pockets. "Who was she?" I ask, lifting my chin, resolving to not get distracted by him.

"Nobody."

"So you allow people you consider nobody to touch you? To whisper in your ear? You put your hands around their waists and listen to them attentively?" I accuse him, my anger and jealousy evident.

"Who were the guys? I mean, I know who one of them was because he works for me." He leans back against the door, his posture and tone relaxed, but the look in his eyes tells me he's furious.

"I asked you first," I murmur, suddenly ashamed of my actions.

"She's Jamison's sister. She's like a little sister to me. If you had stuck around to watch, you would have seen Jamison come over. He actually wanted to say hi to you."

*Oh.*

Well, it may be true that she's like a sister to him, but I'm not sure it's the same for her. Not with the way she leant into him, or how her hands ran over his body as if memorizing every line of him. We stare at each other for a moment.

I don't want to admit I may have jumped to conclusions and retaliated in a very immature manner.

"What were you doing, Meghan? And don't try to bullshit with the whole 'just dancing' thing. You were practically fucking them in the middle of the dance floor."

"I'm sorry," I sigh, hoping I can leave it at that, even

though I know deep down that it won't be enough. "I made an assumption about you and reacted. I shouldn't have." I try to downplay my reaction.

"You're right, you shouldn't have. I meant it when I told you nobody touches what's mine."

"And nobody touches what's mine, either." I blurt out, my eyes going wide at the confession.

"Okay."

"That's it? Okay is all I get?"

"Yes, because you jumped to conclusions and did something you shouldn't have done. Out of the two of us, I have done nothing wrong."

Okay, so he has a point and I don't know what exactly just happened, because I was supposed to be the one mad at him, but I think all is... forgiven. I really hope it is anyway, because I don't want him to be mad at me. Our whole thing was supposed to be about pleasuring each other.

*That gives me an idea...*

"What do you need from me, *sir*?" I ask in my most sultry voice as I remove my coat and throw it over the back of the couch, my eyes never leaving his. I watch his eyes darken with lust and so, with an extra sway in my hips, I make my way toward him.

"Cut the crap, Meghan. When we aren't in the office, you call me Cooper. Especially when you're about to be on your knees, choking on my cock like a good girl." He continues to lean against the front door, his hands in his pockets as if he hasn't just uttered the dirtiest thing I've ever heard from his lips.

I stumble slightly as my legs turn to Jell-O in anticipation. He reaches out and snakes an arm around my waist, tugging me tightly against him. My eyes dart down from his eyes to his lips as I silently beg him to kiss me. I want to taste him and take back some of the control in this situation by bringing him to his knees.

When he doesn't give me what I want, without saying a word, I push out of his grasp and drop to my knees onto the soft carpet. Reaching up, I undo the buttons of his jeans before tugging them down his legs and helping him to step from them. His hand goes into my hair, lifting my head back and stealing my concentration as I'm about to put my hand into his boxers.

The look on his face is one of pure lust, and so I continue with my exploration, causing him to let out a hiss as I reach into his boxers and grip his already hardening cock.

Stroking him once and then twice before pushing his boxers down to his ankles, my eyes are mesmerized by his perfect cock. Cocks are not pretty things, but my words just won't do him justice. He's perfect in length and thickness and his swollen head has a drop of precum, just begging me to lick it off. My tongue darts out and licks the salty bead off before I wrap my lips around his shaft and suck him deep into my mouth.

"Fuck. Baby, your pretty little mouth feels like heaven," he pants, his hand tangling in my hair as he guides himself in and out of my mouth. "Don't forget, it's only for me."

I hum in agreement, unable to speak with him filling my mouth, and it causes him to let out a guttural moan. The pace is slow as my mouth adjusts to his size. I can tell he's trying not to fuck my face, but that's what I want him to do. I want him to use me.

Sliding my mouth off of his cock with a popping sound, I lubricate him with my saliva as I stroke him up and down. Using my tongue, I lick the underside of his cock, from his balls to his tip. I flick the tip of his throbbing shaft with my tongue, alternating with licks and kisses. Looking up, I gaze into his eyes as I guide his cock to the back of my throat and thank God for having no gag reflex.

"You're such a good girl for me, aren't you?" he whispers as he caresses my cheek tenderly.

I hum in confirmation, and the vibration causes him to throw his head back against the door and let out another groan. His hips buck as he presses further into my mouth. It's then that he loses control and starts to really fuck me, his hands in my hair, almost painfully gripping onto the strands.

It doesn't take long for the saliva to drip from the corners of my mouth onto my exposed chest and my eyes to water. The sound of my mouth being pumped into fills the room and mingles with his grunts as he uses me to get himself off.

"Baby," he gasps, "I'm going to come."

He goes to pull himself out of my mouth, but before he has the chance, I place my hands on his ass cheeks and force him to explode in the back of my throat. I swallow the salty taste of him down and look up at him, our eyes connect as he stares at me with a look of wonder on his face.

Pulling back and out of my mouth, he strokes a thumb over my lips, moving the come dripping from the corner of my mouth back into it. "I can never last long with you," he murmurs, helping me to my feet.

Once he's pulled his boxers up and his shirt off, he lifts me, forcing me to wrap my legs around his waist as my dress rides up and my bare pussy rubs against his stomach. Resting my head on his shoulder, he carries me upstairs to his bedroom.

"What just happened doesn't get you off of the hook for your antics tonight, Meghan." Cooper grunts, causing me to lift my head and look into his eyes for some sense that he's messing with me.

"I don't know what you're talking about. I didn't get up to any antics tonight," I reply coyly.

"Those guys you were dancing with…" His jaw clenches as he forces the words past his lips.

"It was just dancing with them. It meant nothing, I promise. And I apologized," I exclaim, snuggling into his neck, dropping little kisses along the column of his throat before continuing, "I don't want anyone else but you. You satisfy all of my needs. That first night we danced and your hands were on my body…" I let out a sigh of satisfaction just thinking about it. "That was everything compared to tonight. You set me on fire, there was no reaction with them."

He doesn't respond to me and instead chuckles as he throws me onto the bed. I lay there staring up at the ceiling as he removes my shoes, dropping them on the floor at the end of the bed.

"Rules two and three..." I whisper into the room.

Cooper's hand drags up my leg, resting it on my hip as he moves up my body and into my line of sight. He stares into my eyes, as if looking into my soul. His silence is loud as I wait for him to say something, anything, to reassure me that I'm getting too into my own head.

"I accept your apology. And for the record, I'm not interested in anyone else but you right now," he says as he settles between my legs and leans on his forearms.

I feel a sense of relief at his words but immediately tell myself not to get carried away. His hands move my hair from my face, bringing me back to the moment before he presses a soft kiss to my lips.

My hands clasp his face and I bring his mouth to my own, returning his kiss, giving him a taste of his own salty release. It doesn't take long for the kiss to become heated and before I know it, we're both lying naked in the middle of the bed, him having stripped me of my dress and himself of his boxers.

Cooper lifts my leg and I wrap it around his waist before his hard cock slips into my hot, wet and waiting pussy.

There's no foreplay now, it's just us and this moment.

I moan into his mouth with satisfaction at the feeling of being filled by him as he keeps a slow and torturous pace, building up the tension inside of me.

This feels different.

Our bodies are connected and our mouths remain fused, our tongues tangling as we make love.

*No, don't get confused. This is just fucking.*

I can't afford to fall for him anymore than I already have—that's just asking for heartache.

Cooper joins his hands with mine and moves them above my head, using the leverage it affords him to increase his depth. We continue like this, alternating between slow and sensual and hard and fast, for what could be five minutes or five hours.

If this is my punishment; I'd break the rules every day for the rest of my life to experience this. I've never felt like this with anyone before. My body feels like it's on fire at his touch.

When I get close to my release, Cooper slides out of me and I whimper with disappointment before his mouth covers my clit and he slides two fingers into my core, stealing the breath from me.

"Cooper..." I breathe out.

*Oh God.*

"You like that, baby? You like when I lick your pussy with my fingers deep inside you, fucking your tight little hole?" he grinds out, his warm breath rolls over my sensitive clit.

"God, yes. Yes, I love it. Don't stop, please," I beg, but the next thing I know, he docs just that and stops.

*The bastard!*

Before I can protest, he flips me onto my stomach, lifts me onto my hands and knees, and slams back into me, setting off my orgasm. My pussy clenches around him as I scream into the sheets, my hands curling into the covers as my body spasms.

When I don't think I can take anymore, his thrusts increase, becoming almost punishing, before he smooths his hand over my stomach and rubs my clit. I try to wriggle out of his reach, but it's impossible in this position. I'm his prisoner.

"Cooper... I can't take it anymore. *Please,*" I beg him, getting only a dark chuckle in response.

His fingers continue their strumming on my clit and before I know it a pressure is building up inside me as I come for the second time. He thrusts into me a final time before he reaches his own release and comes deep inside me.

Collapsing onto the bed as he withdraws, he places a gentle kiss on my shoulder blade. I watch him from my position as he goes into the bathroom, closing the door behind him.

I hear the faucet running briefly, before he returns with a warm washcloth that he uses to clean me up. My body feels spent and, in all honesty, I'm content to just lie on his bed and watch him as he moves around the room, going over to the hamper and disposing of the cloth, turning off the bathroom light.

He saunters back to the bed in all his naked glory and lifts the covers, nodding for me to get in. I obey his silent command and shuffle—not so elegantly—up the bed to climb under the covers.

"We need to talk about protection in the morning," he murmurs as his arms come around my waist and he pulls me closer to him.

I hum in agreement, because we do need to talk about it. I'm on the pill, but even I know it isn't one hundred percent effective. Just as my eyes drift closed and I snuggle deeper into Cooper's embrace. Rule six flashes through my mind.

*No sleepovers.*

I tell myself that I'm just going to close my eyes for five minutes before I leave.

TWENTY

# Cooper

S unlight peeks through the gap in the curtains when I wake and I don't need to open my eyes to know that she's gone... again. Stretching my arm out, I feel around for any sign of warmth, just to be sure, but the other side of the bed is stone cold.

Letting out a sigh of frustration as I climb out of bed, I run over the rules we agreed to the other day. I only agreed to them because I want *her*. To me, they are unnecessary because she has all of me, even if she doesn't realize it.

Thinking back over last night causes me to drop my head and a small smile to grace my lips. Last night was different. At least it was for me. Seeing her dancing with those guys made me jealous and I'm man enough to admit that. So when I dragged her from the club, I had one thought on my mind... to make her *mine*. At the time, I didn't care that anyone could have seen us. I still don't.

*I want everyone to know who she belongs to.*

Last night I fell asleep with ease for the first time in a very long time. With my arms wrapped around Meghan, everything just felt... right. When I ran out on her the other week, I had the exact same thought run through my mind, but this time, when I thought about how I could get used to falling asleep like that every night, it didn't incite panic in me.

*I was at peace.*

Using the bathroom, I get ready for the day, showering and dressing in a white dress shirt, navy blue chinos, and matching navy blue blazer. I'll pair it with a pair of brown Oxfords. My plans for the day include a lunch date with my mom at one and some work in the office.

My parents' marriage ended because, ultimately, my father loved his work more than he loved my mother. Catherine Jackson has embraced her newly found singledom and has been going on date after date, giving me unwanted updates. It should be illegal for a mom to share details of her escapades with her child. I love her, but that's a step too far.

It's a little after ten, so I head downstairs for a breakfast of coffee before setting up in my home office to go through my emails and review some files for court next week. Leaning against the countertop, I wait for the coffee machine to brew my much needed caffeine fix, my gaze looking around the space with fresh perspective.

My kitchen is, for the most part, untouched as most

of my meals are either takeout, reheated meals made by my housekeeper or dining out with clients. Glistening cupboards that, annoyingly, show any fingerprint marks hold china and cutlery that has been largely unused in the five years I've lived here. There are modern appliances, but other than the coffee machine, I couldn't tell you if they've been switched on.

It's not a home.

It's cold and lacks love and laughter.

Briefly, I wonder what I can do to make it more inviting for Meghan. I want her to come over and not want to leave. It's as my eyes are bouncing around the room that I notice the slip of paper on the otherwise clear kitchen island. Leaning across, I snatch up the handwritten note, barely resisting the urge to hold it to my nose and see if her scent lingers.

*What the fuck is wrong with me?*

*Get a grip, Cooper.*

I skim my eyes over the note the first time before going back to read it again, word for word:

*Good morning, sir.*

*I'm sorry I ran out, but rule number six—no sleepovers! Maybe you can punish me again...*

*See you on Monday. I know I'll be thinking about choking on your perfect cock again all weekend.*

*Meghan*

*P.S. Even though I'm on the pill, I vote for condoms.*

She's crazy if she thinks I'm waiting two whole days to see her again. Pulling my phone out of my pants pocket, I bring up her contact information, opening a new message, I type out a reply to her.

COOPER

I got your note. Last night wasn't your punishment, Meghan.

Be at my place tonight at nine sharp. I don't care what you wear, but be warned, I may rip it off.

They will know to let you up and the door will be unlocked. I want you naked and on my bed when I find you.

As I watch the text bubbles appear as she types, I think about the fact that I haven't ever texted her before and that we've always kept our correspondence profes-sional. It's crazy to think how much everything has changed in such a short space of time. I never would have thought I'd act on my desires for her, but I also wouldn't take any of it back.

My eyes are glued to my cell as I watch the dots dance before disappearing and reappearing, unable to tear myself away as I wait to see what she has to say.

MEGHAN
Yes, sir.

More dancing bubbles, before another message comes through.

MEGHAN
My legs will be spread and my mouth open and ready for you.

*Fuck.*

My cock twitches at her words and I adjust myself, briefly considering if I should get her to come over now. I need to have more self control when it comes to her, so I put my phone down and busy myself with making coffee. Heading to my home office down the hallway, I hope I'll be able to distract myself until tonight, but I can't help the smile that spreads across my face at the prospect of seeing her again.

Of tasting her again.

Of making her *mine* again.

At five minutes to one, I walk into a restaurant called Amour. My mom likes to dine here for our bi-weekly lunches. I address the hostess as my gaze roams the room before landing on my mom. Pointing her out to the hostess, I make my way over to her table, a smile on my face.

"Mother," I greet as I kiss her on both cheeks before taking the seat opposite.

She assesses me, her gaze intense before she says, "Cooper, you look good, my dear. Have you met someone?"

*Jeez, already going in for the kill.*

She's like a bloodhound when it comes to sniffing things out.

"How are you, Mom?" I ask, avoiding the question.

I don't know what Meghan and I are at the moment. I know what I want us to be, but I also know what Meghan wants to classify us as, and I refuse to label what we have as *that*.

Before I share anything with my mom, I need to sort through my confusing thoughts. I'm not about to tell her I'm fucking my assistant and that we have rules, but that I would rather scrap them and give a proper relationship a try.

"Okay, we'll circle back to my question soon, my dear..." I knew it wouldn't be that easy to get out of answering her. "I'm having fun, as always. I've been on three dates since we last saw each other. Harold is my favorite, because he knows what he's doing," she says with a wink.

"Okay, I don't need to know about this," I exclaim. "Why do we have to go over this every single time?" I jump in before she can go into any more detail, holding my hands up as if that will ward off her words.

*Tsk*ing at my question, she squints her eyes at me, assessing me before she speaks. I drop my eyes to the menu, if only to avoid her all knowing gaze.

"You know, you should get a nice girl like your assistant. Maybe even your assistant... Meghan, isn't it?"

My eyes snap up from the menu I've been perusing, and I attempt to school my features into a mask of indifference. She's looking at her own menu, her face completely blank, not giving me a hint as to why she would bring Meghan up.

"Why do you think that?" I ask cautiously, my eyes on her, looking for any clue that she knows.

*She can't know what we're doing, surely?*

I guess if she's figured something out and brings it up, it's technically not me that's broken the rules by telling her.

"She seems like a nice girl. She has good manners. When I show up unexpectedly, she always takes care of me. Plus, I think she's gorgeous and I think you'd make beautiful babies." She laughs, like what she's just said is an insignificant thing and not the equivalent of throwing a grenade in my lap.

I respond without thinking. "Yes, she's a nice girl and

beautiful, but that doesn't mean she'd be interested in being with a guy like me. Let alone have children with me. I work too much for me to even consider starting a relationship with someone."

Is that what I want though? A relationship with Meghan. Would Meghan even want more than what we currently have? Would she want *me*?

I know I want more with her but, realistically, is that something I can give her or is it a pipedream that will always be just that, a pipedream?

I'm contemplating this when my mom reaches across the table and grasps my hand in hers, holding on tightly. On her face is a look of motherly love and I turn my hand over to squeeze hers in return, letting her know I'm okay.

"You would be a prize, my darling boy," she whispers fiercely, squeezing my hand back. "You need to realize that not every relationship ends like mine and your father's. My biggest regret is that we may have made you think that if you work hard, you can't have a happy and fulfilling relationship. You aren't your father. Just because you went into the same field as him doesn't mean that you won't be able to find that balance. You already have more balance than he did. Look at you, you're making time for your mother and I know you would make time for any woman you had a relationship with." She looks at me with sadness in her eyes and I wonder if it's there from having lost her husband or from a fear that I might follow his same path.

I don't respond to her because I'm not entirely sure

what to say. I know I'm not my father, but one wrong decision could have me ending up the exact same man that he is. My eyes go back to the menu in my hand as I try to get my mind to focus on what to eat and not where my life is going.

My mom's only looking out for me and I don't want her to be upset, or have her thinking that I'm going to be single forever, but I also can't tell her about Meghan and whatever the hell it is that we have going on.

I spend the next few hours having lunch with my mom before I see her to her car and then head into the office. Although it's Saturday, I have some work that I need to catch up on, especially after my week has seen me preoccupied with Meghan.

Climbing into the back of the town car, I replay my conversation with my mom and try to remind myself that I'm nothing like my father. Yes, it's the weekend and I'm working, but it's not like I have a wife and kid who I'm leaving behind.

The drive to the building passes in a blur and before I know it, I'm exiting the elevator, and making my way to my office, pausing as I pass Meghan's desk.

Moving to the chair behind her desk, I look over the items she has neatly laid out, picking up the picture she has of her and an older couple that I assume are her parents. Running my finger over her smiling face, I wonder what her parents would say if they saw her with me.

*Would they accept me?*

*Would they think she can do better?*

I don't know how long I sit at her desk staring at her picture, even when she's not around, I'm lost in thought about her, but it's going dark outside by the time I even contemplate getting up. Putting the picture back in its place, I stand and walk into my office, determined to at least try and get some work done.

How my father became addicted to working and became one of the best attorneys in Manhattan, when he was with my mother, is beyond me.

I'm not even officially with Meghan and she's all I seem to be able to focus on.

It's late by the time I get back to my place and as I ride the elevator to my floor, I contemplate the thing that's been on my mind since my conversation with my mom —what am I doing with Meghan. There's no doubt in my mind that I want her.

I want to take her on dates.

I want to fall asleep with her in my arms and wake up with her still in them.

The thing that has been eating away at me is whether she wants that too. I know she wants me physically but does she see me as more than that?

Walking through the front door, I drop my keys on the console table by the door and move over to the sound system, putting on a playlist and filling the room with the soothing voice of *Yebba*.

I go to the kitchen and pour myself two fingers of *Macallan 18*. The contents are gone quickly, and I pour myself a fresh glass then make my way upstairs. Switching the shower on in my ensuite, I strip out of my clothes, not bothering to put them away and instead leaving them in a pile on the bathroom floor as the room fills with steam.

As I step into the shower, I take a sip of my drink before placing my glass on the alcove shelf near the entrance. Under the spray, I drop my chin to my chest, leaning my palms on the wall in front of me, the water slashing down on me from the powerful shower head. I feel an overwhelming sense of emotion, I want to shout, scream, cry, beg her to be mine. I don't know what to do with her, I'm at a loss.

I want to bare my soul to her and have her bare hers in return.

I want to tell her... to tell her that... that I love her.

In all my thirty-two years of life, I have never had the urge to tell a woman I wasn't related to that I love her. Ultimately, I know that's because I've never felt this way about any of the women I have dated. Meghan is special.

I sense her presence in the room with me, but I'm not entirely sure it's not just a figment of my imagination. It wouldn't be beyond the realm of possibilities for my mind to play tricks on me with the one thing I crave.

I truly feel like I'm about to lose my mind because of

this woman and I fear I'll lose her one day when she finds someone else.

*Rule number three.*

Someone she loves and wants to start a family with —I can give her all of that. I'd tear down the world for her, because she consumes my every thought and from the moment I met her I wanted her, I just didn't realize that's what this feeling was.

I'm at a loss as to how to convey my feelings to her when, if she doesn't feel the same, they have the ability to scare her away.

When her hands wrap around my waist from behind, I release a sigh of contentment—that she's here, where she belongs. She's placing soft kisses on my back and as I pull her around to my front and under the spray of the water, she looks up at me with nothing but concern in her eyes. She's naked, her make-up and hair are being ruined by the water, but she doesn't seem to care. Even with mascara running down her cheeks; she's never looked more beautiful.

*I'm her main focus.*

"Cooper?" The way she says my name has me closing my eyes and resting my forehead on hers, my hands holding her head. "Are you okay? Has something happened?" she whispers.

Pulling away from her to look into her eyes, she uses her hand to move a piece of hair off of my forehead before cupping my cheek. As my eyes roam over her face searching for a hint of reciprocated feelings, three little words nearly tumble from my mouth.

Looking into her big green eyes, I realize I'll take whatever she is willing to give me. Even if that means I have to be the man to *temporarily* warm her bed.

Maybe, given time, she'll give me her heart, soul and mind too.

TWENTY-ONE

## Cooper

**M**eghan stayed with me for the remainder of the weekend, so I guess that means rule number six—*no sleepovers*—has gone out the window. After she found me in the shower, and we made love against the tiles, I carried her to my bed and practically begged her to stay.

Sunday morning, I woke her up by eating my favorite thing for breakfast. *Her.* We then spent the rest of the day having sex on every available surface in my apartment before she begged me to let her leave so she could look semi presentable for work tomorrow.

Reluctantly, I agreed and sent her with Christopher in the town car.

This morning, I'm excited, almost giddy, as I get ready for work. My funky mood from Saturday has gone, and I feel rejuvenated, like I could take on the world.

Even though I've seen Meghan all weekend, I can't wait to see her, to be in her presence again.

Whenever I'm around her I seem to forget I might not be good enough and allow myself to just enjoy the way she makes me feel.

She invigorates my soul.

Using the drive to the office to do some research, I reach out to a couple of reputable therapists via email. As I watched Meghan sleep on Sunday morning, I decided I should see someone about my feelings of inadequacy because realistically, I can't give Meghan what she wants, or needs, if I'm constantly second guessing myself.

I want to be the man she deserves.

Strolling from the elevator toward my office, a grin spreads across my face as I get closer and closer to her—I'm sure I look like a damn fool, but I couldn't care less. I pause when I get to her desk, finding it unoccupied causes my features to pull into a frown. Her coat isn't on the rack and her bag isn't underneath the desk like I would expect it to be if she'd stepped away to get a coffee or into a meeting. She's normally here before me, getting set up for the day and as it's already eight am, I know something isn't quite right.

I continue into my office, placing my briefcase on my desk, and pull out my cell to call her. It goes straight to voicemail. Hanging up without leaving a message, I type out a text to her instead. I'm sure I'm worrying over nothing.

COOPER

> Hope you're okay. Just checking you're on your way in? Call me when you get this.

Putting my phone away, I begin setting up for the day, the knot of worry in my stomach building. I'm due in court this afternoon and have some last-minute prep to do.

I'm sure she'll turn up soon.

When I still haven't heard from Meghan by lunchtime, and a call to HR confirms she hasn't called in sick for the day, I decide to swing by her apartment after court. All of the worst case scenarios rush through my mind and the knot of worry that's been growing in my stomach all morning continues to churn.

This is just so out of character for her.

*Judge Michaelson is a dick.*

Despite me agreeing to opposing counsel's request for a continuance, he declined and instead ordered us to settle this matter out of court *today*. This means that instead of finishing at five, it's after seven by the time we're through.

I'd briefly wondered earlier if I should have asked her friend, Alex, to check on her, but I got rid of that idea almost as soon as it formed. If I reached out to her friend,

I might give us away and I don't know for certain that something is wrong.

*Yes, it is. Something is very wrong.*

Jogging down the stairs at the front of the courthouse, I spot Christopher parked in a no parking zone and sprint toward him. Jumping into the backseat, I demand he drive me to Meghan's and if he wants to keep his job, he'll make sure I get there at double speed. Pulling my phone out of my inner suit pocket, I switch it on and check for messages from Meghan—there's still nothing from her.

*Dammit.*

My leg bounces with worry, and my fist is clenched in frustration at this whole situation. I should have delegated for someone else to go to court. She needs me, I'm sure of it. I don't think I'll ever forgive myself if it's something bad, and I wasn't there for her.

I can't lose her.

Thankfully, Christopher makes quick time in getting to her place and I can see from the car that the lights are off and the curtains are open.

Christopher smirks at me in the rearview mirror as I jump out, not waiting for the car to come to a complete stop. If I had the time, I'd be having stern words with him about his all too knowing look.

As I'm racing up the stairs to her building, I thank whoever is watching over me for the fact that the old lady from my first visit is coming through the door.

The damn elevator is still out of order and as I take

the stairs two at a time, I hope she just took the day and forgot to tell me about it.

*But she would have texted me back if that was the case.*

When it comes to Meghan, I'm so attuned to her, it's uncanny, and I just know something isn't right. My gut has been telling me this all day and the closer I get to her, the more and more angry I get with myself for not coming here sooner.

Arriving on the second floor, I swing the door open and it smacks against the wall on the other side. Barrelling into the hallway like a possessed man, my legs carry me as fast as they can toward her door. Just as I raise my hand to knock, I hear a whimper on the other side of the door, causing my stomach to drop.

"Meghan... baby?"

My ear is pressed to the door, listening for any sounds coming from inside. It isn't long before I hear a soul-destroying sob. My body is pulled into action by the sound, my heart rate picks up and a sense of urgency takes me over again. Trying the door handle, I send a silent prayer to the Gods as I find it unlocked and tentatively step into the darkened room.

As my eyes scan the space, I note that everything looks to be in place and I release a relieved sigh at the realization that it doesn't look like she's been broken into.

That relief is quickly wiped away when I find her sobbing on the floor, her back pressed against the wall, her legs pulled up to her chest and her arms wrapped around them. She's still dressed in her PJs and tears rush down her cheeks.

"Meghan..." I murmur as I crouch down in front of her.

She looks up at me, as if not realizing I'd enter her apartment, before scrambling into my arms as she buries her face in the crook of my neck. With one arm wrapped around her waist, I throw the other behind me to keep us upright from the force of her body plowing into mine.

I hold her for the longest time, trying to ease her tears enough that she can explain to me what's happened. With every tear that drips onto my exposed skin, my heart aches a little more for her. I realize at this moment that I hate seeing her tears, seeing her in pain and I'll do whatever it takes to make sure she's never hurt again.

"What happened, baby?" I keep my voice as soft as possible, trying to keep the irrational need to inflict pain on whoever hurt *her* at bay.

She cries into my shoulder, her sobs even more guttural, as I stand and move us to the couch. She wraps her legs around me, hanging onto me like a koala bear. There's nothing I can do but hold her, my hands stroking her back.

When her sobs don't seem to be easing, I run my hands over her shoulders, and barely register that her tears have soaked through my shirt. Pushing a strand of her hair away from her face, I cup her cheeks and dry away the tears as she takes in deep, hiccuped breaths.

"Talk to me, Meghan," I plead. My heart is breaking for her from the pain etched across her beautiful face. After a pause that makes me think she won't tell me, she opens her mouth to respond.

"She's... gone... S–she had pneumonia..." she breathes out, her voice cracking and her face scrunching in pain at the words, as if it physically hurts her to voice them.

"Who's gone?" I whisper, my hands smoothing up and down her arms before moving down to grasp her thighs.

She roughly wipes the tears from her cheeks with the back of her hand before pulling in a deep breath and looking away over my shoulder at a picture on the wall.

"My-my mom. She... s-she... di-died." She breaks down just getting the words out and I don't need her to say anymore. "Cooper," she wails before burying her face into my shoulder.

I can't even imagine what she's going through, but I want to take all the pain away for her. I just have no clue how to ease a loss like that.

My hold on her tightens as I pull her closer to me, and do the only thing I can. I hold her until her sobs ease again, my mind running through the support I can provide.

"When do you leave?" I ask after a while, knowing she needs to be with her father—if I remember correctly, her parents live in California.

"Tomorrow morning," she replies with a hiccup.

"Okay. I'll stay with you tonight," I murmur into her hair, taking control.

My words cause her to pull back, her eyes scanning my face before she averts her gaze and speaks.

"You don't have to... I know I'm a mess right now and you didn't agree to any of this." She motions to her rumpled state before continuing. "It wasn't part of the rules and we... we're supposed to only be fun. And this isn't fun."

When she goes to move out of my lap, I grab her thighs and hold her in place before tipping her chin up so she can see that I mean my next words.

"As far as I'm concerned, the rules have gone out of the window. You don't get a say in whether I stay or go right now. I'm going to take care of you and then make sure you get to the airport on time tomorrow. It might have started as some fun for you, but it was never that for me. You can rely on me, Meghan. Okay?"

She only nods in response, but I'm not sure she fully understands the weight of my words. I'm certain she doesn't know yet that I'd slay her demons and that comforting her in her time of need is what I *want* to do.

I want to be close to her, to be her life raft in her most difficult times.

My suit jacket and tie are long gone and Meghan is in the shower while I order food for us—I've kept it light and ordered wonton soup, kung po chicken and a side of lo mein from the takeout down the block.

I'm pouring her a glass of wine when I hear the bathroom door open, and after a moment, she steps into the entryway of the kitchen. Her face is scrubbed clean and some of the puffiness has reduced around her eyes.

I imagine she's been holed up in her apartment all day dealing with her grief alone. It hurts my heart to think that I wasn't there for her. Picking up the glass of wine, I hand it to her while pressing a brief soft kiss to her forehead.

My hand grasps hers, and I lead her to the living room. "Let's sit down. Dinner should be here soon."

"Thank you. For everything," she mutters as she takes a sip from her glass.

She sits down on the couch, her legs curled up underneath her, and I take the seat next to her and rest my hand on her knee.

"Anytime." I squeeze her knee, reassuring her and myself with the touch.

It's such a non-response and so I'm not surprised when she stares at me with her brow furrowed for a minute before shaking her head and leaning across the coffee table to pick up the TV remote. I'm quite literally saved by the bell when the buzzer rings with the food.

As much as I want to tell her I'd do anything for her, right now isn't the time to declare my feelings. When she comes back, we can sit down and have an honest conversation but for now I'm just going to keep her company.

"I'll get it." I smooth down her hair as I stand and place a soft kiss on the top of her head before going to the door.

With the food in hand, I walk to the kitchen to dish up. After opening nearly every cupboard, I find what I need to be able to dish up without bothering her. On a tray, I load up a container of soup, a plate of noodles and some chicken for her, carrying it out to her on the couch. She's still flicking through the channels in the same position I left her in, and as I settle her tray in her lap, she stops on *The Great British Bake-Off*.

We eat in relative silence, with only me asking questions to determine what time she needs to leave and will land.

It's late by the time we've finished eating, so I send her to bed as I tidy up our mess before I text Christopher, asking him to pick us up at six in the morning.

As I walk into her room, in the dim light of the bedside table, I can see she's lying on her side, facing away from the door. The sounds of her soft sobs are muffled by her pillow, but she can't hide the way her body trembles with each one.

Undressing, I climb under the covers next to her, pulling her body into my own so that I'm curled around her. She turns around and buries her head in the space between my collar and jaw. When her cries die down, she starts dropping soft kisses across my chest.

"Meghan... baby..." I plead as her hand reaches down past the waistband of my boxers. I encircle her wrist, bringing it up between us, before she can grab my cock, smoothing her hair out of her face as she looks up at me.

"Please Cooper, I need you. I need you to make me forget. Just for a moment." Her voice is quiet, almost a whisper as she pleads with me.

It's the vulnerability shining in her eyes that makes me give in. I don't want to take advantage of her, but I do want to comfort her and help her through this difficult time. I roll her onto her back and slowly peel off the fresh PJs she's put on after her shower. We spend a while just kissing and exploring each other's mouths like it's our first time.

*I could spend an eternity kissing her.*

Moving to the sensitive space between her jaw and shoulder, I move down her body, past her breastbone in a straight line to her perfect mound.

"Are you sure you want this?" If she told me to stop, I would.

"Yes, I'm sure. I need you. I need this."

Her hands find my hair as she lifts her hips toward my mouth and I take my first taste of her, my tongue sweeping through the already damp folds. Her back arches off of the bed as she lets out a low moan of satisfaction.

Sucking on her clit, she grinds her pussy into my face and I bring a hand up to palm her breast. The nipple hardens and I use my thumb and forefinger to tweak the hard bullet. Her hips buck against me as I continue sucking and flicking her clit, using my teeth to nip at the sensitive bud before soothing it with my tongue.

I ease a finger inside her tight channel and start a steady pace, my thumb circling on her clit. Making my way up her body, I take her nipple into my mouth and suck on it before flicking it with my tongue. Adding another finger and slowly fucking her pussy, I give each of her breasts equal attention before capturing her mouth, giving her a taste of herself as I devour her.

"Cooper..." she gasps. "I want you. Please," she begs.

I move back down her body, replacing my thumb with my tongue, and she comes on my fingers as I continue to lap her up, crying out at the force of her orgasm. When she goes limp and languid, I crawl up her body toward the head of the bed, placing a soft kiss on her shoulder before I move to lie beside her.

Pleading eyes look up at me, and even though my cock is unbearably hard, and I want nothing more than to slam into her, this is about her tonight. About giving her a reprieve from her thoughts.

"I want you," she cries out as she grabs at my boxers.

"I want you too, so much, but not tonight, baby. This is about you," I reassure her as I pull her into my side.

I roll out of her reach and just as I'm about to move so that I am behind her, she has me on my back as she straddles my hips.

"It's not just for you. It's for me. Please."

In the dim light of the room, my eyes roam over her face before I give a nod of consent.

"Thank you," she whispers, her hands smoothing over my chest.

Pushing my boxers out of the way, she eases herself onto my throbbing cock and I release a hiss at the sensation of entering her. It feels brand new every time. I grab hold of her hips as she slowly rocks back and forth, adjusting to my size.

*It's torture of the best kind.*

Her head falls back as she plays with her breasts and gets herself off on my cock. I can feel her orgasm building by the tremors rocking through her body and so I flip her onto her back and lift her leg to my waist, increasing the pace and pressure to bring us both to completion—her with a screamed moan and me with a grunt of release.

"Thank you, thank you," she chants, tears brimming in her eyes.

Instead of saying what I want to say, that I love her, I've shown her physically how much she means to me. It's not enough. Still inside of her, I kiss her before pulling back to look into her eyes, hoping what I feel is conveyed in the depths of my gaze.

I hope she can see all the things in them that I'm too much of a coward to say.

## TWENTY-TWO

# Meghan

I wake up cocooned in Cooper's arms, his warm, solid body pressed against my back. Blinking to clear the sleep from my eyes, I glance over at the clock sitting on my bedside table and see that it's just past five in the morning.

For a brief moment, I forget the events of the previous day as I relax back into Cooper's embrace.

As if not wanting me to be happy, my mind hits me all at once with the flashbacks from yesterday—my dad's phone call and his quiet and shocked voice breaking the news to me. It never crossed my mind that I would one day receive that call.

As pain assaults me, I close my eyes in an effort to ward it off. Nobody ever tells you that the pain caused by grief can physically hurt. I don't want to *feel* anything.

*Oh God, my mom's gone.*

As if sensing my anguish, Cooper tightens his hold

on me as I cover my mouth to muffle the sob threatening to erupt. I don't know why he came here, or why he stayed, but I'm grateful he's here. Lying in his arms, I listen to his steady breathing mingled with the sounds of Brooklyn outside of my window, allowing them to soothe me for what feels like hours.

Before I know it, my alarm is going off and I'm moving on autopilot to get ready for my flight at nine. It'll take me about an hour on the subway to get to the airport.

Leaving Cooper behind in my bed, I walk into the bathroom and turn on the shower before taking in my reflection in the mirror. My eyes are bloodshot and puffy, my nose is red from wiping it so much, and my complexion is pale, like I've been avoiding the sun for years.

I stand in a trance, staring at myself until the steam from the shower causes it to disappear and Cooper walks in. Any other day I would have ogled his physique, but instead I gaze at him with tears brimming in my eyes that I'm praying don't fall.

He doesn't say a word, just smooths his hand over my hair, placing a soft kiss on the top of my head, as his other hand rests on my hip and pulls me into his embrace. I inhale his scent, using it and the way he holds me in his arms to comfort myself.

We move in a comfortable silence as he helps me undress, taking the lead like I need him to, before guiding me into the shower. Removing his own clothes, he steps in behind me, taking my washcloth and squeezing my strawberries and cream body wash onto it before lathering it up and smoothing it over my body.

It doesn't feel sexual, just like he cares about me—to what extent I'm not sure, and I don't have the capacity to delve into right now. When he's finished, he rinses the suds off of me before cleaning himself and I stand under the stream watching him. The tenderness of his actions both this morning and last night has my chin trembling and silent tears coursing down my cheeks as he rinses himself..

In my time of need, Cooper has been here taking care of me. In my mind, I know he isn't mine, not in the sense of me being able to rely on him like I have been. So why is he here? Why is he doing all of this for me? Normally, I'd talk these things through with my mom and she'd laugh, telling me I'm overthinking before giving me some sound advice, but I can't call her.

*I can't ever call her for advice again.*

If I'm truly honest with myself, I want him to be mine and I have since our first meeting. I want him to want me as much as I want him, but I'm almost certain I'm nothing more to him than his assistant.

*Then why is he here?* Isn't that the million-dollar question?

My tears continue to fall, both in grief for my mom and because Cooper is here taking care of me. Pulling me into his arms, he's right there to wipe them away, a pained look on his face.

He picks me up and I wrap my legs around his waist, burying my face into the crook of his neck as my sobs get louder and at the same time he presses my back against the tiles for support. He grounds me and allows me to take comfort in his embrace until eventually my tears stop flowing.

Still in his arms, Cooper carries me out of the shower and places me on the counter, before taking care to dry every inch of me. I watch, mesmerized, as he dries himself next.

"I'm going to miss you," I whisper into the silence of the room. Almost immediately, I want to take it back, wishing I hadn't opened my mouth. I don't want to burst the bubble we're in.

He freezes for a split second while drying his hair and I wish the towel wasn't obscuring his face so I could get a read on him. I open my mouth, ready to apologize for stepping over the boundaries of our... situationship, but he removes the towel with a blank expression on his face and I snap it shut.

"I could come with you? If you want," he suggests and I really want to say yes, but not only is that not what we are, but I know he's got a lot coming up at work.

Shaking my head, I look down at my fingers sitting in my lap. "You can't. You've got too much going on. Anyway, I should really be there for my dad."

Hanging the towel on the rail, he steps between my legs and brushes my hair from my face before cupping my face. "I'm going to miss you too, baby. But you're going to call me every day. If you need me, you call me and I drop everything and get on a plane to you." Placing a gentle kiss on my lips, he steps back, holding his hand out to me. "Come on, let's get dressed and get you to the airport."

I place my hand in his before jumping down from the counter and following him into the bedroom to get dressed.

Cooper ends up taking me to the airport, upgrading me to first class and then buying a ticket just so that he can wait with me until I need to board my flight. He didn't listen to my protests when I said that I could wait by myself, instead he silenced me with a kiss and took my hand as we went through security. I don't know what any of it means, but he intertwined his fingers with mine and didn't let go until I had to get on the plane.

When I board my flight, I buckle into my seat and sleep until we touch down in Sacramento. I don't want to dwell on why I'm visiting home, especially when I was supposed to visit over the holidays but wasn't able to get away. Work was just too busy and even though Cooper said I could go, I didn't.

Although I speak to my parents, in some way or another, nearly every day, my last visit home was nearly a year ago. I was going to visit at Easter and had promised my mom, even with my poor baking skills, that

I'd help with the bake sale she does at the local church every year.

Grabbing my luggage, I make my way to the terminal exit where I see my dad in the crowd. The sorrow on his face that surely matches my own makes my chin tremble and tears tumble down my cheeks. I'd managed to hold myself together since leaving my apartment. I'd drawn my strength from Cooper and he'd willingly given it to me, but seeing my dad brings back the reality of why I'm here.

My parents were childhood sweethearts and so my dad has lost the love of his life. My mom was everything to him and he showed her that every day. Everyone always joked that they were meant to be. Warren and Rosie Taylor. They'd been together since they were fourteen-years-old and got married at twenty.

I didn't come along until they were both in their mid-thirties, and they've always told me they wouldn't have had it any other way as they got to spend their younger years making mistakes and having fun.

I was their miracle baby after having tried for many years unsuccessfully to have children. My mom was only sixty-three, and I thought she would be around to see any children I had—to at least see me get married.

My dad pulls me into his embrace and we hold each other in our own bubble of grief, oblivious to the crowd around us. Both of us sob and take comfort from the other. I pull away first and look into eyes so similar to my own and note that he already looks older than the last time I saw him.

His signature scent of sunshine and cinnamon lingers in the air around us and I give him a trembling smile as my eyes roam over his features, soaking in his familiarity.

"How are you, sweetheart?" he asks, wiping his eyes, and I can see he's trying to pull himself together.

"I'm okay. How are you?"

"Better now you're here, sweetheart." He tucks my hand into the crook of his arm and I rest my head on his shoulder as he grabs my bag, walking us toward the parking garage.

The ride back to the house is quiet as the radio plays old soul classics in the background. I spend the ride to my childhood home looking out of the window as we get closer and closer. Everything looks familiar and yet so different.

*She's not going to be there to welcome me home.*

One of my biggest regrets is that I didn't visit home more often. *I didn't see her in person enough.* Resting my elbow on the window ledge, I place my chin in my hand as I try to keep my emotions in check. I can't help but feel like maybe if I'd been here, she would have been okay.

A single tear slips out and rolls down my cheek before I dash it away. My dad squeezes my other hand as we turn onto their street, sensing the cloud hovering over me as we draw nearer. Parking in the driveway, he shuts off the engine as we both stare up at the house in silence, neither of us willing to move to go inside but still connected by our touch.

Pulling in a deep breath that I release in a heavy sigh, I open my door and jump out of the truck. I can't stay sitting in the car forever. I grab my bag from the backseat and walk toward the front door, hearing the sound of my dad following behind me.

When he opens the front door and I move past him into the hallway, he squeezes my hand, comforting me. The memories I wish I could have avoided just a little bit longer assail me all at once.

Pictures of our family line the hallway walls and my mom's shoes are still by the front door, her coat and scarf hanging on the hook just above them.

Stepping into the living room, I glance around and spot her favorite chair sitting in the corner. She liked to sit in that particular spot because she could look out of the window, watch the TV or do her knitting, with the perfect view. Balls of yarn sit in the basket on the floor under the side table, a half finished project stuffed on top.

Closing my eyes, I take in a deep steadying breath as the memories continue to flit through my mind.

There was the time she comforted me on the couch after my high school boyfriend broke up with me, or when she'd waited up for me after I snuck out to a party with Alex and she'd sat in her chair with the lights off and scared the crap out of me when I tried to sneak back in.

All the times she brought me bowls of ice cream when I was off 'sick' from school and she told me later that she knew I wasn't sick but she wasn't about to pass up time with me and my grades were good so she wasn't concerned. My final memory of her in this house was from the last time I visited home, when she'd rushed me as I'd walked in the door. She'd been *so* happy to see me.

"Why don't you get washed up and we can sort something out for dinner?" My dad interrupts my reminiscing and I nod as I turn toward the stairs with my bag in hand.

Walking into my childhood room comes with its own set of memories. Not much has changed since I left to go to college. My queen size bed sits in the corner against the far wall and my desk is under the window with the chest of drawers standing next to it. A small closet is on the wall opposite the bed and a rug is spread across the floor.

I smile as I remember Alex and I having our dance contests when we were in middle school. We'd force my mom to come in and watch us as we danced around to our favorite songs, usually something by Britney Spears. She was always our biggest cheerleader and we'd both be awarded a cookie as a prize. Even though I was her daughter, there was never one winner.

I wonder for a moment what Cooper would think of my childhood home. It's nothing compared to the grandeur of his penthouse, but then neither is my apartment, and he doesn't seem to have any complaints about that.

I love that he doesn't flaunt his wealth. In fact, the only clues that tell he's a billionaire are that he has a driver, wears nice clothes and has expensive watches. Placing my suitcase at the foot of my bed I sit down on the edge and pull my phone out to text him.

MEGHAN

> I've just arrived. Thank you again for everything you've done for me. I'll let you know when I'll be back soon. I'm sorry to leave you in the lurch at work.

I try to keep it business-like. I don't want to come across as needy, no matter how much I want him.

I'm very aware that when he told me I was to call him while I was away, he was most likely just telling me what he thought I needed to hear after my declaration to try and alleviate some of the awkwardness.

Putting my phone down next to me, I flop back on the bed, thinking he won't respond for a while, if at all. When my phone goes off with the sound of an incoming text message, I grab it immediately, like a teenager waiting for her crush to text.

COOPER

> I'm glad you've arrived safely. Take as much time as you need. Even though nobody can do what you do, I can get a temp in while you're away. I don't want you to come back sooner than you're ready.

I meant what I said this morning, I'll be
waiting for your call tonight.

A small smile graces my lips as I look down at my phone and read his message over again. An overwhelming urge to tell him I love him rushes through me —him being there for me in my time of need solidified it for me—but I don't want him to think it's my grief talking.

I'm certain of my feelings, but I don't want him to brush off a declaration of love because of this life-altering event.

I couldn't take the heartache that would inevitably follow.

## TWENTY-THREE

## Meghan

I've been with my dad for the past two weeks and in that time, we've organized my mom's funeral, sorted out her accounts, and attended her service. Alex came for the service and stayed for a week to help out.

We gave my mom a beautiful send off with all of her favorite people there, dressed in their brightest outfits. She'd always said when she passed, she wanted her funeral to be a celebration of her life with not a single lick of black in sight—we just didn't know she'd be gone so soon.

I've agreed with my dad that I'll stay in town for another week and then I'm going back to New York. He wants me to live my life. I don't want to leave him just yet, but deep down I know that my mom would want me to continue living my life too and not to put it on hold for her or my dad.

Since arriving I've built a bit of a routine; in the mornings, I get up and make us breakfast, then go for a long hike out on the trails. Anything really to distract myself from everything going on.

I'd have lunch at home before sorting through some of my mom's things. Initially, I wanted to avoid doing it. Going through her things so soon after her death seemed a bit... cold, but it has made me feel closer to her in a way.

Cooper and I spoke every night for the first week and he sent flowers for my mom's funeral, but I haven't spoken to him for a few days outside of text messages. I know he has a big case that's just started, so it's to be expected, but I can't help feeling like things have changed between us, like we're more distant than before I left the city. Obviously there is distance between us. I'm on the opposite side of the country to him, but this is different.

I should be in the best shape of my life, what with hiking for hours each day, but I've felt off for the past week. It's like all the energy has been zapped out of me.

When I couldn't gather the strength to move from the couch, my dad insisted I make an appointment with my old doctor, so that's where I'm currently sitting.

Another thing that's been worrying me, but my dad isn't aware of, is that I'm late. It wasn't until the day of my mom's funeral, when my Aunt Kath had mentioned my niece had started her period, that I realized I'm at least a month late with mine. I'm not normally super regular, but I've never been this late before.

I have no doubt that the doctor is going to confirm how I've been feeling can be attributed to stress or depression at the loss of my mom.

The nurse calls out my name, pulling me from my thoughts, and I follow her down the corridor to the exam room in a daze. I feel like I've been in a constant haze since I got the call from my dad. Like nothing is clear, nor will it ever be.

"Hi Meghan, it's been a long time since I last saw you," Dr. Weston greets me as I walk into the exam room. "I'm sorry about your mom," he continues, sympathy etched across his face as I take a seat in the chair next to his desk. "How has New York been treating you?"

I was a patient of Dr. Weston's from before I was born, right up until I moved to New York. He's in his early fifties, with dark salt and pepper hair that is cropped short, and chocolate brown eyes hidden behind a pair of tortoise reading glasses. I guess some people may find him attractive for an older man.

"Thanks, Dr. Weston. And it's been good, still finding my feet, even after all this time," I reply, not wanting to go into too much detail about my mom for fear I'll break down. It's been happening more frequently than I'd care to admit. I haven't been unable to keep a lid on my emotions since I got the call. A lot has changed since then.

Dr. Weston finishes typing up something on his computer before he turns his chair toward me, removing his glasses to give me his full attention.

"So, what can we help you with today?"

"Well, I've been feeling run down and my period is about thirty days late. Although, as you know, it's never been consistent."

"Okay, so there could be a couple of reasons for this, stress being one." He looks at me sympathetically before he continues. "Is there a chance you could be pregnant?" he asks, turning back to his computer so he can type up his notes.

"I mean, there's a possibility, but I'm on the pill and haven't missed a single one." Panic creeps into me at the possibility.

*I can't be pregnant.*

"Okay, although the pill alone isn't one hundred percent effective, we can quickly rule this out as the cause of your symptoms. Given the reason for your return... it's very possible your body could just be reacting to the stress." He tries to placate me, noticing my barely concealed panic.

My mind is running a mile a minute with questions. The biggest one being, *if I truly am pregnant, will Cooper want anything to do with us?*

I had a plan. It involved going back to New York and speaking to Cooper, telling him how I feel—because life's too short. That plan goes out the window if I'm pregnant. I'd need to feel him out, see if he wants kids at all before I drop the bomb of a baby.

I'm interrupted from my wandering thoughts when

Dr. Weston hands me a cup and directs me to the bathrooms.

Handing over my sample, I wait in the waiting room for what feels like hours. With nothing to do but go over an endless loop of what if's, I'm practically hyperventilating when the nurse calls me back. The walk to Dr. Weston's office is simultaneously the longest of my life and far too quick.

"Thank you for waiting, Meghan. So the test is showing as positive for pregnancy. We can do an ultrasound to see how far along you are. If that is something that you would like to do today, or you can come back tomorrow... if you need time," Dr. Weston announces, as if he hasn't just turned my life upside down.

My first thought is that Cooper and I made a baby. I want to smile and be happy at this little being growing inside of me.

My second thought is I'm going to be a mom and my mom isn't here to help me. This causes me to break down in Dr. Weston's office and he comforts me before calling my dad when I become inconsolable.

*I don't know what to do.*

I don't want to get rid of my baby or give it away. I wish my mom was here. She'd give me one of her famous hugs, the ones that ease all worries, no matter how big or small they seem.

"Sweetheart?" my dad calls from my doorway.

Although Dr. Weston called him, he couldn't tell him why, and I didn't have the capacity to divulge that information to him on the drive home. Understandably, he's been worried and sporadically checking in on me since we got home two hours ago.

I shut myself in my room, trying to process the news.

"Hi, Dad," I murmur as I sit up on my bed. It's the first words I've spoken to him since he picked me up.

"Are you okay? I've been worried." He makes his way further into my room and I hold a hand out to him as I pat the spot next to me with the other.

*No time like the present to tell him he's going to be a grandpa.*

"So... I guess I should tell you why Dr. Weston called you," I mumble as I fiddle with my hands in my lap.

"That would be nice, but only if you're ready," he says, covering my hands with his own.

Pulling in a deep breath in an effort to give myself the strength needed, I look up at his soft face. I don't want to disappoint him. I genuinely have no idea how he will react to his only child getting pregnant after having an illicit affair with her boss.

"I-I'm... I'm pregnant," I blurt out.

"Oh, that's... wow," he stutters.

"I'm sorry," I cry. Tears stream down my cheeks and I angrily brush them away. "I didn't mean to disappoint you."

He pulls me into his embrace, and I inhale his unique

scent, taking comfort in him. "Oh, sugar, you haven't disappointed me. I'm just surprised that's all. This is good news."

"Are you sure?"

"I'm certain. I'm just sad your mom isn't here to hear the news. We didn't even know you were seeing someone."

"I... well, that's the thing. It was only a... casual thing. He's... he's my boss." This is such an awkward conversation to be having with my dad. I want to bury my head in the sand and pretend everything is as it should be.

"Oh, okay. And he doesn't want a relationship with you?" he asks with no judgment in his tone.

"That's the thing, we agreed to keep it casual, but it hasn't ever really felt casual for me. I had planned to go back and tell him how I felt, but I'm not sure that's such a good idea now."

"Why not? Your feelings haven't changed since you found out, right?"

"Well, no, they haven't," I mutter, looking down at my fingers as I play with the hem of my sweater.

"So nothing should change just because you've created a life together. If you both have feelings for each other, then this baby will just make your bond stronger. If he doesn't reciprocate your feelings, then at least he will know and you can both make a decision on how to proceed together. Either way, he deserves to know about the baby and you deserve to not hide your feelings."

I don't respond to him, just letting what he's said sink in.

Standing from his spot on the edge of my bed, he drops a kiss on the top of my head before leaving me to think over my next steps.

Deep down I know he's right, there is only one thing to do when I get back to New York.

## TWENTY-FOUR

## Meghan

I've spent the past week with my dad, arranging for relatives to receive items my mom had expressed they get, and stocking up the freezer for him with homemade meals.

He's been a godsend, making sure I'm looking after myself and the news of my pregnancy has done nothing but bring us closer to each other.

I explained to my dad in more detail my relationship, or lack thereof, with Cooper and expressed again my worry about telling him about the baby, but he'd just pulled me close and whispered in my ear that I'd always be welcome home. Which, of course, sets off a stream of tears. I'm hormonal with my pregnancy but also emotional with grief.

Now I'm sitting in the back of a cab on my way to the Jackson and Partners offices after catching a redeye flight from LAX. I haven't bothered to go home, instead opting to go and see him first.

After another heartfelt conversation with my dad, I'm feeling better about my decision to lay all of my cards on the table and tell Cooper how I feel. If he rejects me, then I'll leave my job and raise my baby back in Sacramento with my dad—at least until I can get myself established.

When the cab pulls up to the curb outside of the offices, I take a moment to look up at the imposing building before exiting the cab. *This is it.*

The cold winter air whips at me as I step onto the sidewalk. Taking a deep breath, I pull myself out of my contemplative mood and head toward the front door, a sense of foreboding building inside of me.

When I reach the thirtieth floor, I stride to my desk, hoping to speak to my temp replacement for a minute, if only to try and give me something else to concentrate on before I have the biggest conversation of my life.

Turning the corner, I come up short when I see that my desk is vacant, whoever's covering me must be at lunch, which means no more procrastinating. Pulling in a deep breath as I walk toward Cooper's ajar office door. Just as I'm about to knock, I hear a woman on the other side.

"Cooper, stop it," she giggles, breathlessly.

Something tells me to hide, so I press my body against the wall as I listen in, praying nobody comes down this end of the office. I'm sure it's not what I think it is, but I have to be sure—he can't really have another woman in his office, can he?

"Mm-hmm, that's good," she moans.

"Tell me about it," he chuckles, his raspy voice coming through the door.

Tears well in my eyes and I smack my hand over my mouth in an effort to stop the sob that wants to break free from my throat. My mind can't process this and my ears can't bear to hear any more and so I spin on my heel, stumbling my way down the corridor to the elevators.

My vision is blurry from unshed tears and I'm dragging my hand along the wall for support as I try to get away from whatever is going on in his office.

I don't see Alfie until I stumble into him, his arm going around my waist to stop me from falling backward. Pushing away from him causes his arm to drop to his side, and I blink up at him in an attempt to clear my eyes.

I *can't* break down here.

I don't want to draw attention to myself. I want to make a speedy getaway without being seen.

"Oh, hey, Meghan. You're back," he says, like I've just been on vacation.

"Hi Alfie," I croak out, clearing my throat to try and clear the emotion currently clogging it.

"Is Mr. Jackson still at lunch with Hayley?" he asks, oblivious to my turmoil. I frown up at him in question and he continues with my unasked question. "You know, his ex-fiancé." He leans in conspiratorially. "Rumor has it, they'll be announcing that they're getting back together any day now."

"Oh," is all I can get out as my world crashes down around me.

Rubbing my palm against my chest, I try in vain to ease the pain Alfie's statement has created there. It feels like he's taken a knife and tried to carve out my heart. My other hand goes to my stomach in an attempt to protect my unborn baby from his words.

"Did you need to speak to him?" Alfie asks, tilting his head to the side in question.

*He really needs to work on his social cues.*

"Um, no. I can email him," I reply as I go to pass him.

"Hey Meghan..." Alfie calls to my retreating back, causing me to stop and face him. "Let's go for a drink soon. Now that Mr. Jackson is off the market, maybe you can stop crushing on him. We've all seen the way you look at him in the office." He winks, an almost devious smirk spreading across his mouth.

I don't need to be close to him to see the malicious intent in his expression and so I straighten my spine as I narrow my eyes at him.

"Fuck you, Alfie," I snap back, trying to keep my voice down. "You never would've stood a chance with me and you know it."

Turning on my heel, I march toward the bank of elevators with my head held high. Out of the corner of my eye I can see a few heads turn my way, but for the most part, people keep their heads down.

*Fuck the men of Jackson and Partners.*

As I ride the elevator down to the lobby, my mind goes back to the reason for my visit and what I just overheard in Cooper's office. A renewed sense of loss overcomes me, and I can't hold back the tears that spill over my cheeks.

Stumbling my way out of the elevator, I all but run to the exit, bursting through the doors as if I have a monster on my heels. My vision is blurred and I don't see him until it's too late to avoid him.

"Meghan?" Jamison calls.

*I just can't catch a break today.*

"Hi Jamison," I murmur, swiping away my tears, praying he hasn't noticed them.

"Are you okay?" he asks, concern evident in his tone.

"I'm fine. How are you?" I ask, wiping away the tears that just won't stop.

"Why don't you come get in the car?" He swipes his arm toward a town car that's sitting idle on the side of the road.

"Honestly, I'm fine. I'm just heading home." I take a step in the direction of the subway, but he anticipates my move and blocks me.

"I'd feel better if you took a seat in the car," he cajoles.

Heaving a sigh out, I walk to his car, throwing the back door open and climbing inside, fully aware I'm behaving like a sulking child. To my surprise, he climbs in next to me, closing us into the small space.

"Don't you have somewhere you need to be?" I ask, praying he leaves.

"It can wait. Do you want to tell me what's upset you so much?"

"As if I could tell you, of all people." I bark out a laugh.

"Has Cooper hurt you? I know he told me to leave you alone, but if he's hurt you, I can help. I won't expect anything in return."

I turn to him and take in the sincerity written across his face. As his words register, I can't help but laugh.

*I must look manic.*

"He's hurt me, but not in the way I'm sure you're thinking. Look, thank you for your concern, but there really isn't anything you can do." I go to open the door, but his hand on my forearm stops me.

"My driver can take you home. I have a meeting for the next couple of hours." I go to protest, but his next words stop me. "Do it for me, Meghan. I'd feel better if you took my car."

Nodding, I relax back into my seat before realizing I've left my luggage with the receptionist inside. Without a word, I get out of the car and walk toward the building I really didn't want to ever step foot in again.

I'm vaguely aware of Jamison calling out to me and my garbled response that I've forgotten my bag, my focus on getting in and out as quickly as possible. I'm gone for a matter of minutes and when I return, Jamison holds the door open for me.

"Thank you for this," I say, stepping into the car.

"Any time. I hope everything gets sorted," he replies before closing the door and tapping on the roof of the car.

Turning to the driver, I give him my address and close my eyes until he calls out to me as we pull up outside of my building.

With a mumbled thank you, I climb from the vehicle, standing on the sidewalk looking up at the building I'd created a home in.

Walking into my apartment, I go straight to my bedroom, pulling out my other suitcases and packing the rest of my stuff.

I'm moving back to Sacramento.

I have two suitcases packed, my dad on standby to pick me up from the airport and my flight booked for tomorrow morning, when there's a knock at my front door.

I put down the shoes I'm organizing and head to the door, checking through the peephole before opening it up to Alex.

"Hey babe. How are you doing? I'm so glad to have you back." She steps into my apartment, pulling me into a tight hug.

I haven't seen her since my mom's funeral, and

although we've spoken on the phone or via text message most days, it just isn't the same.

"Hey. I'm as good as can be expected. How are you? I have so much to tell you," I mumble as I pull back from her embrace to look at her.

"I'm good. Let's get some wine before you tell me anything. It's been a long week." she replies, dragging out the word long.

Alex heads into the kitchen, and I follow before leaning against the doorjamb. She pulls a wine glass from the cupboard, holding it up and silently asking if I want one. I shake my head in response.

It's time for me to come clean.

I haven't told her everything that's been going on in my life, not since we went on our shopping spree.

*Rule number one.*

I shake my head to clear it, angry with myself at thinking about the stupid rules that did *nothing* to protect my heart.

Walking to the couch with Alex following in my wake, I take a seat, turning to face her when she sits next to me. She takes a sip of her wine and I wait for her to swallow before dropping the first of my *many* bombs.

"I'm pregnant. About two months, to be exact," I blurt, no longer able to keep it contained.

"Oh my God!" she practically screams at me.

I cover my ears and break out into a cheerful grin as she places her glass on the coffee table and pulls me into a tight hug. I knew I could count on her to be happy about this news.

"I have more..." I brace myself, pulling out of her arms as I continue, my eyes dropping to look at my fingers playing with the sleeve of my sweater. "It's Cooper's baby."

Lifting my gaze to her, I catch the moment her jaw drops and her mouth opens and closes a few times, like a fish out of water as she digests the news. Her silence encourages me to continue, but I drop my gaze, unable to look her in the eye. Not yet.

"After our shopping spree, I agreed to keep seeing him. We had an arrangement, one of the rules was that we wouldn't tell anyone. It was one of *my* rules and I'm sorry I didn't tell you before."

Alex takes my hand and gives it a squeeze, causing me to look up at her. "You don't need to apologize. I thought you might have still been seeing him. I saw you with him the night we went out with Alfie and his friends."

"You did?" I whisper.

"I think everyone did." She chuckles. "He practically dragged you out of the club. It was hard not to see."

"Maybe that's why Alfie was a dick to me today." I huff, folding my arms over my chest.

"Ignore him. I never really liked him anyway. He gave off such a weird vibe. What does Cooper think about the baby?" When I drop my eyes to my lap, she continues, "He knows, right?"

"I... I went to tell him today..." My chin trembles as my eyes well with tears. "He had his ex-fiancée in his office. I heard them..." I whisper as a single fat tear slips free, sliding down my cheek.

Alex closes the distance between us and holds me while I cry, rubbing my back in soothing motions as she comforts me.

"I'm moving back home," I cry into her shoulder, and she pulls back to look at my face for confirmation. Sadness is etched into her features and in that moment, despite knowing I need to be with my dad, I hate that I'm leaving her.

"Do you have to leave? You can stay with me. We can raise the baby together," she says, tears welling in her own eyes.

"I can't do that to you. You're young and single and I can't cock block you with my baby." I chuckle, trying to lighten the mood as I wipe away her tears.

"Are you sure you don't want to tell him?"

"Maybe when I've had some time away to think about it and heal my heart. I won't make him choose me and the baby. I don't want us to be an obligation to him." I rest my hand on my still flat stomach before continuing. "The fact that I left town to bury my mom and he brought another woman into his office hurts. I need some time to get over that."

"I get that you feel like that, but I just don't want you making any rash decisions. Moving to the other side of the country is a big deal when it could all be a misunderstanding. I really think he deserves to know about his baby."

"I know he does, but right now, I don't want to be near him. I heard her with my own ears, giggling and moaning in his office. And I heard him. I'll always hear them when I think of him now. I can't stay and work with him or raise a baby with him, not now," I plead with Alex to understand this from my perspective.

"You know I'll support you with whatever choice you make," she assures me as she pulls me in for another hug.

"Thank you. I want so badly for this to have gone in a different direction, but it is what it is and I need to do what is best for me and my baby. You've always been the strong one out of the two of us, doing what needs to be done to protect yourself and those you love. That's just what I'm trying to do."

"I'm just going to miss you, that's all."

"And I'm going to miss you too, but you're still going to be my baby's godmother."

"I better be," she laughs.

We spend the rest of the evening eating takeout, watching sad romance movies and crying over them, painting our nails and pampering ourselves. I wanted my last night in Manhattan to be spent with my best friend, doing nothing, and that's exactly what I got.

Alex agrees to stay over and when she goes to get into my bed, I take my cell out of my bag and type out an email to Cooper.

## TWENTY-FIVE

# Cooper

I'm out at dinner with a new client and the restaurant he's chosen is abuzz with chatter and the occasional sound of cutlery scraping across plates and glasses being clinked. I've never dined here before and it wouldn't have been my first choice for a client meeting, but I'd definitely bring Meghan for a romantic dinner.

I've missed her while she's been away and just thinking of breaking rule number four—*no dates*—brings a smile to my lips. Admittedly, I haven't spoken to her as much as I should since she's been away, but she seemed preoccupied with helping her dad and I've had a couple of big cases come in since she left.

My phone vibrates in my pocket, and although I would normally leave it until after my meeting, Mr. Kincaid is in the bathroom and I haven't heard from Meghan for a few days.

*I need my fix of her.*

Pulling my phone out of my suit pocket, I check the screen—it's blank. My brow pulls into a frown as I stare down at my phone. Going to put it back in my pocket, I pause before I do, instead opening the mail app. I find an email from Meghan at the top.

She hasn't sent me an email the whole time she's been gone. *Something isn't right about this.* I open her email and my eyes scan the screen as my stomach drops.

**To: C Jackson <c.jackson@jandp.com>**
**CC: HR <hr@jandp.com>**
**From: M Taylor <m.taylor@jandp.com>**
**Subject: Resignation**

**Dear Mr. Jackson,**
**Please take this email as my resignation, effective immediately. It has been a pleasure working with you and I have learned a great deal in my short time at the firm. I wish you the best of luck in your future endeavors.**

**Kind regards,**
**Meghan Taylor**

*Something is definitely wrong.*
*Has something happened to her dad?*

Opening the phone app, I'm about to press her name when my client returns to the table. I exhale a silent sigh of frustration as I pocket my phone and return my attention to Mr. Kincaid and what I can do for his case.

Meghan remains in the back of my mind throughout discussions and I want nothing more than to leave this restaurant and track her down.

*To demand some answers.*

My dinner with Mr. Kincaid lasted much longer than I would have liked, which means it's after ten when I leave the restaurant and can try and reach out to Meghan.

Climbing into the back of the town car, I pull my phone out and dial her number—it goes to voicemail. Hanging up, I try again before deciding to send a text message.

COOPER

Call me, Meghan. I'm worried about you.

It remains undelivered, and I barely resist the urge to throw my phone out of the car window as my anger builds. How could she just up and resign like that? No conversation, nothing.

I call her again and for a moment I contemplate going to her place, before I realize it's redundant because she's in Sacramento. The car pulls up to my building and as I climb out, I wish Christopher a goodnight.

With my phone clenched in my hand, I ride the elevator to my floor, my eyes watching the numbers, willing it to go faster. The doors have barely opened when I rush through them, making my way down the corridor to my door. I'm still in the doorway when I try to call her again and am greeted by the sound of her voicemail. Again.

*Fuck.*

*What is going on?*

I need to know that everything is okay. I don't understand why this is happening, but I want to make whatever is wrong, right.

COOPER

Answer the fucking phone, Meghan.

I'm about to dial her number again, but a text comes through that causes me to pause. At least I know her phone is on and working now.

I breathe a sigh of relief as I press her name to open the message, but it's short lived as I read the message. My chest constricts and I feel like I'm drowning except I'm making no effort to swim to the surface. I drop onto the couch as a another message comes through.

MEGHAN

Please don't call me again, Cooper. I have nothing to say to you right now.

I text her back almost immediately.

COOPER

I don't understand. What's happened?

She doesn't respond and the bubbles don't move to show she's replying. Reading her message again, it dawns on me that she's broken up with me—in a fucking text message.

*How could she do this?*

A strangled sound of pain that I've never heard myself make before escapes me, and I throw my phone at the wall in frustration. I listen to it smash as my head tips back and I get choked up by the tears welling in my eyes.

*This is what it feels like to have your heart broken.*

*She's broken my heart, and she didn't even know she had it.*

Standing from the couch I head to the kitchen, pouring myself a generous glass of whiskey, downing the contents before pouring another one. I don't understand what's happened, what's gone so wrong.

She's left me, in all the ways she possibly could've—she's quit her job and ended what we had.

My heart is telling me something must have happened and I should find out what it is but my logical head is telling me to walk away and leave her alone.

Maybe I should listen to my heart for once. I could track down her friend tomorrow and see if she knows what's going on. Maybe.

*Tonight, I'm getting drunk.*

A banging sound in the distance rouses me from my sleep. Maybe they'll go away, if I ignore them. I'm not in the mood for company. Rolling over onto my back, I throw an arm over my eyes to ward off the daylight. *Why didn't I close the curtains last night?* Dammit, my head is pounding.

When the banging continues, I roll out of bed with a groan, throwing on a pair of sweatpants as I move toward the front door. Not caring who could be on the other side, I swing open the door without checking the peephole. Nobody can get up that isn't on my list anyway.

My list currently consists of my mom, Jamison, Sebastian, and Meghan... Ah, Meghan. *Fuck.* I'm hungover, but not enough to forget that I've lost her.

"Oh, thank God." Jamison breathes a sigh of relief. "Yeah, he's answered the door. I'll call you later," he says into the phone and some of the worry that was etched across his face dissipates as he takes in my disheveled appearance.

Letting go of the door in his face, I stalk toward the kitchen with Jamison hot on my heels. Last night I drank far too much, tried to call Meghan, with my smashed up phone, a bunch more and eventually vowed to follow my head and leave her alone.

"Are you okay? You missed our two o'clock meeting, and they said you hadn't been in all day. I, uh... heard about Meghan."

I turn to him and narrow my eyes in suspicion. "How

did you hear about Meghan?" I ask, my gaze intent on him. He looks to the floor sheepishly before straightening his shoulders and facing me, coughing into his hand before he replies.

"I saw her yesterday when she was leaving your office."

"What do you mean you saw her? She was in New York?" I ask, desperate for information.

His brows pull into a frown as he replies. "Yeah. I had my driver give her a lift back to her place."

*Fuck.* She was here, and at the office. *I should have gone to her place.*

"What did she say?" I practically beg.

"Nothing, just that you'd hurt her and I couldn't help."

She was at my office and didn't come and see me, instead choosing to send in her resignation? *And tell me to stop contacting her.*

There's no point in trying to figure out what this all means. She wants nothing to do with me.

I busy myself with getting some water because my tongue feels like I've spent the night licking a carpet. Gulping down the water, I turn back to Jamison, eyeing him over the rim of the glass.

"You want to talk about it?"

"I'm not sure what there is to talk about. She resigned, I tried to call her, and she said she didn't want me to contact her again." I lift one shoulder in a shrug as

I turn away from him and bring a hand up to rub my chest.

It hurts that she cared so little to tell me to my face that she was leaving me—especially when she was in the city. And it hurts that she didn't give me a chance to make right whatever was wrong. It will continue to hurt until she comes back.

*Or I can move on.*

The thought of moving on makes my stomach turn in protest and I rest my hands on the counter top as I will away the bile threatening to rise in my throat.

"What's the plan for the rest of the day?" Jamison asks, oblivious to my state.

"I'm going to work... I need to find a new assistant," I reply, making my way back upstairs to my bedroom.

Jamison follows me like a puppy, wanting to comfort his owner in his time of need. I don't need this right now. I don't need him hovering because he thinks I'm hurt.

*I am hurt. I'm fucking broken.*

"You don't want to maybe go out, get drunk and talk about it?" His voice sounds almost hopeful, which causes me to huff out a laugh and shake my head.

"Some of us work during the day," I snap, moving toward my bathroom where I turn on the shower before going back to my room.

"Right... but it's like three in the afternoon and the work day is almost over, right?" he calls to my back.

My stride falters at his statement before I continue to my closet to select a suit. I didn't realize that was the time. Thankfully, I didn't have court this morning and my day would have been spent preparing for my upcoming trial.

Or, more aptly, sitting at my desk staring at hers, going over everything that possibly could have happened to have us end like this.

"Well, I guess my day's just starting... I'm serious Jamison, I'm going to work. I don't want to talk about her, so just drop it. We fucked, and she left... That's the end of it."

"You forget I know you, Cooper, and I saw the way you were looking at her in Miami."

"You're full of shit," I reply with an emotion rising in me I can't quite identify.

She's gone and I'm never getting her back. I love her and I *need* her, but deep down I know I can't force her to want or love me back.

"Keep telling yourself that, but you practically dragged her out of that restaurant," he replies.

*I hate that he knows me so well.*

"Did you gossip with Seb about that?" I ask angrily, because how dare he use my feelings for her to goad me.

I'm frustrated with him, and I haven't ever been before, but I don't want to talk about how she left me and broke my heart. I don't want to admit to someone else that I love her and that she was it for me—that nobody compares to her.

Nobody will *ever* compare to her.

*Maybe somebody said something to her?* I scrap that

idea when I realize that she would have talked to me about it, she wouldn't have run away and cut all contact with me.

This is something else, maybe something she thinks I've done, and as much as I want to find out what it is and fix it for her, I'm going to respect her and leave her alone like she's asked me to.

"It changes nothing," I affirm with as much conviction in my voice as I can possibly inject, before walking into my bathroom and shutting the door on him.

*Why does it have to hurt this much?*

Tears well in my eyes and I blink them back, refusing to let them out over someone who could walk away so easily.

*In the end, it doesn't mean shit to love someone when they don't love you back.*

"I think you should fight for her," Jamison calls through the door.

"I don't take on cases I know I won't win, and I've already lost her," I whisper to my reflection in the mirror before dropping my chin down to my chest, leaning against the bowl of the sink.

She made her choice and I'm going to have to live with that as best I can.

## TWENTY-SIX

## Meghan

### SEVEN MONTHS LATER

I'm walking down the street when I catch another glimpse of him through the crowd of shoppers. This has been happening on and off for the last couple of months. I could be on the bus and think I see him walking past, or see a flash of him while grabbing groceries.

I've thought about him every day since I left.

I've regretted how I turned tail and ran and that I didn't tell him about the baby, but I haven't had the guts to call him. What if he hates me or refuses to take my calls?

It's an excuse, I know it is, but I promised myself when the baby comes I will call him. Or maybe write to him.

I'm sure it's just my hormonal body playing tricks on me, like the first time I thought I saw him, and ended up running after some random guy. It's safe to say he wasn't pleased, nor was his wife, that a pregnant woman was chasing him down.

I've since learned to ignore the tricks my mind plays on me, so even though my green eyes have connected with his brilliant blue ones and it feels oh-so-real, I continue walking down the sidewalk and into *Cute as a Button,* the baby store I'm headed to.

Over the past seven months, I've cried countless times as I've prepared myself to become a single mom. Today, and for the last three months, I've had an overwhelming sense of guilt that he won't get to meet his child if I don't reach out, especially as he stopped calling the day I left New York.

Sometimes I listen back to the voicemails he left the night I resigned and told him to stop contacting me. I know he was drunk when he called, his slurred speech and the times of the calls were a giveaway. The messages alternated between begging me to reconsider and not leave him, to him expressing his anger at me for being a coward and not discussing whatever had caused me to leave.

I shake my head to clear the thoughts of him, because it only leads to my mood plummeting and me devouring at least a pint of ice cream. Instead, I try to focus on happier thoughts, like the fact my baby will be here soon.

I'm due in less than a week, which I'm sure my dad will be thankful for. My nesting phase started at the beginning of my eighth month and he's been an angel, putting up with my crazy hormonal demands. He welcomed me home with open arms and has said I'm welcome to stay as long as I need, although I don't plan on staying forever. I have some savings left that will see me through for the next six months. My plan is to look for a job in about a month and then start looking for my own place.

I'm looking at the tiny sleepsuits when the bell above the door chimes, announcing another customer. I don't look up to see who may have entered, instead, I pick up a sleepsuit for a newborn. I admire its beautiful lemon-yellow color and white scrolled text with *'Daddy's Baby Girl'* embroidered across the front, at least until tears well in my eyes, obscuring my vision. I soothingly rub my hand across my large bump, wishing them away. I really don't want to break down in public. Putting the sleepsuit back on the rail, I continue looking through the rack of clothes as I compose myself.

*I wish things could've been different.*

I stick to the neutral colors as I peruse the rails—I don't know if I'm having a little boy or girl. When the doctor asked if I wanted to find out the gender I chose not to, but when I see outfits like the sleepsuit I just put back, I kind of wish I had. A part of me didn't want to find out because I wished we could've found out together. As my pregnancy progressed, I realized how stupid I'd been because it wouldn't have ever just been me, Cooper and our baby.

*Hayley.*

Her name pops into my mind and with it, the now familiar ache in my chest. During the countless nights I cried myself to sleep, I would wish I'd been enough for him, that he would've chosen me over her. For a while after I left, I kept an eye on Cooper in the media until I couldn't take the possibility of seeing him out with her. To see them so in love, him looking at her how I wish he could have looked at me, it would have been too much for me to handle.

I refused to do that to myself. To allow him to have that kind of hold over me.

"Meghan?" I hear whispered from behind me, and I close my eyes in pain at the voice that has haunted me for the past seven months.

*It can't be him.*

Taking a deep breath, I turn around and come face to face with Cooper Jackson. Staring up at him in shock, I exhale a shaky breath. I can't believe that he's actually here, that it's really him. I want to reach out and touch him just to be sure.

*It can't really be him, right?*

He looks good, wearing all black in a polo shirt, jeans and a bomber jacket. His eyes look tired and he looks like he's lost some weight, but aside from that, he looks just as good as the day I last saw him.

It takes all of my self-control to resist the urge to reach out and touch him. We stare at each other for what feels like hours before he shakes his head and diverts his eyes to my bump. A look of pain crosses his face but he's quick to hide it.

"I came to get you. To bring you home. I went to therapy to make sure I was the man you deserve. I couldn't stop thinking about you, and I come here and find you like this..." He runs a hand through his hair while gesturing to my stomach with the other.

I can't quite figure out what the look on his face is; the pain has gone, and it's now replaced with a mixture of disgust and... regret.

"You met someone else and you're... pregnant. Wow," he scoffs, shaking his head, before turning on his heel and walking out of the store.

It takes my mind a minute to register what he's said, as I'm still in shock that he's actually here.

*He came for me.*

Blindly, I drop the items I'm holding onto a nearby counter and race as fast as my feet will carry my very pregnant body. I want to cry tears of joy that he's here... *for me.*

"Cooper," I call. "Wait. Please..."

He pauses on the sidewalk and looks up at the sky before turning around. A fat raindrop falls and lands on my shoulder but I pay it no mind as I continue waddling toward him, pausing when I'm about two feet away from him.

In a matter of seconds, rain has started to fall and big droplets descend from the heavens, coating us both. My rain jacket, that doesn't zip up thanks to my bump, is barely protecting me and so my loose-fitting floral paisley dress doesn't take long to become soaked through.

"I can't do this, Meghan. I can't stand here and listen to you explain away how you met someone else and you're having their baby. I won't beg for you—not when you've so clearly moved on."

He looks at me as if I've broken his heart, which is laughable. I know that can't be true because I heard him in his office with Hayley.

It's on the tip of my tongue to tell him how wrong he is, that I haven't moved on and he's the only man I want but I refuse to be his second choice, when a pain rips through my lower back and abdomen. It causes me to cry out and as I do, he closes the distance between us, grabbing a hold of my arm as I double over in pain.

"Are you okay?" he asks, the urgency and worry in his voice coming through clearly.

The pain passes after about a minute, and I slowly straighten, resting a hand on my lower back.

"I'm okay... I think maybe it was a Braxton Hicks contraction or something." I wave him off.

"Are you sure?" I nod and he steps away, his hands dropping from my arms before he continues. "Maybe you should go home and rest. I'm going to go back to New York."

"We should talk, Cooper," I say, placing my hand on his arm while I beg with my eyes for him to not leave. Not yet.

Rain runs down my face and I'm sure I look like a crazy woman with mascara tracks on my cheeks and my wet hair plastered to my forehead. I don't want him to go. Now that he's here, it's my chance to tell him about the baby.

"It's not going to achieve anything. It was a mistake for me to come and I think it's best if we go our separate ways," he mumbles with one last look at my stomach.

Just as he's about to shrug off my hand, another contraction hits me, and I grip his arm as I double over, crying out from the pain.

*Okay maybe these aren't Braxton Hicks.*

"I'm going to call an ambulance. Something might be wrong." The worry is back in his voice as he pulls his phone from his jacket pocket.

I keep my tight grip on his arm as I remember my breathing techniques from Lamaze classes.

"No," I say, more forcefully than intended, once the contraction has passed. "I'll take myself... I just need to get to my car," I rasp out.

Not all of us are billionaires that can afford a newborn baby and an ambulance ride.

Standing straight, I turn in the direction of my car and tentatively make way toward it, hoping by the grace of God that another contraction doesn't hit me. My hand trails along the wall next to me as I use it for support, the remnants of my previous contraction still lingering. I can feel Cooper trailing after me.

"Promise me you won't leave town until we've spoken?" I beg through clenched teeth.

"Meghan," he all but shouts, causing me to pause in my mission to reach my car. "Something could be wrong. I'm going to call you an ambulance." He barely gets the words out when my waters break, right there on the sidewalk.

Maybe if I keep moving, because the ground is wet anyway, he won't notice. Thankfully, it's quiet on the sidewalk, other shoppers having opted to take shelter in the nearby stores.

My panic sets in as another contraction hits me, keeping me frozen in place as I breathe through it. Okay, I'm actually having this baby *today*. This tiny human, the size of a pumpkin, is going to come out of me.

Out of my tiny vagina.

*I can't do this.*

"Have you seen the size of a pumpkin, Cooper?" I blurt out. "I can't push a pumpkin out of my vagina. My vagina is tiny... you've been in it, you know it won't fit a pumpkin." Cooper looks at me quizzically, probably wondering where a pumpkin has come into the conversation, but I ignore him as I continue rambling. "Oh God, I'm not ready for this. I thought I was, but I'm really not." I cry out as another contraction rips through me.

The rain continues to pour down as if taunting me for my predicament. Like someone's having a laugh at my expense.

"Look at me, Meghan." I raise my eyes to him. "That's

it. Keep your eyes on me. You've got this. We'll get you to the hospital and they'll be able to help," he declares before looking back at his phone.

"Cooper?" I whisper, causing him to pause from calling 911. "Can you call my dad?" I plead, my eyes welling with unshed tears.

"I will once you're in the ambulance," he states, going back to his phone. I snatch it out of his grasp, holding it out of reach with a look of purpose written across my face.

I lift my chin in defiance, telling him to just try and wrestle with a pregnant woman. I'm not sure it comes across as that, not with the way my chin is trembling, and the tears that have started tumbling down my cheeks, mingling with the rain drops.

"I'm not going in an ambulance. I need you to call my dad. I can't do this without him," I practically shout at him.

"Okay, I'll call him," he soothes. "I'll need your cell." He holds out his hand for me to place my phone into. "Will he get in touch with your baby's dad?" he asks, searching for my dad's contact information, his gaze avoiding me.

"No," I whisper, causing his jaw to clench.

"Do you need me to call him?" he asks through gritted teeth.

I shake my head before breathing through another contraction as Cooper calls my dad. This pain is unbearable. None of my classes prepared me for this.

My dad knows all about Cooper, but I don't think he'd say anything to him, not given the reason for Cooper's call. I watch as Cooper speaks to my dad. He introduces himself before telling my dad I'm headed to the hospital. There's no conversation aside from that before Cooper hands me back my phone.

"Who's your baby's dad, Meghan?" he asks, his voice strained.

*Shit.*

Did I read this wrong. Did my dad tell him? I don't answer him, so he lifts my chin, forcing my gaze to connect with his. My features tense as another contraction overtakes me.

*They're so close—too close.*

Cooper drops my chin like I'm on fire, a look I can't quite decipher swimming in the depths of his eyes before he blinks and it's gone.

"I need to go." I rush out as I turn back toward my car, hiding the pain that his reaction to touching me caused. Before I can make it more than two steps, he grabs my arm and halts my progress.

"I'm going to take you to the hospital, Meghan. But you need to tell me who the father of your baby is on the way," he demands as he guides me toward his rental car.

Opening the door, he helps me into the passenger's seat before reaching over to buckle up my seatbelt. I can't help but inhale his glorious scent; it's Cooper but mixed with the freshness of the rain.

*I've missed the smell of him.*

He stiffens at my obvious inhalation before pulling away, shutting the door and walking around the car to his side. When he's settled in, he starts the car, enters the hospital address in the GPS and pulls out onto the road.

It's not until we're two contractions into the journey that he breaks the tense silence.

"Who is he, Meghan?"

## TWENTY-SEVEN

*Cooper*

When I first saw her walking down the sidewalk, I hadn't fully taken in her appearance. I was too stunned that she was really there in front of me. It wasn't until she'd turned into the alcove of the store that my eyes had drifted down to her very obvious bump.

For a moment, I thought it was a mistake to come here, to see her when I didn't know what to expect. My stomach dropped and my heart shattered into a million pieces at my feet. People walked past me on the busy sidewalk, some knocking into me, oblivious to my torment.

I'd stayed rooted to the spot in shock, unsure how to proceed, until I came to the realization that I needed to confront her. I threw myself into action. She'd seen me after all and I'm not one for running away from my problems.

The last seven months have been the worst of my life without her. I was drunk nearly every night for five months and worked all hours of the day, trying my hardest to rid her from my mind. Everywhere in my apartment and the office has reminded me of her, to the point that I even considered relocating.

I was halfway through a case of whiskey when Seb and Jamison came over and staged an intervention, kicking my fully clothed ass into the shower and telling me to get a grip. They said if I didn't think I could get over her, which based on the previous five months they didn't feel was likely, I needed to go and get her.

They were right. I did need to go and get her, but I needed to work on myself first. If I didn't think I was good enough or able to provide her with everything she deserves, then why should she?

I found a therapist I clicked with and started having sessions. For the last two months I've been twice a week, and mentally I'm in the best shape of my life. Even though my mom has told me often, I know now that I'm nothing like my father. I won't make the same mistakes as him. Meghan is the only woman I could see myself being with. She's it for me, but seeing her today... everything just crashed and burned in front of me.

Now I'm here, sitting in the car with the woman I love, taking her to the hospital so she can give birth to another man's child. Her contractions are getting closer and closer and each time, even though she tries to hide it, I can feel her pain. It's like a knife being plunged straight into my heart.

I want to make it better... to soothe her. I want to hold her and tell her she's doing great, but that isn't my role in her life anymore. I'm not sure it ever truly was my role, no matter how much I wanted it to be.

"Who is he, Meghan?" I demand, my grip tensing on the steering wheel. Something her dad said to me has made me think I'm not quite aware of the full picture.

*"It's about time you showed up."*

She's so quiet that when I stop at a red light I flick my eyes away from the road to look at her. She's looking out of the window, the backs of her fingers pressed against her lips as she leans her elbow on the door. Her blonde hair has gone dark from the rain and strands are plastered against the sides of her face. I sigh, prepared to wait her out.

*She's never looked more beautiful.*

"It's you," she murmurs, barely above a whisper.

"What did you say?" I ask, my eyes darting to hers again. She sits up straighter, clearing her throat as if to give herself the strength needed before responding.

"I said... it's you. You're my baby's father," she affirms.

She lifts her chin, as if daring me to argue with her, before rubbing her hand across the expanse of her bump as if to soothe her child... *our child.*

"That can't be true," I say in disbelief, but I don't

really believe my own words, because I know she wouldn't lie to me.

"It can be, and it is. I found out when I came back for my Mom's funeral. I wasn't feeling great and so I went to see my old doctor."

I'm about to ask her why she left, why she didn't tell me, if she was ever going to tell me, but a car honks behind us and another contraction takes her over. Now isn't the time to interrogate her, despite the million questions racing through my mind.

When *our* baby arrives, we'll have time to talk, but right now isn't the time. My focus needs to be on getting us to the hospital. A weight I didn't realize was on my shoulders lifts, as it dawns on me that there isn't anybody else in her life. Only to return at the realization that if I hadn't come for her, she might never have told me. I need to put aside the feelings stirring inside of me, at least for now.

It doesn't take long for us to arrive at the hospital and once I've parked, I help Meghan inside and to the front desk.

"How can I help you?" a friendly nurse who looks to be in her sixties asks.

"I'm in labor. My water broke," Meghan breathes out.

"Okay, my dear, let's get you checked in. And who might you be?" the nurse asks as she types away on her keyboard.

"I'm... I'm the baby's dad," I declare as a feeling of awe blooms inside my chest.

*Fuck.*

*I'm going to be a dad.*

A small part of me and Meghan has been growing inside her for the last nine months.

I have a family of my own.

I don't even know if we're having a boy or girl.

The nurse smiles up at me, a look of understanding on her face as I try to process everything, before turning to Meghan to continue checking her in.

Once we're seen to a room and Meghan is checked over, there isn't much to do except wait. She's about five centimeters dilated and has been administered an epidural to help with the pain. The sound of our baby's heartbeat is the only sound in the room. She's lying back in the bed, one hand rubbing her stomach and her eyes closed.

"Were you ever going to tell me?" I ask, unable to keep quiet any longer.

Opening her eyes, she stares over at me with a look of serenity on her face. Her gaze roams my features, for what I'm not sure.

"Cooper..." she murmurs.

The door swings open and in rushes a man that looks so familiar I can only assume he's Meghan's father. Hurrying to her side, he smooths back her hair before placing a kiss on her forehead.

"Sweetheart, how are you doing?"

"I'm okay, dad. I was scared, but now that I'm here and the doctors have checked me over, I'm feeling ready," she replies and he pulls her in for a hug.

Clearing my throat, I stand from my chair and extend my hand toward her father.

"Afternoon, sir. I'm Cooper Jackson. We spoke on the phone."

He places his hand in mine. His grip is strong and sure as he looks me up and down before shaking it.

"I'm Warren. I've heard a lot about you, Cooper. Surprised it took you this long to come."

"Dad, now's not the time," Meghan admonishes.

"I would have been here a lot sooner had I known, sir." My eyes dart to Meghan and she looks away, guilt written all over her face.

It's the truth. Had I known we were having a baby, I would have been here right away. He doesn't respond to my statement, he just nods before turning back to Meghan, whispering in soothing tones to her.

Returning to my seat, I watch the heart rate monitor attached to Meghan's stomach as they have a private discussion.

"Cooper?" Meghan calls, bringing me out of my reverie. "Would you like to stay in the room for the birth?" she asks, fiddling with her hands in her lap.

"If that's okay, yes I would."

"I would love that," she says, sincerity coating her words.

Her father leaves to grab a coffee and when he returns, it isn't long before things start moving quickly. Before we know it, Meghan is ten centimeters dilated, and it's time to push.

Although I'm grateful that I was able to witness the birth of my first child, a still tension fills the room. I'm in awe when my little girl is placed on Meghan's chest, but the feeling is quickly replaced with anger at Meghan, that she ran away, that I could have missed such a momentous occasion.

If I'd missed this moment, would I have been able to forgive her?

I want to say I would have, but if I'm being honest with myself, I can't be certain I would.

Elizabeth Rosie Jackson was born at seven-fifty-five in the evening on October fifth, weighing a healthy seven pounds and six ounces.

She's gorgeous and I still can't believe that Meghan and I created her. She has her mom's blonde hair, button nose and feminine features, and my blue eyes—although Meghan thinks she looks more like me than her.

Not long after her birth, when everyone had left us to bond with our newborn, Meghan had pulled out a list of name ideas. She gave me the privilege of choosing Elizabeth's first name, her only stipulation was on the middle name.

When we introduced Elizabeth, or Lizzie for short, to her Grandpa Warren he cried at her name. He thanked us for giving her the middle name of Rosie and said that he loved that Lizzie would always carry a part of her late grandma with her.

While Meghan and Lizzie slept, I reached a decision. I'm going to ask Meghan to move back to New York and live with me. They're my family after all, and I'll be damned if I let them go. I might be mad at her because of the last seven months, but realistically it doesn't change my feelings for her.

*Love isn't that easy to erase.*

The nurse has just left after helping Meghan give Lizzie her first feed of the day and she's now swaddled up in her crib. Meghan has a post-birth glow about her. Her cheeks are still flushed from the delivery, and a beautiful smile graces her plump lips as she looks down at Lizzie.

"She's so tiny, nothing like a pumpkin."

"She's perfect," I whisper back and after a moment of silence, "We need to talk... about what happens next."

Dragging my gaze away from Lizzie and up to Meghan—she's still looking at Lizzie, but nods her head in agreement.

"Why didn't you tell me?"

"You really want to go straight into this?" Meghan chuckles while shaking her head. Her face grows serious as she turns to me, leaning over to rest one hand on

Lizzie in her crib, as if she might be taken away if she isn't somehow connected.

"I didn't think you would want to know... it was never a part of what we had. We never talked about it. I didn't know if you even wanted to have children. We were just supposed to be fun."

I might not have seen her for seven months, but I know her well enough to know when she's lying to me. It's the way she's looking somewhere over my left shoulder, as she robotically states her *rehearsed* lines that gives her away.

Resting my elbows on the arms of the chair, I rest my chin on my right hand as I stare at her. "Want to tell me the truth now?" I ask. When she drops her gaze, I continue, "Look me in the eye and tell me those lies again, Meghan," I demand with a growl.

Her eyes dart to my own and her shoulders deflate for a brief moment before she straightens her spine.

"Fine," she huffs, folding her arms across her chest. "I contemplated not telling you at all because I had no interest in being a toy for you to pick up and play with whenever your latest conquest bores you. I wasn't going to put my child in a position to witness you dipping in and out of our lives. All of that being said, I decided last month that it wasn't my decision, and I was going to come to you after she was born, so you could at least be involved in her life. If that was what you even wanted." She draws in a deep breath as if the next words out of her mouth are the ones that pain her the most. "Not that it matters now, but I heard you in your office with your ex... sorry, your *girlfriend*, the day I resigned. Does she know you're here, by the way?" she asks, tilting her head to the side, as if daring me to lie to her.

A smirk spreads across my face as I lean back in my chair and I barely resist the urge to laugh at the fact that she almost didn't tell me about my child because she thought I was cheating on her—it's almost comical.

"I don't find this even remotely funny, Cooper," she practically hisses as she glares at me before darting her eyes to Lizzie.

The smirk that was forming falls from my face before I reply. "Neither do I. You have to believe me when I say what you heard... it wasn't what you think."

I remember the day, but for an almost entirely different reason. Hayley had brought me lunch from my favorite Italian place. We talked about my new woman, she gave me some sound advice, and then the conversation moved on to her new *woman*. Meghan throws a pillow at me, but I dodge out of the way before it can make contact, chuckling at her misunderstanding.

"I heard her fucking moan, Cooper," she whisper-yells, closing her eyes and taking a deep breath, releasing it, before she looks at me. "Look, it doesn't matter," she says before I can explain. "We're done, I'm over it. Yes, we have a daughter, but you'll go back to New York and visit when you can, I'm sure. No doubt getting on with your life." She averts her gaze away from my own, as if it hurts to think of me leaving her.

"I'm not going anywhere without my daughter," I snarl, my nostrils flaring.

She looks at me with fear written across her face and I almost immediately realize my mistake.

*Fuck.*

I didn't mean it to sound like that—I'm not going anywhere without both of them.

"You can't take her away from me. She needs me... I need her," Meghan cries out, tears well in her eyes and she turns away from me but not before I see the first one fall.

I drop my gaze from hers, shaking my head at my poor communication as I try to sort through my thoughts. "That's not what I meant—I didn't mean it like that." I pause, trying to get my words out right. "Come back to New York with me?" I plead, my eyes lifting to look into hers, hoping and praying she can see all that I'm not saying.

"I can't... I don't have a job and I can't afford to rent a place in New York by myself, not with a newborn baby and no job." Sadness is reflected in her tone as she drops her head, causing her hair to fall in front of her face.

Standing from my chair I sit on the edge of her bed. The movement causes her to tense ever so slightly, but I don't let that stop me. Instead, I tuck her hair behind her ear and cup her cheek as I lift her face to me.

"Move in with me? You and Lizzie," I murmur. "I want my baby close to me."

*Both of them.*

She closes her eyes at my declaration, pressing her cheek further into my palm before moving away from me. "I can't be with you, Cooper... not like how we were. I was kidding myself before with all the rules. I'm not going to be the other woman."

I don't know what she means about the other woman or kidding herself before. I don't want her with the rules we had agreed to all those months ago either, but now isn't the time to delve back into what we had.

Now isn't the time to try and figure all of this out, she's just given birth to our daughter and if I'm exhausted, I can't imagine how tired she must be. I need to focus on getting her and our daughter to come *home* with me—where they belong.

Everything else can be figured out later.

"I'll take care of you both," I blurt out and as she looks up at me, a protest on the tip of her tongue. "Until you get a job. You can stay in one of the spare rooms." *For now.* "I don't want to miss a thing with Lizzie," I plead, hoping to God that she doesn't deny me this.

She considers it for what feels like a century and I can see her warring with the idea of living apart from me and us having a custody agreement, splitting Lizzie between us equally, before she replies.

"Okay... I don't want to keep you from your daughter." Her tongue darts out to sweep across her lips, bringing my attention to the fullness of her mouth. "But I meant what I said about us not resuming what we had before I left. We'll be co-parents, nothing more and nothing less." Her voice is husky, as if I'm not the only one affected by our close proximity.

She holds out her hand for me to shake. I'm grateful she's agreed to come back to Manhattan with me but I'm not shaking her hand as if this is some business deal.

Ignoring her still outstretched hand, I bring my hands to her cheeks, tilting her head up before bringing my lips down to graze across her own. Pulling away, I stare down into her slightly dazed gaze as her lips part and I barely resist the urge to kiss her again. In that moment, it felt like the most natural thing to do.

My eyes focus on hers and I try to get a read on whatever it is she's thinking. Her eyes darken and I'm about to act on the feeling she's stirring within me, but hurt flickers across her face and she turns away, causing my hands to drop from her face.

"That can't happen again. Co-parents, Cooper," she asserts breathlessly.

The only thing I can do is nod in agreement, afraid that if I argue the point now, she'll change her mind about coming home with me.

## TWENTY-EIGHT

*Meghan*

### SIX WEEKS LATER

**B**efore I returned to New York with Cooper, I promised myself that I wouldn't want more than to co-parent with him. We even signed an agreement, not a legally binding one, that said that it was all we would ever be and that he would provide anything Lizzie needed.

*I needed the boundaries.*

As if I could switch off my feelings for him and not want to jump him every time he walks into a room. I realize now that infatuation, lust, love or hate—no emotion can be turned off. No matter how much I wish for that to be the case.

Cooper, Lizzie, and I have been living in Cooper's Upper East Side penthouse for the past four weeks and seeing him walk around topless, cradling our newborn baby against his toned chest or in those goddamn gray sweatpants is really testing my resolve.

So far I've managed to stay strong, but I'm not sure how much longer I can last before I beg him to just hold me. My longing for him has grown tenfold with each day we live in the same house. He's so close yet so far, and I can practically feel my barriers crumbling.

I should be putting my focus into finding a job and a place for Lizzie and I to live, but he's not gone back to work yet, and he's very distracting. It seems like every time I get my laptop out to start searching, he walks past with Lizzie cradled against his bare chest.

*Lord, give me strength.*

We stayed with my dad for just over a week so that he could see Lizzie for a while before we had to leave him with the promise that we would visit as soon as we were settled in.

It was hard for me to leave him behind, especially as he had me for the last seven months, but he assured me he would be okay and all but strapped me into the car when it was time to leave for the airport.

As we arrived at the airport, I was shocked to find Cooper had chartered a whole damn plane. I know he's rich, but it was the first time I'd really experienced it for myself. He's usually so reserved with his spending.

Sitting on the couch in Cooper's apartment with Lizzie cradled in my arms, soothing her to sleep, I wait for Alex to arrive. Cooper's out to lunch with his mom. I went to lunch with Catherine Jackson when we arrived back in New York.

She welcomed me with open arms, gushing over her

Lizzie and saying how she always thought I would be the perfect match for Cooper. I left it with him to clear up her misunderstanding, not wanting to be the reason the twinkle in her eye died.

Even though I kept in constant contact with Alex while I was back in Sacramento, we haven't had a chance to meet up since I returned to the city—so a much needed catch up is on the cards today. When the doorbell rings, I make my way to the door, swinging it open and whisper-screaming at her, so as not to wake Lizzie.

"Oh my God, girl. You look amazing. Motherhood agrees with you," Alex compliments, as she pulls me in for a side hug. "She's the cutest baby I have ever seen. The pictures just don't do her justice," she exclaims, looking down at a sleeping Lizzie in my arms. "I can't wait to hold her when she's awake."

"If you mean the look of exhaustion agrees with me, you are correct." I laugh, causing Alex's eyes to narrow.

"Is he not pulling his weight?" she quizzes, and before giving me a chance to respond, she continues on. "You know I'll punch him in the d-i-c-k, if needed, just say the word."

"Of course he is. He's been amazing. I'm just messing with you because I don't feel like I look amazing." I laugh, shoving her shoulder and turning so she can follow me into the apartment.

Leading us into the living room where I've set up a bassinet to pop Lizzie in, I gently place her inside and turn around to motion for Alex to follow me into the kitchen.

"How are you?" I ask as I busy myself making coffee. Alex takes a seat on one of the stools at the kitchen island before answering me.

"I'm good. I'll be even better when I can hold Lizzie." She gazes over at her bassinet longingly before continuing. "I've mostly been working, especially since they gave me more responsibility. I'm enjoying the challenge, even if it means my social life is pretty much non-existent."

"I'm so proud of you, Alex. You've come so far since you moved here and I just know you're going to go even further. There's nothing to stop you from one day becoming a managing partner yourself."

"This is why I keep you around, you're good for my ego," she chuckles.

"Are you seeing anyone?" My back is to her, but I can tell by how long it takes her to answer, that there's something she isn't telling me.

"Not anymore, if you can even call it that," she murmurs, sounding defeated, which causes me to turn around and look her in the eye.

"Want to tell me about it?" I ask, smiling softly with compassion.

Her head drops, and she shakes her head before reaching up to wipe a single tear away. I wrap my arms around her as we cry together.

"Why are you crying, mama?" she chuckles as she pulls away and looks into my eyes.

"I'm sad for you. You deserve so much, and whoever he is... well, he's an idiot for letting you go." I practically wail. "Plus, I'm still *really* hormonal." I laugh, which causes Alex to break out into a loud laugh before we both shush each other, not wanting to wake Lizzie. I'm glad to have been able to put a smile back on Alex's face.

"Come on, let's go drink some coffee and watch movies while we pretend to not just stare at your beautiful baby girl. And you can tell me all about living with your baby daddy," she calls over her shoulder as she grabs the coffee mugs and heads into the living room.

"It's the worst," I moan as I flop onto the couch next to a giggling Alex.

She's put our coffees on the table and so I reach forward and pick mine up before curling my legs underneath myself, taking a sip.

"Why is it the worst?" she asks before tapping her finger on her chin as she continues. "It wasn't that long ago that you were telling me how much you loved him," she teases me.

"First of all, I never said love, not at the time. Secondly, that's the problem now. Coming back to the city and living with him has just confirmed to me that I do love him. I've tried to fight it, but he's been nothing but attentive to me. He's a great dad to Lizzie and, God, every time I see him, I want to climb his body and devour him. Our time apart did nothing to minimize my feelings for him."

"Has the doctor said you can... you know?" she asks,

wiggling her eyebrows as she hides her smirk behind her mug.

"Yes, but that doesn't mean I can or will. We're sleeping in separate rooms, and he hasn't made a move. Not since we were in the hospital, which was a whisper of a kiss, and I then told him we couldn't be more than co-parents. For all I know, he's still seeing Hayley. He hasn't mentioned her, aside from telling me I misunderstood what I heard, and she's not been over, but that doesn't mean he's not talking to her." My stomach clenches at the thought of him being with her, being with anyone that isn't me.

"And you haven't spoken to him to ask what exactly it was you misunderstood?" Alex asks.

"No," I reply sheepishly.

"And why is that?"

"Because I haven't had the guts to bring up that day. I don't want to relive my heartache again."

"I think you should. Do you not think you should have a conversation with him to say you would actually like to give it a try again?"

I laugh at her question, because I've thought about doing just that so many times in the short time I've been here.

"No, I can't ask him if he wants to give a relationship with me a chance because I can't face the rejection that would inevitably come when he says he's not interested. I'd want to leave, and that won't ever be an option now that we have Lizzie. I won't be his fuck buddy again, either. It's better for everyone if I keep how I feel to myself."

My chest feels tight at the thought of having to leave, even if just to my own place. The truth is, I don't want to move out of his place. I like having him around, even if it's down the hall and not next to me in bed.

I want to keep our family together. At least that's what I tell myself.

"I get that, but how are you going to feel when he moves on?"

My heart grows heavy at the thought and tears well in my eyes.

"I'll be fine," I say around the heavy lump in my throat.

If I'm being honest, I'll be destroyed when he moves on—if he hasn't already. At least at the moment I can pretend it's not true. I truly believe that Cooper is the one and it hurts me to even think about him with anyone else. If I have misunderstood the whole situation like Alex said, eventually he will move on.

How would I feel when he starts seeing someone?

Or even worse, when he brings someone home?

When he introduces her to our daughter.

Or he gets engaged to her.

What about when he gets married and has more babies? A family of his own.

No longer able to hold the tears back, my face scrunches up at the pain in my heart as they come tumbling down my cheeks.

"Oh, babe. Come here." Alex takes my mug from my hands and places it on the coffee table with her own before pulling me into her arms.

We sit like this for a while, my sobs muffled in Alex's shoulder as she soothes my back. Eventually, I pull away from her and roughly wipe my cheeks before exhaling harshly.

"Tell me something. Anything to distract me from the disaster that is my life," I beg.

"Promise you won't tell anyone?" she murmurs, a sad smile tilting the corner of her lips.

"I pinkie-promise," I swear, holding out my pinkie finger for her to shake. She laughs at the immature gesture but does it anyway, knowing I would never break a pinkie swear.

"I slept with Sebastian Worthington," she blurts out.

"As in, the owner of Passion? Cooper's friend, Sebastian Worthington?" My eyes practically bug out of my head and my jaw goes slack with shock.

I'm sure my face is a mirror of hers when I first told her about me and Cooper.

"Yes, and it was amazing. It was supposed to be nothing more than a one time thing, and certainly not more than just amazing s-e-x. And even though I knew we were nothing, it still hurt when I found him in his office with another woman on her knees and his c-o-c-k in her mouth," she whispers dejectedly and I gasp in surprise at her confession.

"One, fuck him, not literally though, more like go and

fuck another guy in the middle of his dance floor." I wink at her, knowing she probably would. "And two, I'm pretty sure Lizzie doesn't understand words, let alone swear words, yet, so you can just say it," I joke, drawing a laugh out of Alex.

Alex left an hour ago and although she tried to give me advice on how to proceed with Cooper, I just can't damage our parenting relationship. As much as I want him, I can't put myself in the position of being hurt by him and then having to continue seeing him because we're raising Lizzie together.

Equally, I won't keep him from his daughter because that isn't fair for either of them. There's nothing I can do about it, I'll just have to suffer in silence when he inevitably moves on and then try to do the same myself.

It's just gone nine and I'm curled up on the couch with a *Hallmark* movie on, waiting for Cooper to come home from his first day back in the office. I guess that's a perk of being the boss, taking as much time as you like off.

I'm not paying much attention to the movie, instead I'm aimlessly scrolling through social media. Before I know what I'm doing my figures have opened up the internet browser and I'm typing out Cooper's name. I hover over the return key, debating whether to search his name, when Lizzie's hungry cries sound from the bassinet.

*Thank you, baby.*

Closing the browser and vowing to never search him, afraid of what I might see, I get up from the couch to feed Lizzie before rocking her back to sleep. I watch her for a while, her beautiful face animated even in her sleep, before I climb back onto the couch and pull a blanket over myself as my eyes grow heavy.

*This day has really taken its toll on me.*

I must've been asleep for at least an hour when I hear Cooper come through the front door, I can hear him chattering to Lizzie as he carries her off to her crib.

I snuggle down on the couch and go back to sleep, too tired to move to my bed.

TWENTY-NINE

## Cooper

I came home last night to find my two girls asleep in the living room and after putting Lizzie to bed, I returned to the living room and contemplated leaving Meghan for all of ten seconds before carrying her to bed too.

She must've been exhausted, because she didn't wake up or stir at all while I carried her to my room. Lately I've been wanting to be near her, to drink her in, twenty-four-seven and it's killing me that she isn't ready for that yet. She's getting there. I can tell in the way her gaze lingers on me for a while when I walk into a room or how her breath hitches when I get too close.

It's been amazing having her here in my space, and I love that she's added love and laughter to my apartment, that had felt so cold and lifeless for so long. The time we spent with her dad and seeing her with Lizzie has really helped me forgive her for not telling me when she first found out she was pregnant. That and talking to my therapist.

When I came to my senses, I put a plan in place to make her mine.

*I want her to be mine in every sense of the word.*

Even though to me she already is, I need her to realize it too.

Meghan is currently curled into the crook of my arm with a leg draped over one of mine. I'm roused from my sleep by sweet kisses being dusted across my shoulder. A hand sweeps up my thigh before rubbing over and squeezing my already semi-hard cock.

Not wanting to disturb her, partly because I'm curious as to what she will do, I stay still and wait for her next move. Her tongue darts out to lick across my nipple, and I bite my lip to stifle a moan.

"You taste so good, Cooper," she purrs with a moan of satisfaction. "I can't wait to ride your beautiful cock. It's been way too long, baby."

*I must have died and gone to fucking heaven.*

Her hand slips into my boxers as she grips my now painfully hard cock in her delicate palm. When she strokes me, once, then twice and I can't help but gently thrust my hips into her hand.

It was a mistake to move because she rips her hand out of my boxers, causing the elastic on my boxers to snap against my skin in her haste. I hiss from the unexpected pain and the arm that's around her waist tightens to keep her in place, while she pushes against my chest in an attempt to move away from me.

"What the fuck, Cooper?" she demands, sitting up.

"What the fuck, what?" I ask, opting to play dumb, but by the look on her face, that wasn't the right thing to say.

She slaps her hand across my chest, making me flinch away as I laugh.

"You know what I mean. Why am I in your bed?"

"Because I wanted you here. It's not a big deal," I reply, simply.

*It is a big deal.*

"That's not what we have, Cooper. And you know it. You should've left me on the couch. We agreed to co-parent, nothing more." She pushes away from me and climbs from the bed, making her way out of the room.

"I'm going to make you see that this is exactly where you belong," I call to her as she walks out of *our* bedroom.

That's it, I'm officially moving to Plan B—operation *Make Meghan Mine... For Good* is a go.

I tried to give her the time to come to terms with the fact that I'm not going anywhere, and that this is the real deal, but she keeps pushing me away. I know she wants me as much as I want her.

Plan B consists of delegating work so I can be home early, sending her flowers and gifts, teasing her with my body because I've seen her staring, rubbing her feet when we're watching movies or TV and just generally going above and beyond for her.

I go to the door and listen to the sounds of her getting Lizzie up and ready for the day, before quietly closing it. Walking to the walk-in closet I open the draw that holds my socks before reaching into the back and pulling out the Harry Winston *'The One'* three carat cushion-cut diamond engagement ring.

I bought the ring before I'd gone to California, my plan being to propose to her and get her to come home, but with Lizzie literally arriving the moment I laid eyes on her, it didn't feel like the right time to ask. Especially after the revelations she made about Hayley—I need to get her to believe that she's it for me.

I regret not setting her straight when she brought Hayley up. The truth is, I was overwhelmed with everything that had happened that day, from finding out I was going to be a dad, to the fact that Hayley was the reason she'd left.

I'm sure if I'd proposed to her in California and confessed my undying love, she would have thought I was only asking because she'd had Lizzie.

It's half past four when I get home that evening and I find Meghan in the bathroom, covered head to toe with water and bubbles. Lizzie's in her tub inside the bath and is ferociously slapping her arms against the water letting out adorable gurgling giggles.

It's the perfect scene and I shake my head as I let out a laugh, leaning against the doorjamb. Meghan turns around and lets out a startled yelp, one hand reaching for her chest, just above her heart, as the other supports Lizzie's head.

"What are you doing here?" she asks.

"Last time I checked, I lived here." I smile back at her.

She rolls her eyes before responding, "I know that. You don't normally get home this early, I wasn't expecting you. I was going to finish bathing Lizzie and start on dinner."

"What were you going to make?"

"I hadn't really gotten that far." She laughs.

"Why don't you finish my princess' bath, I'll get her dressed and then you can have a nice long soak, while I figure out dinner?" I suggest.

She assesses me for a minute before her head tilts to the side in question. "Are you okay? Do you have a temperature? Is that why you're home early?" she asks, turning back to Lizzie to finish her bath.

"I'm fine," I reply, my brows drawing down in confusion.

"If you insist. But when I worked for you, we never left the office this early," she says, shrugging as she pulls Lizzie from her tub and wraps her in a towel, turning to face me.

She walks toward me, and it takes great effort not to

drop my eyes down her body to watch the sway of her hips or to stare at her puckered nipples visible through the now wet fabric of her t-shirt. When she's in front of me, she places the back of her palm to my forehead, causing me to let out a low chuckle.

"Huh, no temperature," she affirms, removing her hand and placing Lizzie in my arms.

I watch, transfixed, as Meghan lifts her wet t-shirt over her head before dropping it in the sink and turning away to run the bath.

"I told you... I'm fine. I just wanted to come home and spend time with you both. What do you want for dinner?"

"Surprise me," she murmurs, looking at me over her shoulder as begins to undo her jeans.

I audibly swallow, before nodding in confirmation and turning away from the door to give her some privacy.

*I'm going to get Lizzie ready, I'm going to get Lizzie ready*, I chant to myself. Meghan is pure temptation and it takes a great effort to not put Lizzie in her crib, walk into the bathroom and carry Meghan to bed.

Lizzie's nursery is decorated in pale pinks and whites, her crib is across one wall, with a mobile hanging over it and in the corner, with a view across the city, is a rocking chair.

Cradling her tiny body against my own, I walk into her closet and grab a onesie and diaper before returning to her nursery and laying her down on the changing table. I drape her towel over the edge of the table, before smoothing over her various lotions and potions, and playing this little piggy with her dainty toes, eliciting giggles from her tiny body.

"I'm going to need my little pumpkin to help me with mommy," I whisper to her as I continue to play with her feet.

Putting on her diaper, she wiggles around on the table, as I continue with my one-sided conversation. "Mommy doesn't know that Daddy loves her..."

When she frowns up at me, I'm quick to reassure her, as if she has a clue about what I'm saying. "Don't worry, I love you too... but Mommy is going to take some convincing that she belongs with Daddy and that she should marry me."

Lizzie waves her arms in the air in what I'm taking as her agreement.

"I'm glad we're on the same page." I chuckle as I get her into her onesie before picking her up, carrying her into my room, and creating a pillow fort around her on the bed. Undressing from the confines of my suit I change into a pair of gray sweatpants, leaving my torso bare.

I contemplate for about half a second whether I should put some baby oil on for good measure, before scrapping the idea. I'm not auditioning for *Magic Mike*. I'd only scare Meghan away if I showed her my dance moves.

Taking Lizzie into the living room, I sit on the couch

and place her on my lap with my feet resting on the edge of the coffee table so she can look at me. We play while I update her on my plan, and I keep an ear out for the sounds of Meghan in the bathroom.

Her *Soul* playlist is on, so I know she'll be in there for a while and long after the water has gone cold.

With Lizzie in her bassinet, I call Meghan's favorite Italian restaurant and order us a couple of dishes—one *Bucatini All'Amatriciana* and one *Orecchiette con broccoli é Salsicce Italiane* with a side of homemade bread and olive oil and balsamic for dipping.

Opening a bottle of red wine, I leave it to air on the kitchen island before placing an order for a pint of strawberry cheesecake ice cream and waffle cones from the ice cream parlor a few blocks over.

I couldn't have timed it better, because everything arrives just as Meghan is walking out of the bathroom. Her slender body is covered by a white fluffy towel and with another wrapped around her hair, she looks like a goddess. Coming to a stop by the front door, I can't help but take in the sight of her.

"It smells amazing," she exclaims as she goes to walk past me to the spare room. "You ordered from my favorite Italian place. I'm starving. I could kiss you," she exclaims and her cheeks go a shade of red at her statement.

"I... uh... I accept kisses. From you, I accept kisses," I stutter like a damn fool, leaning back against the door, as if I don't argue cases in court for a living.

I want to tell her that for nearly two years, it's only ever been her I'd accept kisses from, but by the time I open my mouth to speak she's disappeared out of the room. In the kitchen I take a moment to lean against the counter, composing myself and willing my cock down from its semi-aroused state.

Meghan arrives ready to eat wearing the skimpiest shorts I've ever seen and a tank top with no bra underneath. I barely stifle the moan she elicits from me—I swear she's trying to torture me.

*Someone send help, and send it now.*

As we eat dinner, I'm further tortured by her moans of delight at the food, as she takes bites in between our steady conversation about our days. I deserve a damn prize for not swiping the dishes off of the table and bending her over it.

After dessert, we move to the couch and I pull her feet into my lap, sure to keep them away from the evidence her torture has created. I massage her feet while we watch a movie and it isn't long before she falls asleep.

Switching off the TV and checking on Lizzie, I carry Meghan to *our* bed, careful not to wake her.

## THIRTY

# Meghan

I wake up in a warm cocoon of solid muscle, convinced I'm definitely dreaming this time, because he wouldn't have put me in his bed *again*. Clearly my body enjoyed waking up next to Cooper yesterday and that's why I'm imagining it again.

*That's the only explanation.*

The Cooper in my dream and I are facing each other, with my head resting on his bicep as he cuddles me into his chest. I feel safe and... loved. I'm a little warm, but it's all good.

Figuring I might as well make the most of this before I wake up, I place kisses across his chest. My hands glide along his flat stomach, and down into his boxers.

*Mm-hmm,* I can't quite decide what to do next and so I caress his already hardening cock and it grows even more with every stroke. A pained groan sounds from him causing my brow to furrow in confusion.

*Okay, that sounded a bit too real.*

Opening my eyes, I gaze up into Cooper's very real ocean eyes only to be greeted by a storm of lust. Neither of us utters a single word and my look of confusion hasn't abated, because I don't understand how I've ended up in his bed yet *again*.

It would be so easy to capture his delicious mouth and satisfy my most basic needs.

*Oh, God. My hand's still wrapped around his cock!*

"Why am I in your bed, again, Cooper?" I mumble, pulling my hand out of his boxers with more care than I did the previous morning.

I'm angry, confused and... very sexually frustrated.

My breasts feel heavy. *Did I sleep through Lizzie waking for her nighttime feed again?*

As I go to pull away from him, he holds me close and rolls on top of me. My legs betray me and fall open wider for him to lie between them and my stupid chin lifts to give him more access as his nose rubs against the curve of my neck, I barely resist the urge to moan at the contact.

"You belong in my bed, Meghan. You're mine, and this is where you belong. Stop trying to fight it... to fight me," he growls.

I've never been more turned on and my hips betray me, along with the rest of my body it seems, as they roll into his hardness of their own accord. Closing my eyes, I try in vain to push him away, even though I desperately want to pull him closer.

It's when I remember how I felt hearing him in his office, with her, and the seven months of my pregnancy that I spent alone that I break.

"I can't..." I whisper, my voice cracking. "I can't be yours... not after everything that happened. I won't put myself through that again. In the end, it would just destroy me and I'd be crazy to sign up for that," I finish, being honest with him and myself, before turning my head away from his intense gaze and praying that he will leave it alone.

Instead, he rolls off of me and lies on his back, laughing at the ceiling.

Tears threaten to spill as I scurry from the room. My heart aching and hurt that he can just laugh at me airing my concerns. He isn't the man I thought he was. I need to protect myself from him and the way he makes me feel.

"I have to go to work right now, but this conversation isn't over Meghan, mark my words. We'll have dinner and talk about this tonight," he calls out to me.

As far as I'm concerned, there isn't anything else to talk about—there won't *ever* be more between us and the conversation *is* over.

Heading back to my room I get ready for the day before waking Lizzie, changing her diaper, getting her dressed for the day and feeding her. We're sitting in the rocking chair in Lizzie's room and I'm humming nursery rhymes to her as she happily chatters away, when Cooper comes to say goodbye before he leaves for the day.

"Don't go out today. You'll be getting some packages and Christopher will be here to pick you up at seven. I've already arranged a sitter for Lizzie." He looks me in the eye, as if daring me to defy him before he bends down, kisses Lizzie and then me on the forehead, then turns on his heel and leaves.

I stay in the rocking chair in a trance-like state until Lizzie pulls me out of it as she cries out for her second breakfast.

The first package arrives at eleven. It's a beautifully wrapped *Jimmy Choo* box, and I carefully peel away the ribbon, lifting the lid to reveal two packages neatly tucked away inside. Taking the smallest of the two, I undo the drawstring bag and reveal a gorgeous clutch with raw glitter in ballet pink.

*It's absolutely beautiful.*

My hands shake as I take out the second package. If I had to guess based on the size, it contains a pair of shoes. Lifting the lid, I carefully peel back the tissue paper as if something is going to jump out at me, only to reveal a pair of *Love 85* shoes. They're three-inch heels with a rose-colored coarse glitter fabric covering them.

The shoes match the bag perfectly and for a moment I wonder who he had buy them for him.

At one, when Lizzie is down for her nap, the second package arrives. This one is a plain white box with the brand name *Berta* written across it. I lift the lid to reveal white tissue paper, which I peel back before letting out a loud gasp as the dress comes into view.

Picking it up, I hold it in front of myself and walk to the mirror in my closet to get a full length view of it. The dress matches the bag and shoes in color so well you would have thought they were from the same brand.

My PJs are quickly discarded as I step into the dress, zipping it up and facing the mirror. It's an asymmetrical gown with one long sleeve on the right and the bodice underneath showcased on the left. The material from the right side of the dress cinches in at the waist on the left side before revealing the expanse of my left thigh.

*Holy shit.*

This dress is sexy... and although I've just had a baby, it fits like a dream and flatters my stomach so I don't feel self-conscious at all.

I take a moment to consider how I'll do my hair and make up before deciding this will definitely require Alex's help. Slipping the dress off, I lay it across the bed and with a look of longing directed at it, I throw on my robe and rush into the kitchen to grab my cell.

MEGHAN

SOS! I need your help tonight.

ALEX

LOL, what's the issue?

MEGHAN

I'll explain later, can you come over tonight at like five?

ALEX
I'll be there.

MEGHAN
Thank you!

Bring your makeup and hair stuff, please.

I breathe a sigh of relief that Alex has agreed to come over and help me get ready.

At two, when Lizzie is having tummy time on a play-mat, a vase of two dozen red roses arrives, with a note. The delivery guy, seeing my arms full of baby, is kind enough to carry them into the kitchen and place them in the center of the island before leaving.

The realization that I've never been sent flowers before and that Cooper sent me a gigantic bouquet brings tears to my eyes.

I want to blame my emotional state on the hormones still coursing through my body but I don't think it's entirely to blame. Removing the note I read over his scrawled handwriting.

*I hope you've received all the packages so far, there should have been three, and that they're to your liking. It's time to get in the shower as Alex should be arriving any minute now to look after my princess.*

*Your next surprise arrives at four.*

*C*

I read it again and again, searching for some kind of hint as to what he has planned. He hasn't given anything away with this note, but maybe Alex knows something and I can grill her when she arrives.

I can't believe she didn't say anything to me, even after my SOS text.

If I'm going to get through tonight, I'll need a drink or five, so with that in mind I go to the living room to pump as much milk as I can.

Alex arrives at two-thirty, just as I've finished pumping and storing my milk in the fridge. I found a bottle of champagne with a sticky note telling me to open it up when she arrives and so after greeting her at the door, I lead her to the kitchen and pop open the bottle.

"Do you know what he's up to?" I ask, taking a sip of the refreshing bubbles.

"Not a clue. He called Sebastian this morning and asked for my number." She shrugs, her eyes darting away from me. There's something she isn't telling me, and I'm not entirely sure if it's just something to do with her casual mention of Sebastian or something more.

"Okay, spill it. I know you know something," I demand.

"I don't know what you're talking about." She tries, unsuccessfully, to play dumb.

She knows exactly what is going on.

"Bull crap. Why are you acting all suspicious?" I ask, my eyes narrowing at her. "Is it to do with Cooper?" My teeth gnaw away on my bottom lip with worry.

"Oh, God. No, it's nothing to do with him," she reassures me.

"Then what is it? I'm your best friend. You should be telling me everything." I give her my best doe eyes and flutter my eyelashes for added effect.

"You mean like you did with you and Cooper?" she asks. Okay she's got me there. "I honestly don't know what he's up to but I will tell you this, because you're my best friend. I was with Sebastian when Cooper called. I saw him again and I'm not sure how I feel about myself because of it," she finishes with a defeated sigh.

"Oh, Alex. I'm so sorry." I pull her in for a hug before continuing. "If he makes you feel like that, maybe you shouldn't see him anymore?"

"It's not that simple. He makes me feel things I've never felt before and as hard as I try to stay away from him, I still end up back on my knees taking whatever he's willing to give me."

"I get that, believe me, I do. But you also told me not that long ago that you saw him with another woman and how that made you feel. You can't let your body's reaction to him make you feel bad about yourself," I say as I pull back from her to look into her eyes.

"You're right. I don't know why I'm doing this to myself. I deserve so much better," she mumbles.

"I know I am. You're an amazing woman and you deserve the world. Clearly he isn't going to give that to you so don't waste your time and energy on him."

We stand in the kitchen hugging and chatting for an hour before the doorbell rings for the fifth time today with what I'm guessing is my next surprise. Hurrying to the door with Alex hot on my heels, I swing it open before the bell can be rang again and wake Lizzie up.

I'm greeted by the smiling faces of two very beautiful men and for a brief second, my brows pull together in confusion as I wonder what sort of surprise Cooper has arranged for me.

"Honey, you are beautiful, but I just don't swing that way. Now Carlos here is partial to a bit of everything," the taller of the two states with a chuckle, throwing me a wink.

He has the clearest skin I've ever seen and I'm slightly dazzled by it.

"Sorry. Come in." I gesture, my cheeks going red with embarrassment that my thoughts went there and were on display for the world to see.

"Don't worry about it, you've made my day. I'm Luca, the make-up artist, and this is Carlos, the hairdresser." Luca introduces them both, and I do the same with Alex and myself.

After some small talk, I lead everyone into the dining

room where I've set up the dress and shoes so that they can get an idea of what look would work.

Taking a seat on one of the chairs at the head of the table, I sit up straight as Luca and Carlos walk around me like I'm their prey.

## THIRTY-ONE

# Meghan

I feel like a princess as Christopher navigates the
car through the streets of Manhattan. All that's
missing is a crown.

Carlos styled my hair to perfection in bouncy curls
that cascade down my back to my waist. Luca did my
makeup with a 'siren' look, as he believes I need to lure in
my man, although he isn't my man right now and I
certainly don't know if he will be by the end of the night.

The dress fits to perfection but it doesn't stop me
from nervously fiddling with my hands as the car cruises
through Manhattan.

"We're here," Christopher announces, drawing me
out of my contemplation about the conversation I'm
about to have with Cooper.

"Oh..." I whisper, turning to look out of the window
at the front of the restaurant. "Thank you, Christopher.

Have a good evening," I call as I climb from the car, not wanting to wait for him to open the door.

I stand on the sidewalk, pulling my fur coat tighter around me, taking a moment to look up at the building.

The restaurant is called The Aviary and serves a fine dining menu—I know because I've booked this restaurant many times for Cooper.

I've never been here myself before. I couldn't afford the cab fair, let alone a meal, but I've heard nothing but good things about it from Cooper's clients.

Shaking my sweaty hands out in nervousness, I head toward the entrance, attempting to keep my head held high. The doorman, who has been looking at me like I'm crazy as I've stood on the sidewalk staring up at the building, gives me a reassuring smile and holds the door open for me as I approach. Thanking him, I move toward the hostess stand and just as I'm about to open my mouth to speak, her face breaks into a wide grin.

"Miss Taylor, welcome. Mr. Jackson is waiting for you. Please, this way." She turns away and leads me toward a bank of elevators.

*Okay, so either she knows what Cooper has up his sleeve or she really loves her job.*

The restaurant is on the ground floor of the building with its own entrance, but it's joined to the hotel next door and they share a rooftop bar.

When we arrive at the elevator, the hostess presses the call button and the doors open almost immediately.

She steps aside, gesturing for me to enter ahead of her. Once I'm safely inside, she leans in and swipes her card before pressing the button for the rooftop.

"Have a good evening, Miss Taylor." She beams at me, just as the doors glide closed.

"Thank you," I murmur, lost in thought.

The ride up is the longest of my life and gives me more than enough time to think about what Cooper wants to talk about.

In my heart, I don't think it's going to be a bad conversation. I mean, he wouldn't have put me in his bed two nights in a row, or sent me flowers, or bought me this outfit, or booked me dinner at a fancy restaurant when he could've asked me to move out at home, or whatever it is he wants to discuss.

The thought that this could be the end brings tears to my eyes and I look up at the mirrored ceiling of the elevator, blinking away the moisture so as not to ruin my makeup and swipe away a stray tear that managed to escape.

I admonish myself when I remind myself that, at my own insistence, we aren't anything other than co-parents anyway and tonight I will ask him one final time to stop putting me in his bed.

*Maybe you should tell him how you feel.*

*Or maybe I should wait and see what he has to say first.*

Both are valid arguments.

As the elevator arrives on the rooftop, I drag my eyes

from the ceiling as the doors slide open. I'm greeted by the sight of a sea of candles. They're everywhere. Flickering in the cool breeze.

With a gasp of surprise, I tentatively step from the elevator, following the path of candles and rose petals further out onto the rooftop. The space appears deserted and for a moment I wonder if I've come to the right place.

Walking around a corner, I find a table set for two in the middle of the rooftop, surrounded by space heaters that make the space comfortably warm. The view of East Village dazzles in the background and I rest my hand on my chest as I take it all in.

*Tennessee Whiskey* by Chris Stapleton is softly playing in the background as my gaze falls on Cooper.

"Hey baby," he breathes.

He looks so handsome, dressed in a black three-piece suit with a white shirt and black skinny tie. Just the sight of him has my pussy clenching and images of him taking me in his arms, and devouring me here on the rooftop.

*He isn't mine.*

"Hi," I whisper, giving him a wobbly smile, rooted to the spot.

"Come here, Meghan," he commands, holding his hand out.

I immediately obey him and walk toward him in a daze before placing my hand in his.

"You look even better than I could've imagined." He

pulls my body flush with his, causing my hands to reach up and rest on his biceps, wary of being too intimate.

"Thank you. It's all so beautiful," I mumble, flicking my eyes down to where our chests meet.

Butterflies flutter in my stomach and my palms become clammy. His finger rests under my chin as he lifts my face up to his before dipping his head and placing a soft kiss on my lips. I moan against his mouth, loving the feel of his lips on mine, but it also only adds to my confusion.

"Come, we've got a lot to talk about, but first, let's eat," he rumbles, taking my hand and leading me to the table.

"I don't know that I can eat right now, Cooper. I'm so nervous." I tilt my head down, hiding from him. He doesn't let me hide for long as he cups my cheeks and lifts my face to his again.

"You don't need to be nervous, baby... there's a lot of stuff I should've told you a long time ago but I was a fool. I can't carry on like this. We need to lay all of this out on the table and then we can move forward." He pulls out a chair and guides me into it.

Once he's taken the seat opposite me, a waiter appears out of nowhere and pours us both a glass of champagne before placing it in the bucket next to the table and disappearing.

"To us." He holds his glass up and I clink my own against it, my eyes locked on his as I try to get a read on what he wants to talk about, on what his plan is, on... anything.

"To us," I mutter before downing the contents. The cold bubbly liquid glides with ease down my throat before Cooper takes the bottle out of the ice bucket and refills my glass.

"Try not to drink this one so quickly. I need you to understand everything I'm saying tonight." He chuckles, eliciting a smirk from me.

The waiter arrives with our first course, a pear and prosciutto salad, just as I'm about to ask Cooper if we can begin the conversation. I don't touch the food, instead leveling my gaze at Cooper.

I can't go through a three course dinner wondering why he's brought me here.

"I need you to talk to me before I can eat anything. I can't stomach anything right now," I insist, folding my hands in my lap to keep from fiddling with them on the table.

Laying down his cutlery, he leans back in his chair, a cocky smile on his face causing me to roll my eyes.

*He's enjoying this. The bastard.*

"Okay... where to start?"

"At the beginning would be nice," I huff, folding my arms across my chest, before turning my head to look out across the city. I can't let him see the devastation he is potentially about to cause when he utters the words he's about to say.

"You want to go that far back? To the day you came

and interviewed for me?" he queries, causing my gaze to dart back to him, where I'm met with a single eyebrow raised in question.

"If that's the beginning," I whisper, captivated by what he's just said.

"It sure was the start of something..." he mutters before continuing. "I obviously didn't love you at that point, we'd only just met, but I couldn't stop thinking about you, that's for sure. Maria tried to warn me against offering you the job, but the moment you walked into the conference room, I knew there was something about you and I wasn't about to let you walk out of my life. Since the day I met you, there's been nobody else, but I tried my hardest to resist you, until I couldn't."

I frown at his declaration.

*Did he just imply that he loves me?*

*Wait... what does he mean there's been nobody else since he met me? That was two years ago.*

"What do you mean there's been nobody else?" I implore. I'll come back to the love bit in a minute.

"Just that. Since the day you walked into my life, I haven't been with anybody else. I haven't so much as looked at another woman sexually," he states, still leaning back in his chair as if the words that have just left his mouth aren't a big deal.

I struggle to fully comprehend what he's telling me as I search through my memories and what I know about him. I mean, I haven't ever seen him with another woman. I've never had to book a table at a restaurant for a date, or send parting gifts, that's what billionaires have their assistants do, right?

"That's... that can't... no. That–that's not true. What about Hayley?" I stutter.

"Like I said, you misunderstood that whole situation. I should've cleared this up when you first asked me about it in the hospital and I regret not doing so, but there was a lot going on that day. Hayley's a friend of mine. She used to go to events with me before she moved to England three years ago... with her now ex-wife."

My jaw drops at his admission and I blink rapidly trying to process what he's just said.

*He's full of surprises tonight.*

"But I heard you in your office... Alfie said you were engaged to her..." I mumble, trying to piece together what he's telling me.

"I was never engaged to her. The media will make things into whatever they choose. And you shouldn't have listened to that guy." The conviction in his tone tells me he's telling the truth.

*Oh, God.*

*He missed out on my pregnancy because I didn't stay for him to explain.*

"I'm sorry. Oh, God. I'm..." My chest feels tight as the weight of what I've done settles on me. Tears form in my throat and threaten to spill down my cheeks. "You missed—my pregnancy. You—could've... Lizzie... birth —" Unable to form a coherent sentence as the panic sets in, I bend my head at the shame of what I put him through—of what I denied him.

"Hey... look at me, Meghan," he commands, my eyes connect with his as I lift my head. "I should have cleared this up a lot sooner for you. I certainly didn't tell you any of this to make you feel bad, I just want you to understand. I want tonight to be special because I love you and I'm honored that you blessed me with Lizzie, and I pray you'll give me a chance and we can have many more beautiful babies." His voice is husky with emotion as he lays all of his cards on the table.

My eyes well with tears as I stand from my chair and walk toward him. I need to be close to him. He makes room for me, scooting his chair back until there's enough room for me to sit on his lap. It feels like home as I wrap my arms around his neck, tucking my head into the space between his collar and jaw as he envelopes me in a hug.

"I love you too," I murmur, pressing my forehead against his, causing a wide grin to break out across his face.

"Say it again," he rasps.

"I love you... I love you, Cooper Jackson and I have for a long time. I was a fool to think I could follow the rules I set, but I needed them to keep me grounded so I didn't fall any deeper in love with you than I already was." I chuckle, my smile matching his.

"I'd hoped you'd say that but I wasn't one hundred percent sure what I was going to get with you tonight. I have a question for you... well two actually." Nervousness is evident in his tone.

"Whatever it is, I'm sure I'll say yes." I encourage him, unsure of what he could possibly ask me.

It's probably to move into his bedroom or maybe to actually date him.

He reaches into his jacket pocket and pulls out a piece of paper. My brows draw together in a frown. That's not what I thought he would pull out.

"We made this agreement when you came home with me." He pushes a strand of hair from my forehead before continuing. "We agreed to be no more than co-parents and I'd like to rip it up, if that's okay with you?"

"Yes. Okay. Definitely," I whisper.

He lets out a laugh at my quick response and I feel it rumble in his chest, before he rips the paper in half, reaching around me to place the pieces on the table.

Slipping his hand back into his inner pocket, he pulls out a small black velvet box causing the butterflies in my stomach to take flight.

"I was hoping to be on one knee to ask you this, but I'm more than happy to have you in my lap." He chuckles, before clearing his throat and growing serious. "Meghan, from the moment I met you, you made me feel things I've never felt before. I tried my hardest to resist you, but I couldn't. When you left, it felt like my world had collapsed around me, but then I found you and you rebuilt it, making it a million times better. I love you. I love that you've given me my own family. I couldn't imagine my life without you."

Wiping a tear from my cheek, he places a soft kiss on my lips before he continues. "You're many things to me —my soulmate and the mother of my child, to name just two. I want to ask if you'll be one more thing..." He pauses as he opens the ring box and showcases a beautiful cushion-cut diamond ring. "Will you be my wife? Will you make me the happiest man alive and marry me?"

"Yes. Yes, of course I'll marry you," I cry out in happiness, my hands coming up to cover my mouth as I look between the box and Cooper, with tears coursing down my cheeks.

"Do you like it?" he whispers.

"I love it... I love you." I declare, my heart full.

Smiling up at me, he takes the ring out its box and slides it onto my finger. It fits perfectly and after looking at it for a second, I grasp his face in between my palms and kiss him deeply. His arms wrap around me tightly as he opens my mouth with his own, before dipping his tongue in.

"And you'll give me more babies?" he breathes against my lips.

"It would be an honor," I murmur before pressing my lips to his again. "Can we go home and make them now?"

He shakes his head in denial and I pull away from him to search his face, a pout on my lips.

"Don't look at me like that, baby," he chuckles as he brings his thumb up to my lips. "I've booked us a room downstairs."

"I love you." I smooth my hand down the side of his face as I press my lips against his own.

Standing from his chair with me in his arms, he carries me into our future.

*Epilogue*

ONE YEAR LATER

Meghan

S itting in my bedroom at the vanity table with a smile on my face, I listen to the sounds of the party floating through the window from the backyard. I need a moment to breathe before I go downstairs and see all of our friends and family.

It's already been a busy morning.

Rubbing a hand over my stomach, I smile down at my growing bump—I'm five months pregnant with our second baby and we've just moved into my dream home. After our first night as an engaged couple, Cooper and I decided to wait to try for baby number two until after our wedding.

We got married six months after our engagement and I fell pregnant almost immediately after the wedding. It was the best wedding gift we could have given ourselves. Cooper was ecstatic to be able to experience the pregnancy from day one.

"There you are. Are you coming down? I need your help to entertain everyone," Cooper chuckles as he walks into our bedroom.

Coming up behind me, he rests his hands on my shoulders. As he bends to kiss the side of my neck and I tilt my head to give him more access, releasing a moan of satisfaction as he finds the sensitive spot he's so fond of.

This pregnancy has been crazy for my hormones. I've been horny non-stop for at least three months. Cooper likes to tease me, saying I'm worse than a teenage boy when it comes to sex. I like to threaten to withhold sex if he teases me too much, which ends up with him worshiping me instead.

"We can't leave our guests downstairs with no hosts," Cooper whispers against the shell of my ear.

When he moves away from me, I grab his hand to stop his movement, my eyes meeting his in the reflection of the mirror.

"Please, Cooper... I need you." I plead as I turn on the small bench so that I'm facing him and my hands reach out to undo his jeans. I can already see his cock straining against the stiff fabric of his jeans.

"Get on the bed, Meghan," he commands, causing a smug smile to stretch across my cheeks as I prance toward the bed.

Stripping my maxi dress over my head in one smooth motion, I drop it on the floor as Cooper locks the bedroom door. On my back in the middle of the bed, completely naked, I'm ready and waiting for him as he stalks toward me.

His hand smooths from my foot, up my calf and to my thigh. I can see the darkening of his eyes as lust takes him over. When he runs a finger through my slick pussy and brings it to his lips, licking it clean, I moan in anticipation.

"So wet for me, baby... you taste like fucking heaven," he growls before kneeling on the bed between my spread legs.

The first swipe of his tongue has my back arching off of the bed and my fingers diving into his hair, as I roll my hips against his mouth. I'm so close already but the need to have him inside of me when I come has me silently pleading with my body to wait.

Cooper's tongue is flicking over my clit at a rapid pace and I'm not sure I can hold back. When I don't think I can take anymore, he sucks my bud into his mouth at the same time as he pushes one finger into my core.

"Cooper... I need more," I beg.

A second finger enters me but it still isn't enough and so I tug on his hair in an effort to pull him up my body and on top of me. Resting on his hands, he hovers above me, dipping his head down to kiss me. I can taste myself on his tongue as it swipes into my mouth and tangles with my own.

Pulling away for a moment to remove his own clothes, he returns to me and settles between my legs before gently sliding into my greedy pussy. A guttural moan releases from me at the deliciousness of being filled by him.

"I love you," he vows, wiping the hair from my face as he starts to move. "God, you feel so good, baby."

I lift my right leg and wrap it around his hip, urging him to go deeper. With my eyes closed, I give into the sensations coursing through my body. Just two more strokes and I'm sure I'll be tipping over the edge into an explosive orgasm.

"Meghan, Cooper—are you in there?" Alex knocks before rattling the handle, finding it locked she calls through the door. "Lizzie's taken a tumble, and she wants you both."

We stay silent for a moment, looking at each other, still connected in the most intimate of ways.

"Coming," I call, releasing a frustrated sigh. I give Cooper one last kiss before he withdraws from me.

*Cockblocked by my own kid!*

"You get dressed and I'll go take care of her," he says, moving from the bed, throwing my dress next to me before getting dressed himself.

"I love you," I murmur, mesmerized by how the muscles in his body pull and contract as he dresses.

Once he's fully dressed and I'm still naked on the bed having been distracted by him, he walks back to the bed and brushes my hair from my face before dusting a kiss across my forehead.

He moves to the bathroom and I watch his reflection

in the mirror of the ensuite as he swishes his mouth with mouthwash, before spitting it in the sink and then washing his hands.

As he returns to the bedroom, I'm still splayed naked on the bed when he growls, "You're so fucking tempting. Tonight, I'm going to eat you for dessert. I love you."

*Cooper*

I walk away from my wife and I still can't believe she's mine. It's the hardest thing to leave, especially when she's pure temptation laid out on our bed.

Adjusting myself one last time, willing my cock to calm down, I open the door and walk into the hallway to be greeted by a grinning Alex.

"Sorry to have interrupted," she chuckles, as a smile stretches across her face.

"No, you're not. Where's Lizzie?"

"Last time I checked, she was in the living room being comforted by your mom. I'm sure she'll be fine, but you know what she's like."

I nod in response and as I go to walk past her, Alex rests her hand on my arm, making me pause. I look down at it and then up at her face in question but she's biting on her lip and avoiding my gaze.

"Is... is Sebastian coming?" I struggle to hear her

whispered question, but Meghan's told me enough for me to know what went on between them.

"He said he would be..." I confirm. "I don't think he's bringing anyone." I continue, answering her unasked question. She nods her head in response before straightening her shoulders and standing taller.

She waves her hand at me to usher me away. "Go to Lizzie."

Downstairs I find my mom and Meghan's dad sitting with Lizzie between them on the couch in the living room. Lizzie is eighteen months old and growing too fast for my liking.

"Hey pumpkin, what happened?" I ask as I crouch down in front of her.

"I-I-I fells. Ha–a–nd," she hiccups as she shows me her little grazed palm.

Pulling her hand toward me, I examine the graze before placing a kiss on her open palm. It doesn't look like it'll get infected, but I'll clean it up just in case. I carry her into the kitchen, leaving my mom and Walter to talk on the couch, placing Lizzie on the counter next to the sink.

"Let's get you cleaned up," I soothe, taking the first aid kit out from under the sink.

It doesn't take long to clean her wound and set her back down to play with the other children. She was a trooper and didn't make a peep as I cleaned her up, instead watching in fascination as I went through the motions.

Meghan comes into the kitchen, followed by Alex as I finish clearing up the counter and I watch her as they talk in hushed tones.

*She's my wife.*

Some might say our relationship happened too fast, but I'd known since meeting her that there was something between us, it just took me a while to realize she was meant to be mine. It's definitely been a whirlwind but I wouldn't have it any other way. She's the perfect woman for me and has blessed me with a beautiful daughter and a son I can't wait to meet.

After pouring a glass of orange juice for Meghan, I grab myself a beer from the fridge before joining her and Alex. Handing over Meghan's glass, I wrap my arm around her waist, dropping a kiss on the top of her head.

My gaze drifts out to the backyard, and I watch Lizzie running around, screaming with her new friends. A content smile stretches across my face at everything we've built together.

I have everything I never thought I would get and I'm never letting it go.

The front door opening has me turning to see who's entered and I'm greeted to Sebastian walking in, a woman dressed in a short, hot pink dress follows behind him on skyscraper heels.

My gaze shoots to Alex, and she meets my eyes before shaking her head, her eyes are glassy, before she turns on her heel and walks out into the backyard.

I can practically feel Meghan glaring daggers up at

me and so I aim my own glare at Seb, who smiles as if he doesn't have a care in the world.

"Did you know?"

I squeeze her hip before responding, "Not a clue. Believe me, I'm as pissed at him as you are."

She releases a heavy sigh, resting her hand on my chest. "It's probably best to give her some space, can you ask him to leave her alone?"

"Anything for you, my Queen," my lips brush against hers pulling away before it can become heated.


Want a sneak peek of Alex and Sebastian's story?

Keep reading for the prologue of Don't Fall in Love...

# Prologue — Alex

I lost sight of Meghan about an hour ago. One second, I was chatting away with Maggie from the tenth floor about her two adorable babies, and then when I looked down onto the dance floor, Meghan was gone.

I figured she'd gone for a drink, or a dance or something, so I didn't start looking right away, but it's getting late now and she's nowhere to be seen.

This isn't like her.

I want to go home but I don't want to leave without her. Or at least without knowing that she's safe. My stomach churns with nerves as I stand at the rail that overlooks the lower floor of the club.

Taking my phone out of my black clutch, I send her a text.

ALEX

Hey, where are you? I can't see you.

It shows as delivered almost immediately but even staring at it, willing a reply to come, doesn't garner me one.

She couldn't have gone too far. I'll search the club and if I have no luck, I'll alert security.

Passion is an up and coming club. I've heard the owner has a few scattered around the world, and even at two in the morning, it's still bustling and doesn't show any signs of closing soon.

I take one last look over the balcony onto the dance floor before I turn and walk to the corridor that leads to the VIP restrooms. As I enter the dimly lit corridor, I notice four doors in addition to the restrooms.

No way she wandered into a supply closet. Unless... she could be getting laid. No, we're talking about Meghan, not me. With my mind set on my mission—find Meghan Taylor—I decide to test the handle of each door. Mystery door number one leads to the supply closet, stacked with cleaning products and smelling of bleach.

Next is the ladies' restroom. I go in and check each stall—luckily for me they're all empty so I don't have to stand around for too long. Moving back into the corridor, I go to the men's restroom next.

I may get unsolicited dick pics occasionally but I'm not actively trying to see some dick right now, so I knock on the door and keep my eyes scrunched closed. Cautiously, I poke my head through the door and call out for Meghan.

Getting no response, I move onto the final three

doors. Two of them are locked and after pressing my ear to them, listening out for any signs of distress, I move on when I hear nothing.

*Maybe she is in there having the time of her life and they just have good sound proofing.*

I smirk at the thought. As if Meghan would be getting it on with some random guy in a club. I'm lost in my own thoughts when I swing open the third door. In hindsight, I should have been paying more attention; who knows what I could've walked in on.

The most beautiful man I have ever laid eyes on is sitting behind a sleek glass desk with a laptop open in front of him. Behind him is a wall of windows looking out over the club below. His head snaps up as I enter, his brow furrows in question at my intrusion.

"I'm so sorry. I was just looking for my friend." I try not to stutter as I stare at him.

God, why am I so nervous? Butterflies take flight in the pit of my stomach and my skin heats under his assessing gaze.

He's set me on edge just by looking at me. It's intense. His full focus on me.

*Watching like I'm his prey.*

I can hear the dull beat of the bass in the club, but it fades away as we continue this silent staring... contest? He smirks up at me as he removes his glasses and reveals his dazzling eyes. They're kind of blue but mixed with the perfect hint of green.

Leaning back in his chair, he keeps his gaze trained

on me. Like a deer caught in the headlights, I stay frozen in the doorway, unable to look away from him.

He's dressed in a crisp white shirt, which is sculpted to his muscular chest and arms. Navy-blue chinos encase thick thighs and navy-blue velvet Oxford shoes, that I can see through the desk, are on his feet.

A thought occurs to me as I take in his long legs that are crossed at the ankle—*what would it be like to sit under that desk and unzip him?*

My brow pulls into a frown at the confusing thought. He's a stranger and I've never had this almost instant attraction to someone that I don't even know the name of. I lift my eyes up his body, taking in his clean shaven jaw, full lips, and tanned skin tone. He has a straight nose and black hair, shaved on the sides but long on the top, that's neatly coiffed.

"That's okay, sweetheart. What does she look like? Maybe I can help?" he asks as he gestures towards his laptop.

*Oh God, he's British.*

I squeeze my thighs together and pray he doesn't notice the movement.

"Um, her name's Meghan. We work together. She was wearing a dusty pink dress. She's blonde..." I scratch my head as I try to think of more identifiable features.

He types away on his laptop and then his delectable mouth lifts on one corner as if he's seen something amusing.

"She went home with somebody."

I stare at him for what feels like forever. With a shake of my head, I timidly move toward his desk, stopping next to him.

I need to see who.

He slams his laptop closed at my approach, and I frown at the action.

*Oh my God, has Meghan been taken by someone?*

*Is he involved?*

"I need to see," I state, looking down at him and trying to keep my composure. "No offense, but I don't know you and you could be in some conspiracy to..." I wave my arm around looking for the right words. "To kidnap her." I fold my arms across my chest in defiance.

"She left with someone from your party earlier. There is no conspiracy here, I assure you." He holds his hands up as he leans further back in his chair.

He returns my stare, but for some reason I feel like he's reaching into my soul and learning every facet of me.

Turning my head from his gaze—which is making me want to do things I never normally would—I stare out of the window at the clubbers below as I think about what he's said.

*Meghan's a smart girl.*

I'm sure she'll be fine. She's an adult after all.

Deciding to text her again and ask her to call me as soon as she can, I make a plan to go home and get into bed. It's been a long week at work and I need to relax.

Maybe I'll even drag out one of my much used toys and *really* relax.

I'm turning away from him when he grabs my hand and I stumble on my heels, falling back into his lap. He's all solid muscles and warm body. Even though we're both very much fully clothed, I still get wet from the contact.

*Jeez, I need to get laid.*

It's been months since I was with someone—the whole needing to have some sort of connection with the person I'm fucking really does screw with your sex life.

Turning my head to apologize for falling into his lap —even though it's kind of his fault—I suck in a breath as I realize just how close we are.

His mouth is inches from my own and it really wouldn't take much for me to close the distance and have a taste. I'm aware of his hands touching my body, one on my waist and the other on my thigh, stroking small circles.

*Shouldn't he be helping me up, not holding me in place?*

I wiggle my ass in an attempt to relieve the ache building in my core.

"Sweetheart, I wouldn't do that if I were you," he murmurs in my ear and I close my eyes at the rumble of his voice as it runs through my body.

Before I know it, our lips connect and his tongue dives into my mouth. He tastes like a combination of honey and mint. It's intoxicating. Moaning into his mouth, I wiggle my ass into his crotch again, this time eliciting a moan from him.

He lifts me from his lap and places me on the edge of his desk. His lips still devour mine even as he stands between my legs.

I should feel intimidated. He's all muscle as he towers over me. He must be at least six foot five. His hand skirts up the inside of my thigh and caresses my pussy through my G-string. I tear my mouth away from his to gasp in a lungful of much needed air.

My body feels like it's on fire and he's the only person that can temper the flames.

I've never been this reactive with a partner before... ever.

He sits back in his chair and lowers it so that his head is aligned to my crotch. And then with no warning whatsoever he buries his face in my pantie-clad pussy and inhales a deep breath. My eyes widen at his forwardness but, as if on instinct, I lean back and open my legs wider for him.

*I don't know what's come over me.*

"God, you smell fucking amazing." He moans, running his tongue over my underwear.

When he pulls away, I whimper at the loss of contact, and my eyes dart to his when he pushes my legs together. His features are dark with lust and they only darken further when his hands smooth up the outside of my thighs and under my dress to grab the top of my panties.

He removes them, and I spread my legs wide for him again as he throws my G-string somewhere over his shoulder. His eyes never leave my bare pussy as he trails a finger through my damp slit, and I moan at the contact, throwing my head back. Rubbing over my clit, he slides one of his long, thick fingers into my core, right to the hilt.

"You're so tight. I'm going to need to stretch you a little to get you ready." He groans as he brings his mouth to my pussy, covering my clit with his tongue and flicking the sensitive bud.

Slowly, he adds a second finger to my pulsing core and slides it in with ease, using my wetness as lubrication.

I don't think I've ever been this turned on, and with a stranger no less.

"I don't normally do this," I pant as his fingers begin to move.

An overwhelming need to make sure he doesn't get the wrong impression settles deep within me, even though I know he won't be bothered. Guys don't care about shit like that.

He doesn't respond to my comment, he just continues to eat me, bringing me to the edge before he pulls away and stands, causing me to let out a groan of disappointment.

"Take off your dress and put your hands on the glass," he commands.

I look up at him in confusion, my eyes moving back and forth between him and the window.

*He wants me to do what?*

I like to try new things as much as the next person, but I'm not an exhibitionist.

"It's a privacy window. They can't see you," he reassures me, tucking a strand of my straight, light brown hair behind my ear.

His words soothe me and for the second time tonight, I take what he has said as fact without seeing any evidence.

Standing from the desk, not daring to look back and see the mess I have no doubt made on it, I walk up to the window, my hips swinging with each step.

Reaching under my arm, I unzip my dress and let it fall to the floor until I'm left in nothing but my black strappy five-inch stilettos. I tentatively place my hands on the window, just as he's directed, throwing a questioning look over my shoulder at him.

He looks... *hungry.*

His gaze devours me like I'm his next meal and his tongue darts out to wet his bottom lip. *I need to kiss him.* I turn from the window and wrap my arms around his neck, pressing my lips to his, my tongue begging for entry into his mouth. He allows me to be in control for all of two seconds before his tongue is plundering my mouth and he's grabbing a fistful of each of my ass cheeks.

Dazed and confused, I pull back, returning to my

position in front of the window. Even with my heels on, he still towers over me and, for a fleeting second, I wonder if I should be fearful of the power he's exuding and the control he has over both my mind and body.

The thought disappears as he moves his chair behind me and sits back down in it, pushing down on my lower back to urge me to bend over slightly. My flushed cheek rests against the cool glass and I watch the crowd. It's exhilarating to see the people below, oblivious to the pleasure I'm experiencing so close to them.

When he spreads my cheeks and proceeds to eat my ass, I tense initially at the unfamiliar contact before letting out a low moan of pleasure. My eyes close of their own volition and I enjoy the sensation of his mouth on the only virgin part of me.

His two fingers return to my soaked core and he slowly pumps them in and out, stretching me as he adds a third. I can feel my arousal running down the inside of my legs, and for a fraction of a second wonder what the view must be like for him.

"Such a good *fucking* girl, aren't you?"

I don't answer, unable to vocalize anything at this moment in time. His hand comes down on my ass cheek, filling the room with a cracking sound as it echoes in the confines of his office. I let out a yelp, the unexpected pain making me clench around his three fingers. He lets out a low moan as his palm soothes the spot he just spanked.

"You need to answer me, sweetheart," he growls.

"Yes," I rasp out.

"Yes, what?" he demands.

"I'm... I'm a good girl," I moan as he continues to pump in and out of me, almost punishingly.

"And what do good girls get?"

"Fucked?" I question a hint of desperation in my tone.

*Please say they get fucked.*

All over, the tingle of my arousal builds with every thrust of his fingers.

"Yes. Yes, they do, baby," he chuckles. He increases the pace of his fingers, moving his mouth back to the puckered hole of my ass.

My vision goes fuzzy as I feel my orgasm building and I let out a cry of release, clenching around his fingers while I come undone.

"Now is the time to get dressed and walk away if you don't want me to fuck you," he warns.

There's a hint of a plea in my tone that I can't quite hide. "No. I need to feel you inside me."

He stands. I hear the faint sounds of his fly unzipping and the foil of a condom wrapper being ripped. It feels like an eternity before I feel the head of his cock pushing into me from behind.

Stretching my sensitive pussy, his hands find my hips, gripping them roughly. In one smooth move, he's seated to the hilt and I let out a guttural sound of pleasure as an orgasm I didn't even know I was on the verge of having, sends spasms through my body.

*Okay, what is he doing to me?*

One of his hands moves across my stomach, past my breasts and up to hold my throat lightly, pulling me back into his embrace. With my body pressed between his and the window, he starts to move in and out of me.

His grunts of pleasure fill my ears as he slowly increases his pace. I'm in awe when a third orgasm starts to build with each stroke of his thick cock. Little whimpers fall from my lips—I don't feel like I can make it through this one. Each thrust has my body convulsing as if a current of power is electrifying my blood.

*What is happening?*

Moving the hand still on my hip to my clit, he rubs it in smooth, precise movements bringing me closer and closer to the edge. I try to wriggle away, but he holds me steady, murmuring words of encouragement into my ear. Before I know it, I'm coming again, and as I clench around him, I can feel and hear his own orgasm taking him over.

He pulls out of me, resting me against the window. When he's certain I'm able to stand on my own, he walks off toward a door I hadn't noticed when I came in, disappearing behind it and leaving me alone in his office.

Catching my breath, I take the opportunity to get dressed and sneak out. I hate awkwardness at the best of times, let alone after coming three times. I'm going to chalk this up to a wild, orgasmic experience with a guy I will *never* see again.

When I get home and I'm tucked in bed, reliving the events of the night, it dawns on me that I didn't even get his name. I suppose I could easily find it out by searching the club, but I'm not going to. There's no need.

It isn't until I see him again on another night out, that I realize he's friends with Cooper Jackson, one of the managing partners at the firm I work for.

This fact alone isn't enough to keep me away from him.

It should be, maybe then I could have protected myself better.

This is the start of our story; of how Sebastian Worthington barreled into my life and turned it upside down, because like a moth to a flame, I'm drawn to him.

Even if it ends in my own heartache.

Don't Fall in Love is available on Amazon now, get your copy here.

# Afterword

Thank you so much for reading my debut novel. If you loved Meghan and Cooper's story, be sure to leave a review.

If you're not quite done with Don't Tell Anyone, you can sign up to my newsletter here (subscribepage.io/HJq3CE) and receive the bonus scene of Meghan and Cooper's wedding day!

If you enjoyed Meghan and Cooper's story, be sure to read KA's second book, Don't Fall In Love, which follows the story of Alex and Sebastian. You can grab your copy here.

# Acknowledgments

Thank you to my team of alpha readers—you know who you are!—for amping me up during the process of writing Meghan and Cooper's story. Although I started writing their story before I met any of you, you were the push I needed to sit down and write—even when I didn't want to.

A special shout out and huge thank you to the Self Publishing Romance Authors Discord group, who allowed me to ask a million questions without feeling like any one was too silly.

A massive thank you to my editing team! First to Allie Bliss, who without her input Meghan and Cooper wouldn't have been anywhere near as exciting or engaging. Then, Jade Church who gave me so many useful tips for future books. And finally, to Sarah for going through and polishing up what Meghan and Cooper's story.

A huge thank you to TL Swan and the Inkers group, who provided me with some many hints and tips throughout the process, even when I felt like a needy newbie.

Finally, I want to thank my friends and family (even though you better not have read this!) for being so supportive throughout the process of writing this book. Especially my boyfriend, Ryan, who supported me through my journey and nights squirreled away in my writing corner as I wrote Meghan and Cooper's story.

# About the Author

KA James is an author of contemporary romance. She lives near London, UK with her partner and their Bichon Frisé, called Mia. Before starting her author journey, KA was an avid reader of romance books and truly believes the spicier the book, the better.

Outside of writing, KA has worked in HR for eleven years but has truly found her passion with writing and getting lost in a world that plays out like a movie in her mind. After all, getting lost in the land of make believe, where it's much spicier is way more fun.

 KA is in the process of writing her third book and hopes that you enjoyed reading Alex and Sebastian's story. Be sure to follow along on one or more social media channels to be kept in the loop.

Printed in Great Britain
by Amazon

48960448R00219